CELINE L. A. SIMPSON

MUSIC TO MY EARS

First edition

ISBN: 978-0-6451611-0-6 (paperback)
ISBN: 978-0-6451611-1-3 (hardback)
ISBN: 978-0-6451611-2-0 (ebook)

Editing by Joeli Woodrow
Cover art by Ashley Quick & Murphy Rae

for everyone who was convinced
that the band on stage
made direct eye contact with them

they did. they absolutely did.

Acknowledgement

I've never written acknowledgements before, so bear with me.

The first person I would like to acknowledge is Joeli. I weaselled my way into your Instagram DM's and it could have teetered into a ghosting, or it could have flourished, but no matter how high I raised my own freak-flag, you've always raised the roof right beside me. The prompt to write this book came from you, and I can confidently say it wouldn't be what it is without the time, effort and care you put into it. I know we don't do compliments and praise, so I'll pretend that I never wrote this and go about my day. And if COVID gave me anything, it gave me you and I am so grateful.

Mom and Dad, I wouldn't be able to verbalize my dreams as a reality by saying 'I am an author' if it weren't for you both. There is only one thing I wish to say, and I know that you will know what I mean when I say it:

> ***"If I have seen further it is by standing on the shoulders of Giants" - Isaac Newton***

Thank you.

Bradley, you are always in my corner. I came upstairs to you today and told you that I'd finished writing the book and your smile matched my own, your excitement matched my own. That's all I'll ever need, so thank you for always being the little voice that says 'yes, you can.'

And last but not least, I would like to thank you, the person who might be reading this. Or even if you didn't read this exact part, but you read the book. I loved writing this book, and I love you for taking the time to read it.

1

Allie

I was 100% one of those people that insisted that the more I pressed the button that illuminated the little walking man, letting me know I could safely cross the road, the faster the light would change. I thought the world was separated into two types of people. There were those like me, who believed in the power of the speedy tapping of the crosswalk button, and there were those who believed it wasn't connected to anything and thus, didn't do anything.

I loved December, but holy cannoli, the wind was so cold I could almost feel the snot I was consistently sniffling up turn into little icicles in my nose.

Rapidly pressing the crosswalk button, I was hopping from foot to foot, eager to make my way towards the light. The heavenly light of the iridescent 'Open-24-Hours' corner store that was a blissful 1-minute walk from my apartment.

I had a shitty day, a *really* shitty day. The kind of day that almost had me thinking that maybe the crosswalk button didn't do anything. Maybe it was all a lie and I really was just your run-of-the-mill idiot who pressed it too much and too quickly. But then the light changed, and I was instantly reaffirmed that that was complete baloney. It might have been the only win I had for the day, and you better believe I was grabbing it with both hands.

Today was another 'I need something so sweet my teeth will fall straight out of my head' kind of day. So, after working late and receiving far too many, and completely unsubtle, ass-pats from my knob of a boss for a congratulations on yet another successful marketing campaign execution, it was all I could do not to crawl into the corner store.

As the light got brighter and my frozen feet brought me closer to the haven I'd been yearning for, I tried to appreciate the quiet calm that was the inner city. The type of quiet that you didn't get often but when it happened, the silence seemed to be too loud.

The melody of Mozart's *Rondo Alla Turca* trickled into my mind. My fingers trilled the air in front of me as if my hands were gliding over the ivory keys of my beloved piano. I could hear the build of my favourite moment, the perfect crescendo, that I almost let my eyes shut, to completely immerse myself into its bliss.

The warm air that so abruptly opposed the frigid wind outside the small corner store hit me, or rather I hit it, and it shook me from the only moment of peace I had found all day. The immediate contrast made my nose sting to the point of making my eyes water, causing my face to scrunch up and look like something I was confident resembled a raisin.

So, it would appear to anyone around me that I was caught in that dreadful in-between moment where you needed to sneeze, but you couldn't. And the sneeze itself has yet to decide whether to just flutter away or come back with vengeance.

In an effort to recollect myself, I quickly unwound my *skeenie* (it was both a scarf and a beanie – a *skeenie*), took off my gloves and threw them both into the tote bag I had slung over my shoulder.

To add onto the almost-sneezing face scrunch, I also felt myself immediately start to perspire thanks to the sudden temperature drop and the ridiculous number of layers I had on.

Running my hand through my hair to give it a bit of life after its own slumber beneath my *skeenie,* I made a beeline for the baking aisle. Throwing a casual wave to the cashier who saw me here so often, and always at the same time buying the same thing, I should've really tried to find another corner store to alternate between. But as I said, this one was a 1-minute walk from my apartment, so, fat chance.

There was only one other person in the baking aisle, unusual, but it had happened before.

The loud whispers from the figure that was bundled behind the upturned collar of his thick, black, almost floor length coat – very *Sherlock Holmes* – was not something that I would've usually concerned myself with.

The guy was keeping to his own business and I was more than happy not to have a witness when I carried more than my body weight of do-it-yourself brownie packs to the checkout. But my completely unabashed admiration for his bright, red hair - long enough to be tucked behind his ears and fashioned in a sort of messy-but-on-purpose way - had me gaping like an opened mouth trout.

There were some people who could just *do* that with their hair, and I was so envious it made me want to hurl. Don't get me wrong, I loved my hair - it fell just to the top of my bum and cascaded in long, light brown waves. I'd never *not* grown it, and it had only ever been short once and it wasn't an experience I wanted to have again. Ever.

I just wished that sometimes I could've been that person, the one who bleached the living daylights out of their hair and then poured on a colour dye, all in the safety of their own bathroom and with complete disregard for all the YouTube 'hairdresser reacts' videos that assured you that you would 100% end up with spaghetti hair if you did the above.

Regardless, the tall guy with the red hair and cool jacket was in the baking aisle, same as me and I understood that, it resonated. Clearly.

Maybe it was the day I had, or that fact that at the end of it all I could admit to myself that I was feeling a little, okay *a lot*, lonelier than usual, but I turned to face him.

"Everything literally looks the fucking same, how are there so many versions of the same thing?" he whisper-shouted to whoever was on the other end of the phone plastered to his ear.

I took a deep breath and popped my best 'hello, I know we're strangers but I swear I'm not weird despite my socks and gross greasy hair. I actually shower often and have a great shampoo and conditioner regime' smile and walked over to help him out.

2

Allie

I lifted my hand up in a half-hearted wave, "Hey," and then dropped it immediately.

I was confident that my smile was the most inviting thing in the world until the tall guy with the red hair whipped his head towards me so fast, I thought I heard his neck crack.

His face was a mask of both shock and horror and made me feel like I had something green in my teeth. It felt like it was a freeze-frame of a moment that held for too long and immediately regretted.

The single second it took for his phone to fall from his face to the ground snapped both of us out of it and had me taking a small step back from what was already a respectable distance from a stranger to start with, while he bent down to snatch it up.

I cleared my throat and tried again, my smile probably looked a bit more forced than before. Because it *absolutely* was.

"I don't usually eavesdrop, but I heard your conversation and thought I could help. I love to bake. Not, like, every day, but I bake sometimes. Maybe, like, once a week and not always on weeknights like tonight. I bake on the weekends too. You know, if I'm not busy," I trailed off.

The confident flow of my explanation fizzled off into a whisper as it became very clear I was rambling, feeding him information he did *not* need to know.

I would've loved to have just wrapped my *skeenie* over my face and waited for this dude to walk away because not only was that completely the opposite of what I wanted to say, but this guy was gorgeous. Like, woah, I didn't realise people like him existed in real life, much less in a simple little corner store by my apartment.

He managed to school his features from what I could only assume for him was the unpleasant view of my 'world's most inviting and I swear I'm not a weirdo' smile, to something that looked like worry.

His head whipped to the other side, leaning back to get a good view of the whole aisle behind him. Then he did the same to the side behind me before his eyes - eyes that were a hazel-green and had me, again, looking sort of like a trout - landed right back on me. His gaze was heavy to the point that any lingering chill from outside disappeared very, very fast.

Gulp.

"What?" he said. Not really a question.

He just kept looking at me as if this entire interaction was the strangest thing to ever happen to him. Who knew? Maybe it was. I didn't know this guy from a bar of soap. For all I knew, I could have interrupted one of the most important conversations of his life.

I pointed to the shelf in front of him but I couldn't follow it with my gaze. I mean, when I told you that he was a sight to behold, a sight like I'd never beheld myself before, I meant it, "I thought I might be able to help you, you know, find what you needed."

10 points to Allie for pumping out coherent sentences.

He looked between me and where I was pointing, and his features softened. A guarded expression still held firm, but it was almost like he had decided I wasn't all that much of a threat, or at least not a threat that could kick his ass. Awesome.

The person on his phone was shouting something which caught his attention and he quickly lifted it to his ear again, but his eyes didn't leave mine.

What the shit is happening right now?

"Yeah, no, I'm still here. Sorry, I dropped my phone—No, it's fine. You don't need to come in, I'll just ask for help. Aspen, it's fine, I'll be out in a minute."

His girlfriend? Or boyfriend? *Aspen.* A name that could apply to any person or gender. Bugger.

He shoved the phone into the front pocket of his black skinny jeans. My eyes tracked the movement with no attempt at being subtle whatsoever. I'll admit, it wasn't my best moment, but it *had* been a long day and let's be honest, that was the closest to stimulating-male interaction I'd had in a very long time. If you know what I mean.

I cleared my throat again and plastered on my smile despite my racing heart and asked again, "So, what were you after?"

He still held onto the bemused expression before he answered, and not with what I thought he was going to say, "Do you know who I am?"

Alrighty. What a giant asshole.

As far as first impressions went, that was not a winner.

I could feel my face scrunching up again but this time it

was sort of like what would happen to your expression when you walked through someone else's fart while shopping. Yep, almost exactly like that.

"Didn't we just meet here, just now, in the baking aisle?" I clarified to him, but also half to myself because I *swear* I'd never seen this guy before.

His eyebrows shot up at that like this was incredibly surreal, "Oh, right. Sorry, I thought—," he paused, then shook his head, "Nothing."

His hand moved up to push his red hair away from his face.

Ah, very good, so it was just the straight up messy-hair look, not the messy-on-purpose look.

I had taken another step back, suddenly eager to remove myself from the situation as fast as possible regardless of the fact that I had just stumbled upon the most attractive man I'd ever seen in my life.

"Baking powder," he finally said. He looked from me to the shelf in front of him. I think I preferred shock-and-horror to unsure-and-awkward if I was being honest, "I'm supposed to get baking powder. My brother likes to bake."

Ah, brother.

My face softened and a genuine smile ghosted over my lips. He didn't need to explain what the baking powder was for, but I took it for what it was; an olive branch between strangers who found themselves in an incredibly awkward first encounter. Maybe he wasn't such an ass.

Maybe.

"Well, you won't find it there, that's all the decorative baking stuff like food dye. The baking powder is down the other end with the flour," I gestured with my thumb behind my shoulder as I started to walk backwards.

Once he had taken his first step towards me, I turned my back and walked as casually as I could down what had just become the longest aisle I had ever been in. It was probably not obvious to the untrained eye, but this was very out of character for me. To talk to random hot dudes and help them find their runaway baking ingredients.

I had never been more aware of my walking style in my whole entire life.

Again, what in the world is going on? It's like, midnight on a weekday.

The soft tapping of his boots behind me was the only indication that he was actually following and hadn't done a 'fakey' and sprinted the other way.

I grabbed the brand I used and handed it to him, making sure not to let my hand touch his, as much as I would have loved to have 'accidentally' touched his hand.

"Thanks. I was never going to find that," he laughed lightly.

Oh, God. Could this get any worse? He had one of those side, half smiles that you always read about, and I'll be damned if it didn't make my insides scream and knot up. I always thought that was absolute nonsense - no single smile could make you want to cry out for mercy, but there you had it. I did manage to, however, maintain enough of my dignity and cry on the inside.

Dare I say, another 5 points?

He looked up only to have the sexy side smile fall from his face, which then had me realising that the good old trout mouth expression I tended to adorn was up, front and centre. Closing my mouth with an audible snap, I cleared my throat – again – and offered a smile. I was 80% sure it looked natural and not at all offensive or creepy.

"I'm Dax," his hand shot out between us and I looked at it for probably a second too long before I reached out and slid my hand into his.

Yep, *definitely* glad I was touching his hand.

It was large and completely swallowed mine, and it was coarse and callused like someone who used their hands in life. Not like mine, which I knew were soft and small.

I looked back up to meet his gaze, "Allie. Alice—I'm Alice."

"Alice. Nice to meet you," his side smile reappeared and my day suddenly felt a whole lot better, "I have to admit, I didn't actually think anyone else would be here at this time," he let out a breathy laugh as he let go of my hand and moved to rub the back of his neck.

Instinctively, I tucked both hands behind my back, but this felt good. This felt like we'd levelled up. That our conversation had gone from horrid to awkward to now normal.

I was going to tally this with another 5 points and not expect anything else from the evening. Quit while I was ahead.

Pointing behind him back the way we'd come down the aisle, I explained my purpose for being present before I thought better of it, "The only place to get a brownie mix box at this time."

"Ahh," he nodded in sincere understanding. It made my smile widen and my hands fall from behind my back to my sides.

He started to walk backwards until I stepped towards him. He turned around and headed straight for the pre-mixed cakes. Grabbing one from the shelf – not my usual brand – and handed it to me.

"Those," he pointed to the box I now held, "are my favourite."

Another olive branch.

So, he liked brownies too.

"I thought your brother was the baker?" I smiled and flicked my eyes to the baking powder he was holding.

He looked down at it and then back up at me. His eyes were brighter than before, like he was completely content to be right in that moment with me.

"Oh, he is most definitely the baker, hence his use of baking powder instead of just a ready-to-go box. You're more my kind of person, Alice."

My stomach felt like it encompassed an entire lightning storm. Every wave and jolt made my body very hot and then very cold.

I laughed in response, my face stretching into a smile that felt far too wide.

"Does your brother dress like you? I don't think I could picture boots like those," I point to his all-ties-and-buckles combat boots, "baking in a kitchen." I lift my eyebrows at him for some extra sass.

"Would you believe me if I said that this is exactly what he bakes in, but also with eyeliner and his hair spiked up in every direction?" His face looked so serious I couldn't help but burst out laughing.

A shuffling sound came from the end of the aisle behind Dax, where the cashier stuck his head around the corner. I slapped a hand over my mouth to muffle the rest of my cackling.

I yelled an apology just as he snapped a photo of us.

That was weird, I really hope the next time I came here my photo wasn't plastered to the sliding doors with a notice declaring me a public nuisance due to my disruptive sound levels.

When Dax turned back around to face me, any humour that

was lighting his features before had all but disappeared and was instead replaced with a deep frown.

"Craig, the check-out guy, doesn't get out much. He probably just took a photo for the purpose of memorising our faces," I laughed again, trying to lift the mood.

For some reason his frown *bugged* me. It didn't have a place in our conversation. A conversation I was really, really happy to be having.

The frown eased a bit, "That is entirely creepy if that's actually what Craig spends his time doing."

"Oh, he's harmless. I think," now it was my turn to frown and Dax's turn to laugh.

I thought that the conversation was going to end there. It felt like if it was going to naturally dwindle, it would've been then. I was, however, pleasantly surprised when Dax asked me another question.

"So, do you always help random guys in the baking aisle?" he enquired.

"Oh, all the time," I nodded in complete sincerity.

I didn't, I never did.

"Really?" he said, eyebrows raised in a mocking show of shock.

"That's actually the only reason I'm here. I don't really even like brownies," I went on, sagging my shoulders in a mocking reply of being found out.

"I knew it," he said while snapping his fingers like he'd just solved a crime.

"You did not!" I gasped.

"Oh, I absolutely did," Dax might be wittier than I was. He didn't stop there, "Especially with that winter get-up you had on coming in here, it *screamed* 'I hit on guys in 24-hour corner stores to pass the time.'"

My own eyebrows hit my hairline and I reached out and tapped him lightly with the brownie box I held, "I was *not* hitting on you!" my face heated up immediately, "Oh my god!" Never mind that he had seen me walk in here wearing my *skeenie.*

"Honestly, I'm just glad you made the first move and not me. I was wondering how I was going to keep away from you with that beanie-scarf contraption you had on."

"It's called a *skeenie,* thank you very much, and it's the most convenient article of clothing I own."

"I 100% believe that," he laughed and I joined in.

I had just thought of a good reply and barely opened my mouth when a loud *hooonk,* that dragged on for longer than necessary, sounded rather abruptly from outside, causing me to jump and my heart rate to spike.

Dax turned to look behind him where you could vaguely make out a black car with someone waving out the back-passenger window. He looked back to me and lifted his hand in a stoic wave as he started to move backwards.

"Thanks again, Alice," he held up the baking powder in my direction in a sort of 'toast' style.

The only thing I could think of to yell after him was, "It's Allie. Just Allie is fine!"

That sexy side smirk made an appearance one more time before he dropped a note onto the counter to pay for his item and hurried outside into the car.

I stood there like an idiot for another minute before I grabbed a second box of brownie mix - this time in the brand I usually got, just in case his choice wasn't up to scratch - and made my way to the check out.

Not an asshole then.
Definitely not.

3

Dax

"Dude, I thought you got absorbed into the aisle or something," Aspen leaned over and shoved me as he sped off down the street.

The rest of the band - Angus, Luke and Rip - were all crammed into the back of the sedan.

It was probably important to point out that this was a small car, and we were five fully grown men. It was also not the only - nor the biggest - car that was owned between the five of us. But since the very beginning, we would always pile into this sedan and head to gigs, sound checks, anything.

So, for fear of breaking tradition, as we left the soundcheck for our show tomorrow night, here we were crammed into the same sedan that took us to our very first gig.

We had wanted to end the tour in our home city, so we were doing one quick show before heading off to do a couple more across the country and then back here for the final shebang.

It felt good to be home, to be in the city that not only we grew up in but that we could stay in our own places and not in hotels or tour buses.

Angus and Rip lived together and were the first to be dropped off. None of us lived particularly close to one another, but if we did a big loop from where we left at the stadium, it worked out.

Sticking my hand out the window we all shook in our standard half-handshake-half-hand-slap manner, really it just looked like a lazy handshake, and set off again.

Luke was next; he hopped out at his building where he shared an apartment with his girlfriend, and I stuck my hand out for the same slap-shake. It didn't really warrant words which suited me fine just now.

Aspen sped off again, circling back around the inner city to our place.

I tore my gaze from the window, looking but not really seeing a whole lot. I let out an exasperated sigh and moved my hand through my hair, pushing it off my face, "There was a girl. She was buying brownie mix," I explained with a mumble, turning my attention back towards the window, "Alice— Allie."

His eyebrows lifted as he cast his gaze at me briefly, "Oh, yeah? She get a picture?"

"Mm. No, she didn't know who I was."

Aspen's laugh was traced with both bewilderment and disbelief, "Ha! Are you kidding?"

See, I wasn't an asshole, and I was entirely aware that she thought I was the world's biggest bellend when I asked her if she knew who I was.

Taken out of the context of my life, I knew how that looked. To assume that everyone was just magically aware of your presence, I mean, I got it, but everyone, *everyone,* knew who I was. I hadn't met anyone in my adult life who didn't. Until tonight.

"Mmm," it was the only response my brain could manage.

"Could it have been the hair? It's never been that colour before," Aspen went on, clearly still shocked that it was possible.

I mean, I understood that this still sounded like we thought an awful lot of ourselves but no matter where we went, or who we were with, everyone knew. The check-out guy from the 24-hour corner store even snapped a photo with me when I walked in. I just asked him not to post it online 'til I left. There was no reprieve, and we weren't complaining. We didn't mind it. Sometimes.

"No, Ap. I'm telling you. I looked her right in the face for a very long time and she had no idea. It was like she'd never met a bigger asshole in her whole life. You should have seen her face when I asked," I had to laugh.

I couldn't *not* laugh. It was sort of like the face you'd make when you stepped barefoot into dog-poop on your lawn, first thing in the morning when you were grabbing the paper. But after that, it went well. Really well.

It was silent between us for a while longer while Ap sped a bit too fast through the too-quiet city.

"I shook her hand," I spoke it out loud for the sake of saying it, just to see how it felt rolling off my tongue.

"Oh?"

"She was funny, too."

"Funny's good, Dax," I could hear the smile in his voice.

Allie. Alice.

I liked Allie better. She just *looked* more like an Allie. The long, dishevelled hair. The seafoam green eyes. Definitely an Allie.

Aspen had a small smile I would have loved to wipe right off his face but I'll tell you, the man had a flare for baking, and there was little that could come between me and one of his chocolate chip cookies tonight.

We pulled into the underground parking lot of our building. Jumping out of the car, a small but loud *beep* sounded as Ap locked it and we made our way to the elevator.

I pressed the call button for the lift continuously until it arrived. There was no doubt in my mind that it made it arrive faster and I'd go to the mat with anyone who said different. We shuffled into the small square space. I scanned my card on the reader and punched the number at the very top; floor 37.

The trip to our apartment could have lasted an hour or five seconds. I was so in-my-own-head I couldn't stop thinking.

She had no idea who I was.

"Dax?" Aspen waved his hand in front of my face. I swatted it away as the elevator doors pinged, opening to our home.

"Did you get her number at least?" he called after me as I headed straight for a hot shower and him, straight for the kitchen.

"Nope. No, I didn't."

Why didn't I just ask her for her number?

4

Allie

"No, Savannah, I'm saying that he looked me right in my face and asked me if I knew who he was. Can you imagine the *cajones* on this guy? I couldn't believe it. I thought he was the world's biggest asshole. No one has a face like his and also struts around being a gentleman."

Or at least in my experience.

I took a long swig of my wine as Sav, my best friend and ride-or-die, looked on while absentmindedly fiddling with the many pieces of metal she had decorating her ears.

"But…" she prompted, hopeful.

"*But...*" I went on, "it did turn out that he was not an asshole. Not at all. I wasn't even sure why he asked, maybe he had thought we met or something. And he was *funny*. And I could have kept talking to him if he didn't have to leave so fast. And he was nice too, not just 'hello, how are you?' nice, but 'buys his brother baking powder in the wee hours of the morning, nice'. Also, he had excellent taste in brownie mix. *Yum.*"

A small, amused *humph* sound left my friend as she tended to her own wine glass, "His name, you said?"

I squinted at her. I'd definitely 'said' it already. She was only asking to gauge my reaction, my expression.

Savannah was one of those 'people readers' who could do so with annoying accuracy. *Insert eye-roll here.* I had no secrets from Savannah, I also had no say in whether I did or not, she just knew.

"Dax, he said," I looked down while my finger idly circled the rim of my wine glass that was being drained far too fast.

Another *hmm* sounded from her direction and I could feel her eyes on me. I dared a look up and a small smile played on her lips that had my hand twitching to chuck my wine at her. In a loving way, of course.

Savannah had been my best friend since we were little more than excreting machines waddling between our parents' apartments. Apartments that were placed directly across the hall from one another. The doors were always open, and we were always going back and forth.

Same school and same after-school tutor – old and barely alive – but where Sav's extracurricular was dance, mine was hours and hours spent playing the piano.

If I had a spare anything, it was spent on the piano. Any time not spent sitting directly at the piano, with Sav or poking our heavy breathing tutor with a stick fashioned from three pencils expertly taped together, was spent listening to all the music I was learning.

Anything classical called to me like a moth to a flame. The peace of it, the complex simplicity that I felt from both playing and listening was one of the few joys of my youth. My life.

My main dudes *Beethoven, Mozart* and *Bach* were my closest companions besides Savannah, egging me on to conquer my self-doubt and become the world class pianist I dreamt of being, or at the very least – because we all needed a backup plan – to be someone who fiddled the keys for a living.

I passed all eight grades with flying colours (internal fist pump), and then all of a sudden found myself alone, in the very same apartment across the hall from Savannah's family – who were still there though mine had disappeared – faced with an eviction notice and completely broke.

The pet shop I had worked at part-time had an opening in their head office for a Marketing Manager, a position that had been open for a long time and they found themselves eager to fill it. So, I pleaded my case, lied a little on my CV, and four years later I was working the same job.

There you have it. Alice Charlotte Jamison summed up in a matter of minutes. Probably less.

Savannah clapped her hands then rubbed them together after setting down her glass of wine. That meant only one thing - she had hyped herself up enough to voice something to me she knew I wouldn't want to hear, see or do. Great.

"Alright—," she started to say before I, with a mouth full of wine and an empty glass in hand, jumped off the couch in her living room and headed straight for the kitchen to refill, all the while furiously shaking my head.

I swallowed, "Nope. No, no, no. No Sav, I'm sorry I won't."

"But you haven't even *heard* what I was going to say!"

She eyed me with a singular, daunting, dark and perfectly shaped brow as I plopped back on the couch, full wine glass in one hand and in the other I held the bottle. The latter I passed to my friend for her own refill.

"Give me 20 seconds to say it. I swear it's not bad. It's something fun."

"Yes, but it's *your* fun. You did the hand-clap-rub thing. I know, Savannah," I might not be a people-reader, but I was a Sav-reader.

"Allie!" she dragged out the last syllable of my name with an infantile whine.

We just stared at each other then. Fighting a battle that was being waged by the severity of our intense gazes. I folded with a mighty exhale.

"Fine. 20 seconds," her responding smile was so big I smiled too. Dammit. Another massive gulp of wine down, she started to plead her case.

"I have two tickets to see *Lady Luck* in a couple weeks for their second last show in the city and my plus one dropped out. I need you to come with me—"

10 seconds to go.

"—They're mosh tickets, right up the front and I LOVE THEM. PLEASE COME. I DON'T WANT TO GO ALONE. PLEASE!" she made it with three seconds to spare. Impressive.

"*Lady Luck* is punk?"

"Rock," she corrected me. "Well, like rock, punk-rock," the smile on her face was so blindingly hopeful that she knew I had to say yes.

"I have something on though, Sav," I said as I picked invisible lint off my jeans. I never have anything on, everybody knew that.

"No, you're going to hole up in your apartment with string-bean-Dean and play your piano in your room that only has one sad little window."

"Hey!" I swatted the air between us, "Dean is—well he pays the rent and keeps to his space. Plus, he's never late with rent and always lets me have his leftovers." Yes, I was aware that I mentioned the rent thing twice but really, Dean didn't have too much else going for him in my books.

Savannah's face scrunched up at the last point. The very same 'I just walked through someone's fart at the shops' look I had worn myself the night before during my interaction with Dax.

Dax. I wonder what that's short for?

"I don't know Sav. Rock concerts are *loud.* And the lights… " I trailed off.

Her eyes took on a sad, protective look which she dropped almost immediately, but her features did soften from ecstatic to understanding-yet-hopeful.

"Allie, it will be fine. I swear. We will be so close to the stage you won't even be able to see the big lights over the audience and you can wear your earplugs to help," she sat there waiting.

No matter how many times I declined, she'd never stop asking. Even if she found other people to ask. I just *couldn't.* I was working through it, be it slowly, but still. I knew if I said no, she wouldn't push it but doing more of this kind of *stuff* would help me. It's what I needed to do.

I nodded. Folding again, "Okay. Fine."

Her answering *whoop* was enough to make me feel a kernel of excitement over the frantic pounding of my heart.

"Awesome, Al! We'll have to leave for it early, like, maybe around 4PM. But I'll message you again closer, don't worry. The concert won't start 'til 7 but we need to make sure we're one of the first in line so we can be right up front."

"Don't you get your tickets from your work though? Can't we just get, you know, *escorted* to the very front?"

Savannah worked for one of those massive business enterprises that owned all the music venues in the city. When I said all, I meant *all* of them. From the little 'indie' holes-in-the-wall to the stadiums. Same company but hitting every single niche. Brilliant, I tell you. It was safe to assume that Sav had tens of thousands of dollars' worth of free admission under her belt.

"We get to go backstage after the concert, but I got the mosh tickets, which effectively means first come first served. I am determined to make direct eye contact with Wyatt or at least Angus. Maybe get Aspen to wave at me. *De-ter-mined.*"

And when she sets her mind to something, there was little that could stand in her way, I'll tell you that for free.

Groaning as I stood up from the couch on relatively unsteady legs, I grabbed my tote bag, slung it over my shoulder, slipped into my Chucks without even casting a second thought to doing up my laces, and wound on my *skeenie*. Sav's was a 15-minute walk from my apartment.

Bundled up, I looked back and tried to channel the same confidence from the night before, urging it to light up my face like a supernova.

"See you later. It will be fun. I can't wait!" I gave her my most enthusiastic wave. Maybe she was at least semi-convinced by it. Maybe.

Her answering yell was much louder than before and laced with excitable profanities that followed me all the way out of her building and onto the street below.

5

Allie

Like most days when I made my way back from work, I thought about how much I really needed to start cooking more meals at home, and the amount of money I would save if I did meal prep like every other responsible adult my age.

The idea lingered for as long as it usually did – about 3 seconds – before it melted away with the rest of the things I knew I needed to do but would probably never act upon.

I pushed open the door to my favourite Chinese restaurant and waved at Wendy who promptly brought my food over from the kitchen at the back.

"Hey, sweetheart. How are you?" Wendy walked right up to me and gave me a big squeezing hug.

She smelt like sugar. Just way too sweet that it made you wonder what her home would smell like if the scent followed her around so aggressively.

Wendy herself was wonderful though.

"Hey, Wendy. I'm good, just a quiet one," I smiled back at her.

"Alright. Well, you eat up. Go on, I'll see you again soon."

I nodded and said my thanks on my way back out, waving to the guys in the kitchen as I left. It was about a 7-minute walk from my apartment which again, suited me fine.

All I could think about was heading home, changing into my comfies and smashing a bowl of Chinese takeaway that was about a-portion-and-a-half too much for what I needed and then playing my piano for a very, very long time.

I was in the process of relearning *Prelude in C Major,* a composition by *Bach* I played relentlessly as a younger teen, and then, like so many things that were once important and special, I forgot about it. I was quite close to finishing it and my fingers ached to run along the keys.

My apartment building was old, and so were their attempts at safety and security. The door heading into the building itself didn't have one of those things you needed to tap a card on to get in, not even a lock. Even better, you didn't need anything beyond the ability to press an elevator call button to reach any of the floors. I was impressed that they had locks on the apartment doors, to be honest.

I kept tapping my finger on the button for the elevator until it arrived. Much like my philosophy with the crosswalk button, it made the elevator arrive faster than if I had only pressed it once and then just stood there. The thought of doing that actually made me all tingly with anxiety.

Insert entire body shiver, and not the good kind, here.

The elevator carried three scents depending on which corner you stood at; an old gym bag, yeast and, the least offensive and thus my favourite even though it had made my eyes water on more than one occasion, onions. But, for all the poor qualities of the apartment building, the apartments themselves were nice. Well, mine and Dean's was, at least.

Unlocking the door, I kicked off my work boots before heading to the kitchen still with all my winter wear on. By the time I walked the small distance down the hall, I was too hungry to even care, so I set about making myself a bowl of food - *skeenie* and all.

I had just sat down when string-bean-Dean got in from work.

"Hi, Allie," he said while he took off his coat, hat and scarf.

"Hey, Dean," I gave him a floppy wrist wave.

Seeing Dean in his coat reminded me that I still had mine on. I took it off, along with my *skeenie,* and let them both drop directly onto the floor behind me.

Dean constantly smelled like packet Mac and Cheese and wore only one colour in varying shades. That colour was orange.

If you're imagining a peach coloured shirt and terracotta pants that zipped off into shorts, then you're imaging Dean to a T.

I asked him about it once. He said that he tried a minimalist lifestyle for a year, but it never stuck. One of the points was to have multiples of the same thing and to only wear that. To remove any dependency on material items so as to fully embrace life.

I got it. I even thought there was some truth in it, but what I didn't get was how Dean looked at that aspect and thought 'yes, the colour I'd like to wear every day for the rest of my life is just a range of different shades of orange', but there you had it. He was particularly proud of the zip option that converted his pants into shorts because 'they were versatile', he said.

Now you see, this was why he was called string-bean-Dean.

He was the ultimate string bean.

"I got some Chinese, want some? Pay back for your leftovers the other day," I motioned to the selection of meals in front of me with my fork.

"Yeah, sure. Thanks, Allie."

"Sure, sure," I said.

Honestly, I didn't know why I even thought about it but, I assumed he would sit at the kitchen island with me. Don't get me wrong, Dean and I weren't really friends, but it wouldn't kill him to step out of his bubble while he was eating the food I bought. When I ate his leftovers, at least I did it in the common space.

He shouted a thanks down the hallway as he headed to his room and sealed himself inside with a loud bang of the door. It caught me off guard making my breath catch in my throat. My heart rate immediately spiked, and my stomach turned.

I squeezed my eyes shut, gripping the sides of the island for support and just breathed. Breathed and breathed and breathed through it like I always did.

In for 10 seconds, out for 10.

I did that 10 times until my stomach stopped rolling like I was on a ship at sea.

That was good, I got control faster than last time.

I sat at the kitchen island just staring at the half-eaten food in my bowl but not really seeing it. My appetite had vanished completely. Damn it.

I huffed a disappointed breath and closed all the containers of food I had fully intended to eat and put them in the fridge. Just as I was placing my bowl in the sink to wash, a knock sounded from the front door.

I frowned to myself. I hadn't invited Savannah over and she

never came up unannounced and Dean, well, he never had friends over.

Picking up my clothes from the floor of the kitchen, I hung them up as another far less patient knock came again. I opened the door and my heartbeat spiked again for the second time and I instinctively closed the door between us a bit more, hiding behind it slightly.

"Ben," I had intended for his name to sound more like an insult rolling off my tongue, but it was barely audible.

He had the audacity to smile at me like we were old friends, "Hey, Al. Just came to pick up my things."

His things? I hadn't seen Ben in 8 months and all of sudden, there he was at my door wanting his *things?*

"Your what?" I said. The anger that was now certainly making my face flushed pushed any meekness away from my demeanour.

"You messaged to tell me about my stuff you had put in a box? I haven't had time until today to come and get it."

Ah, this 'message' was sent the night we broke up. *8 months ago.*

"Are you *kidding* me, Ben? I sent you that message when we broke up. What makes you think I haven't thrown it out?"

"Have you?" he asked, his eyebrows knitted together as if the thought had genuinely not crossed his mind.

That even though he cheated on me for the better part of our almost 3-year relationship and then, once he was found out, explained that it was in fact *my fault*. That each one of his unfaithful encounters was because of something I had said or done, and that perhaps it was high time that I took a good look in the mirror at the kind of person I was. To have made someone I 'loved' feel like they needed to seek that 'love' somewhere else.

I found it hard to remember any of the good times we had now that it was over. I had considered moving out of the city and moving in with him come the end of the year. He knew I didn't drive but he refused, and I mean *refused,* to move in with me. Dean had even been open to finding somewhere else to live.

All I could say was that I counted my lucky stars that none of that ever happened. I counted them double time that I listened to the little niggly voice in my head that kept on saying *not yet, not yet, not yet* whenever a conversation came to pass about taking the 'next step'. To 'growing' in our relationship.

I was going to puke. I could feel the emotion pulsing behind my eyes and my throat started to constrict. I hadn't thrown out his stuff, it sat under my bed.

I rolled my eyes, closed the door and locked it.

"What the hell, Allie?!" his shout was dampened by the door between us, but it was still very much a shout.

"I'll get your box of shit, Ben, but there is no way in *hell* that you're stepping foot into my apartment," I huffed back at him as I walked down the hall to my room.

I grabbed the box from under my bed making sure that everything was in there. It was. I had made sure the first 5 times I opened the box after I'd initially packed it; I just didn't want to leave anything to chance because I really, *really* didn't want to see him ever again. Ever.

Grabbing the box, I had resolved not to say another thing to Ben when I handed him his shit and watched him leave my life forever. In the 10 seconds it took to walk from my room to the front door, I had once again found strength in the anger that was coiled in the centre of my stomach.

I stopped short, almost dropping the box.

Dean was leaning against the kitchen island talking to Ben. Dean had let Ben *in* and was talking to him in the kitchen.

"What the actual fuck Dean?!" They both turned to look at me like my reaction was completely unwarranted, "Why did you let him in? Did you not think my locking him in the hallway was a clear sign that I didn't want Ben in this apartment?!" my voice was rising with every word that left my mouth and it was but mere minutes before I began to cry, I could feel it.

I wouldn't give Ben the satisfaction. Nope, over my dead body, Ben.

I walked over to him and shoved the box at him.

"There, now please leave."

"Are you sure this is all of it?" he gave me a quizzical look like he wouldn't put it past me to keep a thing or two as a memento. You have *got* to be kidding me.

"Oh, bite me, Ben. That box of crap has been under my bed for the last 8 months. If I hadn't forgotten about it altogether, I would have tossed it out. Now, you have your stuff, and I won't say it again, you are not welcome in this apartment. Now *leave.*"

He just looked at me like he couldn't fathom the disrespect I was hurling at him, like the end of the relationship had taught me nothing. Oh, believe me Ben, it had. I could've written a freaking book on all the things I'd learned.

With one more look down his nose at me, he glanced at Dean and reached a hand out around the box, balancing it on one of his knees.

"It was good to see you, Dean. Let's grab a drink sometime," he offered him a warm smile that I had never been on the receiving end of. Not once.

"Yeah, sounds chill, dude. Let's do it," Dean shook his hand and flashed him a smile in return. I could have popped right out of existence in that moment and neither of them would have noticed.

Ben left my apartment without another word and I walked right up and locked the door, pressing my weight against it until I was sure I could make it all the way to my room before falling apart.

I pushed away from the door and kept my eyes on the floor as I walked back down the hall to head to my room.

"Hey, Allie, you really shouldn't—"

I whirled on the spot, "No!" I yelled, my voice cracking in the process. Well, I clearly didn't make it back to my room before losing my cool as I stood there, a finger pointed directly at Dean, who had never heard me yell in the whole time we had shared an apartment.

"No, Dean," I collected myself and lowered my voice. I didn't yell, I wasn't a yeller, "You had no right to let him in here. This is *my home* too. If I lock someone out in the hallway, you don't let them in. Not without at least asking me first. It is none of your business what has gone on between Ben and I."

"Allie—," Dean tried to start back up, but if I knew Dean – and I did – it would've just been a reworded version of what he was going to try and say to me the first time, which was that I really shouldn't be so rude, and that Ben was a nice guy.

I walked away completely ignoring him, and when he called my name one more time, I called back down the hall, "Poor form, Dean!" before sealing myself inside my room to sit at my piano and play.

And play and play and play.

* * *

I didn't sleep well. I didn't sleep at all really, until the sun came up and I dozed off for about ten minutes before my alarm rang.

I dragged my feet all the way to the kitchen where I sorted out the drip coffee machine to do its thing while I scaulded myself in the shower. I stood there for so long that I thought I actually fell asleep and then I ended up with no time to wash my hair. Yay.

Tying my robe around me, I made my way back to the kitchen and grabbed the largest mug I owned, filling it all the way up before going back to the bathroom to dry my hair and apply a small amount of makeup. I didn't usually wear make-up, but the bags under my eyes were large enough to store a small fortune so today was an exception. The thought had me looking at the expiration date of a lot of the things I had in my makeup bag. Most of which I had owned since I was 18. Now being 25, let me verbalise your exact thoughts: *Nasty*.

Did I put it on my face anyway? Of course.

I drained my coffee and threw on some black stockings and a blue dress before running out the door, still hopping into my boots and wrapping on my *skeenie*. I was late. I blamed the shower-snooze moment I had. Well, really, I blamed Ben.

3 years of my life. I had made peace with it now, but mostly when I looked back on that time and saw everything I so stupidly looked over, I got angry. Angry at myself, angry at him, angry at Dean (just because he was there). Everyone, really.

The world was my enemy when I reflected on those 3 years

of my life and it took a long time to stop blaming myself for his endeavours. Because I had believed him, I had thought there was something wrong with *me.* I didn't think about Ben anymore.

It was colder this morning than usual, and a fine mist hung in the air like a big cloud had fallen all the way from the sky overnight and fell asleep along the city streets. I gripped my tote over my shoulder a little tighter than usual, hoping that the tightness in my muscles would warm me up.

The reality that there was a coffee machine at work that was, most importantly, free for staff members was the only thing powering my steps. Darting in between the other busy on-foot commuters, I tried to get from point A (my apartment) to point B (my office) as fast as possible without rubbing shoulders with too many strangers as possible. I hated it, walking in a crowd and having person after person rub *their* shoulder on *yours.* A shiver of repulsion went through me at the thought.

I was about to cross the road, consistently tapping the button for the little man to light up, ignoring the stares of everyone around me who thought I was a lunatic, when I saw him across the street.

The shoes were different, the pants and jacket were different too and his collar was down. But there was a guy walking the way I had just come on the other side of the street with red hair and my stomach flip-flopped. It flip-flopped and started doing the tango with the rest of my organs.

I started pressing the crosswalk button so fast that my arm began to cramp. And before you ask, no, I didn't cross the street unless the man illuminated. I was a law abiding citizen.

I was going to run after him like a crazy person. I really, *really* didn't want to. I even tried to make a pros and cons list in my head to try and work through it, but I just felt like this was my chance, you know? Maybe it was meant to be that I saw him again.

Dax, from the baking aisle.

The light changed and I sped walked across the street back the way I had come from, away from my office. That's when he stopped and turned to speak to the person who was walking just behind him. I hadn't even noticed he had been walking with someone. As he turned, I saw his face.

I felt my whole-body droop, just totally deflate like a balloon.

I turned myself back around and walked the last couple minutes to my office building.

I was absolutely losing it.

I was just about to run after a *complete stranger* who I thought was someone I literally didn't even know. Someone I met for 20 minutes and that was it, story over. What would I have even said?

It didn't matter anyway. It wasn't him.

6

Dax

I could see every single person in the crowd.

I was looking for her. I was looking before I even *realised* I was looking.

Anyone with hair a similar shade, or really anyone at all. I looked and looked, in between every single song, and I had absolutely no idea why. She didn't know who I was.

I feel like a massive french fry.

The boys were insane tonight. As a unit, we always complemented one another. But everything, *everything* went so right tonight. It was the perfect way to kick off the end of our last leg.

After the show, as usual, we all packed up in Aspen's black sedan, and at this point I was honestly surprised the car hadn't died - it was over 20 years old. So old that it shouldn't even be on the road, but no matter how many times we piled in and the ancient suspension let out a back-cracking groan, we always arrived safely and in one piece wherever we were headed.

Ap called the car his lucky charm, which I thought was kind of nice. It had been my car first, before I passed it down to him when I left home for college. Needless to say, that was an experience that was short lived.

Dropping the boys off at their houses, we all had to be packed and at the airport in two hours. We were flying across the country for two shows back to back before we got to come back home, decompress for a couple days and then finish off the tour here.

This had been our biggest tour yet, and it felt like it too. We had been to more places than ever before, played more shows – bigger shows – and were on the road for longer.

When they asked us if we wanted to start or end the tour at home, we all said 'end' without hesitation.

I shoved enough clothes for a few nights into my duffle bag, chucking in my essentials and then packed my backpack with things for the plane. It was going to be a long flight and I couldn't sleep on planes. I wished I could, but I always liked to look out the window. To see it all.

In a life that was as loud as mine – a life I loved – but one that was overwhelming, it reminded me that it could end at any time, that I was so *small* in the grand scheme of things. It gave me perspective. It reminded me that I was lucky. So, I could never sleep because I was always looking.

Aspen yelled for me from where he was waiting in the living room.

"Coming!" I called back, then grabbed a notebook and pen to throw in my backpack for any last minute lyrical inspiration that flew my way.

When I say that it happened anywhere, I seriously mean it. My notes section on my phone was full of lyrics, but when I could, I preferred pen and paper. And let's not even approach the voice memo app. If anyone were to play them all one after the other, they would have a hard time believing what I did for a living.

"We're gonna be late, Dax," Aspen said, giving me an exasperated sigh as I walked into the living room.

Aspen was always on time. He was the reliable, planned, scheduled, responsible person in the band. So, being even a minute behind schedule was like a deflated soufflé to him. Those were his exact words.

We walked out to the front of our building where a car waited for us. Our driver was new, so we didn't know his name, but he seemed like a nice guy. He complimented our music and mentioned his daughters were big fans then requested a photo op before we boarded our flight.

Ap and I talked about a few things from the show that we thought were especially good, like Rip throwing in a random new riff into one of our songs and how it had elevated the entire pre-chorus. Aspen thought we could re-release the song as a single with the altered guitar, and as usual, my kid brother was on the nose. His ideas were always amazing, and I made it a point to tell him exactly that as often as I could.

Ap and I had snapped a photo with the driver before we grabbed our bags from the boot of the car and walked inside the terminal.

We were dropped at a different part of the terminal than the main entry, a bit more private where we were also taken through a private security screening room. Even though we tended to fly late to avoid the bigger crowds, there were always concerns for everybody's safety anytime we moved from one place to another, so we got used to the precautions that were put into place. I don't think I even remembered what the regular front of an airport looked like anymore.

We walked into a private room where we waited until our plane was ready, and we'd be seated after all the other passengers had boarded.

Also, I'd like to clarify that no, private jets weren't always ideal or economically sound ideas, regardless of what our profession was. So, we took regular commercial planes the same as everyone else.

Angus was sitting down, on his phone. In front of him was a pile of bags that Ap and I added to. There was a lot of space in the room they had put us in but we tended to huddle, hence the pile of bags.

Rip and Luke left to get something for us to eat - my request for just a packet of chips - while I sat down in the chair next to Angus and waved at a rest of the crew. Some of the team had already left on a previous flight.

I pulled out my phone and scrolled through Twitter. I sent out a message letting everyone know that we were heading out for the following final shows and we couldn't wait to see them. I settled in and fully intended on spending the rest of our waiting time to board responding to fans who were commenting on my tweet.

I was so absorbed that I didn't even notice Jenna come into the room and sit right next to me. Not until she bumped her shoulder into mine. Angus, the not-so-subtle prick, pretended he got a call and walked out of the room. Aspen said he saw something out the window that he needed to get a closer look at from outside of our waiting room. There was literally nothing to look at except for an empty tarmac, dickhead.

"Hey, stranger. You're a hard guy to get alone!" she said, holding her cold beverage in both hands and sipping it through a metal travel straw.

I gave her a small smile and put my phone away. I didn't particularly want to speak to Jenna, but I also wasn't a jerk.

"Ha, yeah," I reached up to rub the back of my neck before pushing the hair out of my face. I really wanted to just pull it all forward and count to a hundred until she left but, again, not a jerk, "It's been crazy these last few weeks with the end of the tour," I responded, leaning forward in the chair resting my elbows on my knees.

"Yeah, absolutely! Oh, that reminds me. You still have something at your place that you wore on stage, Phoebe keeps asking me to get you to bring it, but I keep forgetting. Next time you remember, bring it, 'kay?" she took another sip of her drink.

"Sure, sorry," I said and silently hoped that was the end of the conversation.

Jenna had been my girlfriend. A very long time ago.

She'd come onboard in the hair and makeup department to help Marco out when things took off for us and, well, Jenna was attention grabbing. That was really the perfect way to put it. You couldn't walk into a room and not look directly to her first, she just *commanded* any space she was in. Something I had experience with too, so I guess I gravitated to her because I thought we stood on common ground.

I tried to stand on that common ground with her for 10 months and then she just called it off. I wasn't surprised at all if I was being honest.

I tried; I really did. I had liked her a lot at the time, but even though she toured with the band, our relationship just fell by the wayside. When we had a break over Christmas time, things were fun. We had a great winter together, but the rest of the relationship just muddled into itself and before I knew it, she had packed her things, called it quits, and went to stay with Phoebe from the outfit department.

Jenna and Phoebe had been in a relationship now for the last three years and I was, and I seriously did mean this, so stoked for them. Phoebe was great, and just because Jenna wasn't for me, didn't mean she didn't have good qualities too.

When Jenna told me she and Phoebe were exclusive, she had really turned up the pity party. I kind of just sat there and stared at her as she assured me that it wasn't my fault and I didn't turn her off men so 'don't think that for a second'. And ever since, she hadn't really stopped with that attitude, as if her relationship continued to wreak havoc on my heart. That she was the reason I was alone. I assure you; she wasn't.

All the above being considered, I still tried to be her friend, but Jenna was *a lot*.

"So, how *are* you, Dax?" she asked.

Her use of my nickname bothered me. It was saved just for family and the guys. It sounded *off* coming out of her mouth more than anything. She alternated though, when she wanted to get deep and meaningful, she called me Dax. When she had no interest in talking beyond your standard 'hi' and 'bye', she used my first name, Wyatt. So, I knew exactly the sort of conversation this was going to be.

"I'm good, Jenna. Thanks. You?" I replied, turning my head to look at her from my position, still hunched over my knees.

"Yeah, I'm good, hun. Really, really good! Excited for some down time with Phoebs, it will be a proper dream." She smiled and then frowned a bit, as if mentioning her girlfriend was a no-no in front of me.

Before I could even reply she leaned closer to me and spoke a bit softer, "How are you *really*, Dax? Is everything okay?"

Please, no. Not this again.

"Yes, Jenna I'm good. I'm keen for some downtime too. Maybe sleep in for once," I laughed lightly to try and emphasise how okay I was, anything to avoid this conversation.

"You know," she went on, not picking up anything I was putting down, "I was thinking, I have a friend who you would really, really like! She also really loves your music, so that's a great icebreaker!"

Here we go.

"Thanks Jenna, but I'm actually pretty good on the whole dating thing."

"Dax," she gave me a pointed look, "You haven't had a girlfriend since we broke up, you know, and that's over 3 years ago now," she put her hand on my shoulder and it literally took all my strength not to shrug it off.

"What are you talking about? I've seen plenty of people since we broke up, Jenna. I've told you before I have no internal squabble about you and Phoebe, I'm happy for you. For you both," I said and offered her another warm smile to show her I meant it.

"Mmm," she said, frowning to herself a bit. Her eyes scanned my face like she was reading me. I wasn't sure what she was reading because there was literally nothing beyond the words I had already spoken to her, "I know you *say* that, but I just don't *feel* like you're being completely honest, you know?"

"Jenna—," I started, but she was committed to the conversation.

"Sleeping with someone is not the same as seeing someone, Dax."

I huffed a breath and leaned back in my seat, scooting all the way down so that my head was leaning on the backrest,

"That's really none of your business, Jenna," I mumbled.

I really didn't want to be speaking to her about this. Like, at all.

"Of course, it's my business, silly! We're friends, and when you're worried about your friends you try and fix it."

"Fix it?" I was stunned, the bite in my voice was hard to keep at bay. I knew she didn't do this to crawl under my skin, but I had told her and *told* her so many times.

She didn't let up, "You're so emotionally unavailable and you weren't like that when we started dating. But towards the end and all the way up until now, it's like you just turned off all your feelings. I'm sure that if you get out into the world and date, you'll see that things don't have to be this way."

"What way?" I asked back.

"You don't have to be so...I don't want to say the wrong thing here, but finding someone might make you better."

"Make me better?" I felt like a parrot.

"Yes! Exactly, oh, I'm so glad you're getting it. Carly is *so fun.* You will absolutely love her," Jenna pulled out her phone, presumably to text her friend that I'd agreed to a date. I was sure I was not the only one here who could clearly see I'd not done that in any capacity at all.

"Jenna, I don't want to go on a date with your friend," I said, trying to sound firm, but still trying my hardest to be civil.

She looked up from her phone wearing a mask of confusion, "But you *just said—*,"

"I said nothing Jenna, nothing," I stood up, not really wanting to be next to her anymore, "I am *fine.* I literally tell you the same thing every time you have these conversations with me. Conversations, by the way, that are not your place to have with me at all. It's been *years,* Jenna, since we dated—"

She cut me off, "That's *exactly* what I'm saying!"

"Then stop talking for a second and just listen to me," I'll admit that my voice raised a little higher than I would have liked, but she just *pushed and pushed.*

She sat there, and leaned into the back of the chair, showing me clearly that the floor was mine with a little head tilt to the side and raised one of her eyebrows like I was delusional and she could humour me if she had to.

"I am not *broken,* Jenna. You do not need to fix me. And even if I was broken, it's not your job, or your place, to try and do it. I am fine, I have been fine since we broke up. We dated for 10 months, not years. It was great, yes, it was a nice time, but it ended and that's fine. I am not mad, or sad, or crushed about it. I feel nothing but actual happiness for you and Phoebs, she's awesome and that's great. It is. But I don't need you constantly, and I mean *constantly,* talking to me and about me – because I know that you do – to other people about the state of my emotions and my personal life. This might come as a shock to you, but our breakup was not the end of the world, for either of us. So, I need you to stop, because I can be your friend, but not like this. You cross a line every damn time you do this Jenna."

"But—," she went to cut in again.

"No, I'm sorry, but no. I'm not having this conversation with you, now or ever again. I'm done, leave it alone. Okay?" I looked at her, hands at my sides just waiting for her to reply.

I was breathing heavily, and it took everything to just keep the anger out of this conversation. I hated how she spoke to me, *hated* it.

She just nodded. That was good enough for me.

I turned to leave the room needing to walk off the ball of

restless energy that now sat in the pit of my stomach. I came up short when the guys and the two security guards that were travelling with us were standing in the doorway just watching it all happen like it was a live theatre performance.

Great. I just put my head back down and kept walking. They got the hint, and all shuffled to the side to let me pass.

"Flight boards soon!" Ap yelled out to me as I walked away.

I raised my hand in confirmation that I wouldn't be long.

Emotionally unavailable.

I wasn't emotionally unavailable. Things worked well when I focused on one thing at a time.

My mind was sort of set up like a storage locker, or maybe like a house where everything was still packed away in boxes, but everything was labelled clearly.

Jenna was packed away tight in one of the boxes that was further towards the back, so to speak. That time of my life wasn't something I thought of or reached for, but it was there, nonetheless. Everything was. Every birthday, every holiday, every girlfriend or break up or studio session.

It was all there. Compartmentalised. I only unpacked a box if there was something in it I needed. I'd always been that way and it always worked. Always. I'd never needed more than that, never *wanted* more than that. The stuff I never reached for? It never came up and I never thought about it.

Some people had journals; some people meditated.

I had my life packed up into boxes, and it worked for me just fine.

* * *

The guys had already boarded the plane, Luke, Angus and Rip

in one aisle and then I was supposed to be by the window, as I always asked to be, with Aspen in the middle and Jake, the security guy, was next to him.

I had to step awkwardly over their knees to get to my seat. I wasn't late but in standard Aspen style, he had everyone board as soon as we were told it was our time, so even though we had another 10 minutes before the doors closed, here they all were.

"Hey, sorry," I said after I had sat down, shoving my backpack under the seat in front of me where more of the tour crew were buckling in for the flight.

I didn't see Jenna, but I also didn't look for her. I didn't feel bad about anything I said, I didn't.

"All good," Aspen said, giving me a smile. He didn't mention anything about what had happened with Jenna, and I'd wager he passed on that advice to the other guys too. They wouldn't have said anything though. They all knew how she was with me and no one particularly appreciated it.

Eventually the captain came on the overhead speaker and gave us more information about himself and the type of plane we were on, how long the trip would be and the flight path they chose while the plane taxied to our runway. And then, just like that, we were off. The lights of the city below were beautiful. That was another reason I loved to fly at night. You could see all the lights that weren't visible in the day.

The seat belt sign turned off when we reached altitude and the cabin crew let us know that food and drinks were coming by soon, and that they would do that twice. I took off my seatbelt and reached in my bag for my headphones and my book. I was reading a mystery-thriller and it was just getting good. I grabbed my chips too, always preferring to bring a snack than buy a snack.

I put down the food tray in front of me to lean my book on and I was scrolling on my phone to find a playlist to listen to when I unintentionally tuned in to the guys' conversation they were having behind me.

"—alley. I've heard so many good things, bro!" Rip said with a hefty amount of enthusiasm.

I yanked my headphones out of my ears and turned around in my seat. Not ideal, as the move caught the attention of most of the other passengers on the plane and since I had started sporting the red hair, people saw me very quickly and recognised me just as fast. A few very audible gasps sounded as those who might not have known we shared their flight now became painfully aware. I offered a small smile to the rest of the plane, but it wasn't at the top of my lists of concerns. Not when Allie's name had just been plucked from my mind and thrown out into the world like that.

"Did you just say Allie? You know Allie?" I asked. My heart was going so fast. The girl from the baking aisle found her way back into my head. How did Rip know Allie?

"What?" he said. He looked incredibly lost.

"You just said you knew Allie," I replied, expectantly.

"I was just saying that there's a huge river and *valley* you can see from a lookout where we're going. It's supposed to be pretty cool and I thought we could all go for a hike while we were there."

I just stared at him while my brain caught up to what my mouth had done. Aspen was definitely going to be telling them about Allie now.

I slid back down into my seat, slouching down as far as I could go and put my headphones back in. My face felt as red as my hair. I was trying to find a song to put on as quickly as possible, but not before I heard Aspen start to sing quite loudly, "Wyatt and Allie, sitting in a tree. K-I-S-S-I-N-G..."

7

Allie

Sav and I had met at our usual Italian place that was right between our apartments. It was just around the corner from work, so I ended up staying a bit longer to tie up some loose ends for the day.

Work had been non-stop for the last few days with the end of our campaigns on the birdseed coming up, and a last minute effort to optimise our ads to surpass our targets meant all hands on deck. Needless to say, I was ready to be swept off my feet by the weekend. Dean was meant to be out of the house which was just an added bonus.

I had ignored him for the better part of the week after his less than impressive foot-in-mouth situation regarding the whole Ben thing. I finally said hello to him yesterday after he greeted me first, then he told me he was heading out of town for the weekend. Maybe he did it on purpose to give me some space, but I doubted it. Unfortunately, string-bean-Dean was a bit too dense to have thoughts like that on his own.

Regardless, I wouldn't be sharing my takeaway with him any time soon.

I got to the restaurant before Savannah so when they seated me at our table, I ordered two glasses of our favourite wine and scrolled on my phone until she arrived. I was so deep in thought that I didn't realise she was there until she grabbed my face in her hands.

"You spend too much time on your phone," she said by way of greeting, and leant down to kiss my cheek.

I waved away her comment. She said it to me all the time and I definitely agreed but, being on my phone for *work* and being on my phone for *me time* were two completely different things. If only my eyes knew that and only generated migraines when it was the work portion of the screen time.

Sav sat down and took a grateful sip of her wine, making an *ahh* sound after that made me smile. She'd had an intense day. One of the things with working at a music venue was that they were constantly battling the rip-off tickets game.

There was a matinée on today and they had over 200 people arrive who had purchased their tickets off a reseller who botched up all the tickets and disappeared from existence. To say that was a shitstorm was an understatement.

"The saving grace and light at the end of the tunnel is seeing *Lady Luck* next weekend. It's what's pulling me through the hard times right now," she said dramatically as she took another sip of wine.

Before I responded back with some news that she was going to find absolutely thrilling, the waiter arrived for our order. We only ever got the same thing, so I ordered two plates of mushroom and truffle ravioli and some garlic bread, as well as a second glass of wine for Sav, which she shot me a grateful look for.

Sipping from my own glass, I set free my declaration, "I

have been listening to some of *Lady Luck's* music this week," I said proudly, smiling from behind my glass as I took a second swig and set it down.

"No!" The smile on Savannah's face was striking.

"Mmhm, I have," I said, matching her smile with my own.

"Which album? Hold the phone, *Allie*!" she gave me a face that translated to 'I can't believe you're listening to music from my favourite band just so you might be able to sing along at the concert with me' then reached over and squeezed my hand.

For Sav, it was always the little things that made her feel loved.

I squeezed her hand back before playfully tapping the back of it to lighten the mood and my sappy friend, "The one with the rose and thorns on the front. There are maybe three or four songs I really like on that one. Though, I have to be honest, the names are confusing because they don't match any of the lyrics," I knew I was frowning at my own thoughts.

Savannah laughed, "I know! What ones?" she prompted.

"Oh, uhm, I like the song *Run.* I also like *I'm leaving with the money whether you give it to me, or I take it right out of your hands,* that's the one that stumped me a bit. And the last two are *Anything to Take You Home,* and one that says something about a cemetery."

"Ooo! *Carve This on My Headstone?* That's my favourite too!" she squeaked.

"Yep! That's the one. I haven't listened to their other albums yet, but I figured a few off the newest one was better than none at all," I said.

Our food arrived on the table and I picked up my fork to dive in. I was starving.

"How did you even get the songs?" Savannah asked over

a mouthful of pasta as she shoved some garlic bread in her mouth. She was not a graceful eater, I loved it.

"I bought their CD," I said around an equally large mouthful of my own food. I was not a graceful eater either.

"You bought a *CD?!*" she was baffled.

I nodded my head with high eyebrows, "Mmhmm," I said as I reached for my glass of wine.

My eyes caught on a figure at the front of the restaurant. Savannah was still talking about something to do with how CD's were a dead technology but all I could do was stare.

A man, a tall man, stood facing away from the main dining area and he was wearing a long black coat that reached all the way to the floor. The collar was turned up and he was wearing a black beanie.

I stopped chewing with my mouth still full of food, and it was like my whole body was in a trance.

After my experience at the start of the week, I had pretty much given up hope of running into Dax again. I had convinced myself that it was one of those missed opportunities that you always see people making movies about, the dwelling on the *what if*, but I took in the figure facing away from me, his clothing and his height. I was convinced all over again that it was him.

Maybe fate heard my pathetic inner monologue and the rapid tapping of the crosswalk button when I thought I saw him on my way to work.

The blood was rushing in my ears and I was breathing heavily through my nose thanks to the gob-full of pasta and bread that now resided in between my pearly-whites. I just couldn't look away from him.

Savannah moved her head in front of my view, obviously

catching on that I wasn't present in whatever conversations she was having with herself. I moved to look around her as she started waving her hand in front of my face, but absolutely nothing could break my stare.

The guy reached up his hand moving to pull off his beanie. As his hand got closer to his head, my ass lifted higher off my seat. I was going to run for it.

He tugged off the winter hat and I landed painfully loud back in my chair. His hair was blonde under the beanie. Any of the bits sticking out were hidden by his upturned collar.

I was actually going insane.

"Earth to Allie," Savannah was now lazily waving her fork with a piece of speared pasta on the end in front of me. Like she had given up using her hand to wave because she'd been doing for so long and it was too much effort.

I quickly chewed and swallowed the food in my mouth and took a quick sip of wine.

"Sorry," I mumbled, my head dropping down a bit as colour no doubt filled my face.

"What was that?" she asked.

"What was what?"

She gave me a look that said, 'it's written all over your face so spill.'

I cleared my throat, "I thought I saw the guy from the baking aisle. He looked the same from the back with the hat on," I said, I winced a bit at the memory of my first episode of thinking I'd run into him again, knowing I was about to tell that to Savannah too.

She knew something else was up, *"And..."*

"And I thought I saw him on my way to work at the start of the week too," I said it very fast and with my eyes closed before shoving more food into my mouth.

Her inhaled gasp was incredibly loud, and what was then followed by a whispered shout, "Allie!"

I rolled my eyes at her, "It's nothing."

"Oh, it's not *nothing.* Someone's caught your eye! This is good, Al! I think it's high time you jumped back on the horse; you've been off it long enough."

"It's not like I decided to jump off the horse myself, Savannah. It reared up, I fell off and then it kicked me in the face as it ran away only to come back every 8 months to steal my damn apples."

She frowned at the last bit; her mouth opened to enquire but I shut down that line of conversation toot sweet, "It's nothing, don't worry. Just being dramatic."

"And you didn't get his number?" she asked, though she knew I didn't.

"Nope," I replied, popping the 'p' at the end.

"Well, you know what you should do?" she points her fork at me again, this time, pasta free. I had just taken the last bite of my own meal, "You should periodically check the corner store! You said his brother bakes, right?" I nodded and she continued, "Well, he will need something else baking related eventually."

She had a point.

"It's whatever, it was just a conversation. I'm just, I don't know, tired, I guess."

Savannah gave me one of her looks again but, mercifully, let it pass. She pushed me, *a lot,* but she also knew when to let it go.

* * *

I was eternally grateful for the walk home if only to try and burn off some of the food. What could I say? I loved having big dinners, it was just so satisfying. So, the 10-minute walk home was welcomed especially as the streets were near empty.

I was happy to walk. Anywhere and everywhere. Driving? Not so much for me anymore. I could be *driven* places, which surprised me too. But driving myself? No.

Three years ago, I was doing just that. I was driving home from work.

As I was merging onto a freeway, I had my classical musical blaring through my car speakers – I knew it wasn't the standard thing to blare but, whatever - and I was loud-humming along to all of it. Every single note I heard was branded into my brain. I noted every dip, every drag and hold. Every rise and fall. It was wonderful and no, I didn't listen to that song anymore.

The drive wasn't too far, 20 minutes to the apartment I lived in just outside the city, all on my lonesome and not too far from where Sav and I grew up. I knew the drive so well that I could've told you the seconds and minutes between every merge, every turn, every stop sign I came to, and whether the road I was getting onto tended to be bumper-to-bumper or not-so-bad at the time of my commute.

I was probably a minute from exiting the freeway when a truck was merging onto the very same road. The breaks had been faulty, and it was a merge from a decline. I didn't see the truck fast enough, didn't hear the loud blaring horn that rang for far too long until I caught the big, massive lights in my mirror. The impact caused my car to flip five times.

The driver of the truck was fine; bruised ribs and a tender face from his seatbelt and airbag, and the impact of his truck hitting my car managed to slow him down. I didn't remember anything after the sound and the lights, but I could tell you that my car was very small, and very old.

I spent 6 months in the hospital and was labelled with so many injuries that it went over two pages. Broken ribs, internal bleeding, whiplash, soft tissue damage, a compressed spine and my whole face was purple from bruising and swelling. My right leg was broken in three different places and I needed surgery on my right hip (yes, every time I went through a body scanner, it beeped). My arm was also fractured. There was more but, you got the picture.

I was very, very lucky. It was weird that I could say that now. That I could feel that way about the accident now.

It was just after I had met Ben, too. The relationship was so new when everything happened. Maybe it was the honeymoon phase or maybe it was that he might have been a totally different person at the start, but he stuck around. I guess for a long time I felt like I owed him something for that, too.

Anyway, after I was discharged, Sav helped me move into the city where I had organised to share an apartment with string-bean-Dean from work. He messaged hoping I was okay, I messaged back saying thanks and asked him what he was up to. One thing led to another and I mentioned I wanted to move into the city ASAP, and he mentioned he was looking for a roommate. The place was only a 10-minute walk to my office. Sav's place was a 15-minute walk away and the corner store was only a minute down the street. So, yes, walking was good, I loved to walk.

There was some trauma that lingered from the experience. Bright lights and loud sounds sometimes triggered my PTSD.

It was like an out of body experience but also like being trapped in your own mind with no doors or windows.

Every time an episode hits me, I see two bright lights behind my eyelids and I hear the aggressive honk of the truck's horn like I'm standing right in front of a semi-trailer. Then I get shooting pains; in my face, my back, my leg, my hip. The anxiety attack that follows makes me feel like I'm shrivelling up like a piece of dehydrated fruit. My hands tingle and go numb and then I can't breathe.

I had learned to manage it, different techniques to calm myself down. Crossing my legs and placing my hands on my chest. To breathe. Sometimes tapping my collar bones helped too, it grounded me. All the things I'd learnt from therapy – western and holistic. I hadn't been in a long time though, things just got to a point and then stopped going anywhere. Stopped helping.

The memory of the accident drifted as the soft melody of *Prelude in C Major* moved through my mind keeping me company, as music often did on my walks. So, when the sign for the 24-hour corner store came into view, it took me a little by surprise.

Savannah's suggestion echoed in my head and I soon found myself standing in front of the automatic double doors which kept opening and closing, sensing me standing out front.

He's not in there.

But he could be. He might be.

He might walk in as I walked out.

What would I even do if I saw him again? 'Hey! I've been trying to find you.' That's not weird at all.

The doors slid open once again and my feet moved of their own volition into the corner store. Craig was there, as usual.

I didn't stop to speak to him, but he did stare at me the whole time which wasn't normal for Craig. I walked around and stood at the start of the baking aisle.

It was empty.

The memory bubbled to the surface and I could see him hunched over and looking for something that was nowhere in front of him, and I could see me, going straight for the brownie section. This was a waste of time, what was I even doing?

I turned to leave, giving Craig a small smile on my way out. That's when he spoke to me for the first time ever saying more than the word 'hi'.

"I didn't know you knew Wyatt Smith, Allie," Craig said. Craig was also apparently from New Zealand. I had been coming into this corner store for over 3 years and I just realised that the only words he's spoken to me were 'hi' and 'Craig' after I introduced myself one time.

I processed that little nugget of information as I answered him, "I don't know anyone by that name, Craig."

"Yes, you do. I saw you talking to him last week," Craig looked at me very intently and I instinctively took a step back because it occurred to me that though I waved at Craig on average twice a week whenever I'd come in for brownie mix for the past three years, I didn't even know he was from New Zealand until tonight. I didn't know Craig at all.

Stranger danger, Allie.

"I think you've been working too many shifts in a row Craig. I have never spoken to a Wyatt Smith in my life," I said, giving him a stern look in return.

"I took a photo of you two in the aisle speaking. I know people get funny when they have famous friends, but you don't have to lie about it," he scoffed like he was genuinely offended.

"I'm not lying Craig, I mean it—," the words got caught in my throat as Craig thrust his iPhone into my face showing me a photo he had uploaded to Instagram with a caption that said, 'Wyatt Smith just came into my work!'.

It was a photo of him and Dax. His red hair was unmistakable.

My insides did a weird thing seeing his face again. My mind had not done it justice.

Craig then swiped to the next photo in the post and it was Dax and I. Me with my hand over my mouth muffling a laugh and Dax looking over his shoulder with a frown.

"Craig, that guy's name is Dax," I said, but my voice wasn't convincing.

"Allie, I think you're the one who's losing it, mate. You spent 20 minutes speaking to the lead singer of *Lady Luck* and you're telling me you didn't know? Yeah, right!" that was apparently the end of the conversation for Craig as he turned around and promptly ignored me.

My brain wasn't working but my body managed to walk me out of the store and plant me in front of my apartment building. I stood outside in the cold just staring at the front door because it had just occurred to me that I had spent 20 minutes in the baking aisle with the frontman of the most popular rock band in modern rock and not only did I have no idea who he was, but I was seeing him live in a week and I was supposed to be right at the front of the stage.

Holy applesauce.

If fate was real and had taken pity on my inner monologue, this was an absolute doozy of a situation.

I pulled out my phone and typed the band name into google. A small gasp left my mouth as thousands of photos of *Lady Luck* popped up. Usually Dax had black hair, but holy guacamole, that was him.

I shoved my phone away and finally took a step into my apartment building.

Holy shit, Dax was Wyatt Smith.

8

Allie

I couldn't feel my hands and it had nothing to do with the weather. I was so nervous I might've actually puked. Lovely.

I couldn't believe I was here. The last week, as one could imagine, consisted of me mapping out how this was going to go down. I couldn't sleep, my brain was so overloaded with plans I might as well have been the blueprint section at your state library.

I was pathetic, which was new for me. I had finally reached the level that I so closely teetered on and usually edged more on the side of quirky, where most people just gave me sympathetic looks and immediately classified me as 'socially awkward'.

One realisation quickly morphed into another as it was never more blatantly clear to me than in that moment of being three hours early for a concert, yet somehow still late, that I just did not get out enough.

The line was already wound around the side of the stadium with easily about a hundred people in front of us. Savannah, however, looked incredibly pleased with the situation and assured me, though I needed absolutely no assurance, that battling them all to the very front of the mosh pit was no problem at all. So close that when Wyatt – who I now knew was Dax – apparently did his signature head shake halfway through their show that we would 'be majestically hit with his sweat'. I mean I really shouldn't have to say this, but ew? Gross.

The hours spent waiting had Sav and I alternating between who would run to the café – not across the street like everybody and their mother was doing – but the one a block over and completely empty, for refreshments and toilet breaks.

Every time it was my turn to duck off it was as if I had never felt such intense relief before in my life. I knew Savannah knew that I was keeping something from her, but I just, I wanted to keep this to myself for a bit, just in case. Just to *see.*

I wasn't sure what I was expecting to find out, but I just wanted to see him first, then I'd tell her. I was sweating so bad, but in saying that, I felt calmer than I could have been. It was either that or I had settled myself so far into delusion that I was now comfortably living in a reality that was no longer my own. Either way, I was fine.

The sun was setting, and the bitter winter wind picked up, making me incredibly grateful for my *skeenie* and my gloves, even though when I met Sav at the base of my apartment building, her face fell with quiet disapproval. I got it, I mean this was a rock concert and I was wearing a *skeenie,* but I'd take it off, of course, and I was wearing something black and ripped under my massive coat, so, I would fit in when the time was right.

Not a second too soon, the doors to the stadium lobby opened and people were being let inside. Tickets were authenticated and scanned, and bags were checked no matter how small they were. Any food and drink purchased outside the stadium was taken and thrown away as contraband, standard, and within 20 minutes we were inside.

My arm being violently tugged by Sav-on-a-mission who went straight for the correct door – perks of working at the venue – and down the stairs, through the gates that sectioned off the mosh area – needing only to wave at the security guard there, Dave, apparently, and used her bony elbows to land us straight at the front of the pit. If I had had my pencil-tower-p oking-stick from our tutoring days, I would have been able to touch the stage.

Holy moly, okay. I wasn't beyond being able to admit that I was a bit excited. I hadn't been to a concert since *Michael Bublé's* Christmas concert in 2011, and at that point, it was riveting. I knew for a fact that I wasn't the only one who claimed that as the 'traditional album of Christmas'.

I tried picturing him up there, the guy I had met in the baking aisle, and I guess I could imagine it, but he didn't seem like a rock star, he was normal? Not that rock stars *weren't* normal, I just meant...I honestly didn't know. This felt very much not like my life.

Out of habit or nervousness, or both, I ran a hand through my hair, fluffing it up and letting the long waves fall to my front. He probably wouldn't even remember me.

The mosh area started to fill up and I really should have known that the 7PM starting time was in fact *not* the starting time, but the 'stage doors open' time, where we would then wait for an extra hour for the lights to dim, and then another

30 for the support band to come on.

The support band was called *Watch Them Burn* – charming – and I didn't really mind them. Savannah sang along with every single one of their songs. Halfway through their set, I took off my *skeenie,* gloves and coat and shoved them into my tote. As predicted, Savannah's approval for my outfit underneath all the layers made up for her initial disapproval, and I did my best to dutifully bounce around with her.

The lights were not flashing nor were they completely turned on but set to cast a medium-lit haze over the audience. The big light show was usually reserved only for the headlining band, and my ear plugs – effective and discrete under my long hair – were completely apt in muffling the sound to where it was completely enjoyable.

I was living in the moment, not thinking about anything else – trying my best not to acknowledge that Dax was in the venue and would be within spitting distance in a matter of moments. Nope. My mind was clear. Very, very clear.

And you know what? I was having *fun.* This was *fun.* An honest to God revelation and the amount of inner pride I felt for myself in that moment was enough to clog my throat with emotion (internal shimmy of celebration).

This wasn't a big thing for everyone, and it never used to be a big thing for me, but it was now. I knew from the glint in Savannah's eyes that it was a big thing for her too. My victories were her victories, and vice versa. The bone crushing hug she dragged me into pushed all the air from my lungs and had me laughing at the same time. It was then followed by my face being squished between her hands and having her yell the lyrics to the song that was being performed right into my face.

I was mind-blowingly stoked, it made me start to get a bit emotional, that was until Sav grabbed my shoulders and mouthed over the music, *"Are you okay?"*

I nodded back to her enthusiastically just as the song came to an end. *Watch Them Burn* took their bow and thanked everyone for their time. They then gave a big, warm, rock-n-roll welcome to *Lady Luck.*

I was crouched down in front of the stage when I *felt* the screams of the stadium reverberate through the floor. A clear sign that the band had walked on stage. My heart was in my throat and I honestly needed to do a nervous-pee so bad that the idea of standing up from my crouch was almost more frightening because of the potential pant-wetting situation that could happen rather than seeing Dax.

I shoved my tote bag just under the gate in front of us and stuffed yet another layer of clothing I was wearing into it. I came to find that mosh pits got very, very, warm. I was now left with my skinny jeans and oversized *'Your face is a work of Moz-Art'* shirt.

I gave myself the world's worst and shortest pep talk. Everything I was going to do and all I had planned went right out the window when I popped up. It was all I could do to slap on my biggest smile and show Savannah I was indeed ready to rock. I probably looked insane.

How was this actually happening though? And why was it so important? If felt important. I shook the thought from my head and tried to convince myself that he would see me and that would be it. No spark of recognition and everything I thought up or perhaps imagined during our meet-cute was just more of me edging towards that 'pathetic' tier I usually lingered just below.

My smile lasted all of a second before morphing into the very same opened mouth trout look that I seemed to have modelled more in the last 2 weeks than in the entire year prior. Savannah, bless her soul, was screaming so loud I could hear the scars forming on her vocal cords despite my ear plugs.

I really wished I could take in her excitement, but my eyes had locked with the frontman of the band. His black boots were laced and buckled halfway up his shins, the skin-tight black jeans that were tucked into them and sat just below the line of his boxers. Seamlessly moving into the faded *Iron Maiden* band-T that he wore and complemented by the weathered – so cool I could choke – leather jacket that also sported a few too many unnecessary buckles (not complaining).

Topping it all off was his face - the very same face that was far too sexy to be in the 24-hour corner store that was a 1-minute walk from my apartment - and the messy, bright red hair.

Dax was on stage and he was looking right at me.

9

Dax

Allie was in the front row.

I was just staring at her, genuinely trying to understand if I was looking at the same person from 2 weeks ago, and how that was possible.

The front row of *my* concert. For the band that *I* was in. The very same Allie that did not know who I was. The same Allie that despite that very real and true statement, I had looked for continuously in every show we had played since we met, since I saw her.

What the hell is happening right now?

She honestly looked like she was in shock, but then her face softened a bit and she smiled, giving me the same quick wave she did in the baking aisle. I might have been on stage, but I could have been anywhere in the world as I gave her a smile and wave back.

My tongue felt like a weight in my mouth and suddenly the probability of my being able to sing and perform seemed entirely out of the question. Allie was in the front row of my concert; I was literally looking right at her.

And then I realised, she'd figured out who I was.

The stadium had erupted with screams so loud the stage beneath my boots rumbled, but my eyes were on Allie, and her eyes were on me. Okay, so, maybe being on stage was a bit of an issue. She without a doubt knew I was Wyatt.

The daze of our intense eye contact was broken when the girl next to Allie grabbed her face in both hands and turned it towards her own before proceeding to scream directly into her face. If I wasn't so shocked, I would have laughed.

It was moments like this where years and *years* of stage persona, performance training and knowledge came into play and without a second to spare or collect my fractured attention, I screamed into the microphone I held, honestly relieved that any sounds came out of my mouth at all.

"ARE YOU READY TO ROCK TONIGHT?!" I held the mic out to the crowd and cupped my ear to show I was waiting for their reply. It was deafening. Even so, and though it was completely untrue, I followed it up with, "I CAN'T HEAR YOU!" and I was certain my teeth shook in my gums from the sheer volume of the crowd, "You might know this one, it's called *Run.*"

Song after song and the crowd kept getting louder. This was why we loved our home city. We were one of them, and they knew it too. My fingers danced along the frets of my guitar as me and the guys got lost on stage, in the electric buzz that filled the air every time we played live.

I ran up to the back of the stage, many times, and stood facing Aspen as he played the drums as I always did, but this time I used it to help keep my attention on the music, to make sure I remembered I was performing live in front of tens of thousands of people.

I tried my best *not* to look at Allie because I desperately, *desperately* needed to focus on the show. But I did, I peeked, and one moment she was there and the next she was gone. Her friend looked worried and dazed, but she stayed put.

After the whole 65 minutes of the concert, the very moment the music ended and the screams from the stadium burst into life, the blonde-haired girl that was standing with Allie, the one that screamed right into her face, made a beeline for the exit. I had never seen someone move through a mosh pit so quickly and with such little friction in my life.

* * *

We set up a meet-and-greet after the show, smiling and signing things from different people, taking photos and asking for names, but I was wholeheartedly thinking the entire time that I had *broken* Allie. Or somehow upset her to the point where she left the concert and it made me *sick*. If she had figured out who I was and then she had run away, well that wasn't saying too much, was it?

Was it because I was trying not to look at her? Maybe I made her feel unimportant. No, surely not, I was playing a show, I was *working*.

Guilt rushed through me then. I didn't lie, but I also didn't really tell her who I was. I mean, I could have but it didn't really feel like baking aisle conversation, and now I had no way to even message her, to find out why she ran out. I had wanted to tell her who I was, what I did for a living, of course I did, but it was 20 minutes in the baking aisle. An easy, effortless, *enjoyable* 20 minutes.

The blonde-haired girl, who had bulldozed out of the mosh

pit and standing to the side with a security guard named Dave, caught my attention.

I stood up abruptly. The kind of stand-up moment where you took everyone off guard, including yourself and all of a sudden everyone stops talking and they're all just *looking* at you, waiting for you to do something.

What is happening? Did I have stage fright? Was that what was happening right now?

Aspen jumped to his feet next to me and leaned in.

"Dax, what are you doing?" he whispered and then leaned around to try and look at my face.

I knew my mouth was opening and closing like a fish out of water. I turned my head between Ap and the girl who was talking to Dave, who was now also looking at me. I managed to convey to my brother in the most incoherent way possible that the girl from the store had been in the front row, and then she disappeared but she was there with *that* girl. At least, that's what I wanted to say, I was almost positive none of it came out except for maybe 'Allie' and 'friend'.

Aspen got the point and asked the security guard to our back, Philip? Peter? Something that started with a 'P' for sure, to grab the girl talking to Dave and see if she could come for a chat after the signing.

With a firm hand on my shoulder pushing me back down to my seat, Aspen patted my back and apologised to the fans waiting in line.

Get a grip, Dax.

The last thing I wanted was for the fans in front of us to think we didn't want to be right where we were, because there was little else that brought me joy like meeting the people that made what we did possible. So, I got my shit together and for the next hour we made every single person who came up to see us feel like they were the most important person in the world, because it was true. They were.

I'd never had to juggle more than one point of concentration at a time. It was probably more accurate to say that I *couldn't.* I *didn't.* I'd always been able to compartmentalise, and probably to a fault. When it was band time, it was band time and I had no problem ignoring everything, and *everyone* else.

Ap was the same and the rest of the guys could split their attention and still got the job done. I guess that's multitasking for you. It's why every relationship besides the one with my brother – and my parents I guess – had never made it to the year mark. Sure, I could have fallen in love plenty of times. When the band was having a break between tours or we were in one spot recording, I was more than capable of being a good boyfriend; loving, doting, spontaneous. But when the band was on, well, it was the only thing that was on.

We all stood up as a unit and waved to everyone before heading back into our dressing room. It was more of a mini apartment with no bedrooms. Just a basic kitchen, lots of couches and to my great pleasure, the blonde-haired girl tagged along with Dave and…Patrick?

* * *

Luke howled as we entered our little back room and was soon joined by the rest of us. Screaming, yelling, making weird noises pretty much just to be loud. You name it, we did it. We met in the middle of the room for our ritual end-of-show huddle, chanted the name of our band three times and then screamed again, and that was that.

We thought as youngsters just starting our band that we needed to do it before and after every show. Now, we just did it because it was tradition and thought it was so stupid that it made us laugh. We tried to drop it a while ago and even though nothing went wrong, the performance felt unfinished until we did it.

I walked over to the girl who was standing next to Dave. "Hi." I lifted my hand in a half-hearted wave.

"Hello!" her responding smile and enthusiasm were very reminiscent of someone who might have met higher profile personnel semi-regularly and held herself together well.

This was a good start.

"I'm Wyatt, and this is Aspen, Luke, Rip and Angus," I motioned behind me to my band mates lounging on the couches.

They all replied with different variations of the same greeting at the same time. The blonde-haired girl leaned around me to wave at the rest of the band.

"Hey guys! I'm Savannah. It's so nice to meet you all, I'm a massive fan," her smile was infectious and bright.

I smiled back with a small nod of my head in thanks. Her own smile dampened a bit as she leaned forward. I leaned forward in reply.

"So, I'm a bit confused as to why I'm back here. Don't get me wrong, I'm stoked and have pinched myself a few times already but, I'm curious," ah, we have a no-shit-Sherlock sort of woman here. Perfect.

This was going very, very well. What were the chances!

"Alright. No beating around the bush then. How do you know Allie?"

Savannah's eyes locked with mine and her hand slowly lifted

to cover her mouth as her eyes widened.

"Oh, my, *God. Oh my god, oh my god, OHMYGOD,*" she began to pace immediately. Okay, so I could deduce that she knew about the baking aisle.

"Savannah—" there was no hope of stopping the inner spiral I could see unfolding before me. All the pieces of this moment, and the moments most likely recounted to Savannah by Allie, were falling into place.

She spun to face me and expertly yelled, "The hair!" right into my face. I will admit I flinched because I knew, *I knew.*

"Wait. Hold up. Who the fuck is *Dax?*"

"Well, I'm Dax," I offered her my least predatory smile. The one that said, 'sure! You can kick my ass if you want to and I won't fight back.'

This was not going well.

Savannah looked at me like I'd grown a pair of boobs right before her eyes.

"It's my middle name. Well, it's a nickname of my middle name. Maddox. Dax, my parents and Ap call me Dax. And the guys too sometimes, but that's just in private. No one knows about that, so..." I pushed my hair back from my face.

I'd not only broken Allie but I'd broken her friend too. She just sort of, stopped. Her eyes got a far-off look and she may or may not have been breathing.

I waved a hand in front of her face but certainly did not go any closer, "Savannah, are you okay?"

"I think I need to sit down," Savannah placed a hand on her forehead.

Dave, the security guard, walked over to help support Savannah as he led her to one of the free couches. I walked behind them and sat down next to Ap. We all just looked at her. Okay, stared.

This couldn't get any worse.

"So, you were at the 24-hour corner store getting *baking powder* for Aspen?"

"Yes, I was. And then Allie showed up and, well, I'm assuming she told you the rest."

A perfect eyebrow rose at that, confirming to me that the whole 'do you know who I am' thing absolutely came up in conversation and Allie thought I was a giant asshole.

Oh, look! How about that, I was wrong. It just got worse. Great.

"I thought she was a *fan*! I didn't know she didn't know me; everyone knows me. Us. It had gone so well after that though. The talking, you know. And I wanted to tell her, of course, but it just didn't come up," I explained to both Savannah and the rest of the guys, all the quizzical looks I got back confirmed that I sounded as stupid as I felt.

Why was this so important? It felt important.

Savannah waved off my explanation, "Yeah, yeah *Wyatt.* I'm not the one that needs that explanation, bucko. Oh my *god,* this makes so much *sense* now. Oh, and she was doing *so well.* Damn. *Shite.*"

"Doing well with what?" I asked, confused. The rest of the guys were still watching this all go down like it was a ping pong tournament.

Savannah waved off my question again.

"Savannah—"

"Sav is good," she interrupted, though her smile was kind.

"Right, *Sav,* well I was hoping for a way to speak to her. Maybe grab her number. I wanted to explain..." I reached up to rub the back of my neck, I was at a loss for words. That had never really happened before.

It was totally the wrong moment, but Aspen reached out and smacked me in the chest with the world's stupidest smile on his face. I shot him a look that promised so much pain he had no idea, but his attempt to muffle his smile had me rolling my eyes. His smile was clearly catching because the rest of the guys were suddenly sitting there with shit-eating grins on their faces too.

Sav looked between us, "*You* want Allie's number?" her expression was pretty locked down, but I could see the similarities to boys' smiles ghosting her face.

"Yes, absolutely. I mean, it would be nice to see her again. Maybe see if she'd want to go out. When we met it was nice—"

Aspen chose that moment to lean over and start to make kissy noises in my ear. I gave him a solid punch in the arm that had him howling out. I offered Sav a pleasant smile and absolutely no explanation. I knew anything that happened here was probably getting relayed to Allie and, so far, I was coming off as the most awkward person ever.

An awkward rock star who doesn't know how to talk to girls. Wonderful. Nice, Dax.

Sav sent over Allie's number with the disclaimer that she was going to, "100% let her know what the name of sweet-baby-Jesus happened, because this was *insane* and not real life and just didn't happen to anyone, like, ever," and wished me good luck. Then proceeded to pass on a direct warning and clear series of events of what would happen to my balls should I do anything wrong by her best friend.

I honestly would have been disappointed had she left without issuing one. Sav seemed like the 'squish my friend's heart and I'll squish your face' sort.

She shot a wink off to Angus and patted Dave the security

guard on the shoulder and headed out, but not before thanking us for the invite to chat over her shoulder and that she'd hoped to see us around. I decided immediately that I liked Sav.

I released the world's longest breath that I didn't even realise I was holding, and let my head fall into my hands. Aspen walked over and stopped before me. His boots, which were pretty much the same as mine, were the only thing in my line of sight and I couldn't be arsed to lift my head from my hands.

"Good luck, *bucko.*"

I lifted my middle finger up to my four band mates who were all happily laughing at what was going to be a very interesting conversation. Even so, there was still one underlying thought that kept coming to the surface of my mind, and that was I couldn't believe my luck.

10

Allie

Work was usually a drag, but today, it was dragging super hard.

My phone buzzed for the first time all day and if there was a world record for 'fastest time to pick up a phone from a desk', I just beat it.

It was Sav.

Savvy: *Hey doll how are you?*

Allie: *Hey, I'm good.*
Just work, you know.
What's up?

Savvy: *Okay, so I have news...*

Allie: *Are you okay?*

Savvy: *yep I'm fine*

it's about the concert.

Allie: *Oh, yeah*
I'm sorry I left early.
I was feeling a bit...
overwhelmed.

Savvy: *No babes, that's fine.*
I understand, but I think you'll
be awfully interested in what I
have to say.

Allie: *Okay, now I'm worried?*

Savvy: *You should come by after work.*

Allie: *Come round to mine?*
I'll be home by 6.

Savvy: *Ugh...but Dean?*

Allie: *...*
Fine
but you're buying me dinner.

Savvy: *Deal. Anything is better*
*than Dean's leftovers. *gag**
Love ya xxx

Allie: *Me too xx*

Well, there was no chance in hell I was going to be able to focus on work now, because I had some pretty massive news for her too, like, 'hey Sav, I randomly met Wyatt Smith at the 24-hour corner store and had *no idea* he was a famous singer and I'm pretty sure he thinks I live under a rock because I was oblivious and then we waved at each other when he was on stage at *his* band's concert and remember when I thought he was an asshole for asking me if I knew him? Well, turns out I was the asshole who not only didn't recognise his life's work and success but also insulted his shoes in reference to baking.'

And then I realised. *Holy fuck knuckle,* she knows. *She knows.*

She knew that I knew that Dax was Wyatt, and that I knew and didn't tell her.

I was going to throw up. This was *a lot.*

I sat with my head wedged between my knees until I calmed down and found something to distract myself with at work.

The pet store Head Office had a relatively large staff base. They rented an entire floor of a fairly new building and I was in the corner for the marketing team. With all our most recent campaigns launched, now we were just monitoring. Seeing how they were performing, making any necessary optimisations to our ads and observing customer feedback and interest. The usual things. We had a lovely large budget for the campaign, so we were just letting it go crazy and I was pretty much free with my time for the week.

I did the tasks that I had to do daily. It was enough to take my mind off the Dax-Wyatt-Savvy situation for exactly 4 seconds.

Emails, social curation for the following day's posts on social media, scheduled those to go up automatically, found a couple of influencers online who would be interested in showcasing a new type of dog shampoo we were selling to their followers.

If you're wondering if people could really be influenced to buy dog shampoo, the answer was yes. People could be influenced to do and buy just about anything and such was the nature of my job.

The best part about living with Dean was that I didn't have to see him at work either. He worked in the I.T. department which lived happily on the other end of the floor. We didn't even commute together. Our whole life-schedules were completely non-conflicting that it practically felt like I lived by myself *except* when Savannah came over.

You would've assumed it was just the leftovers situation and his incredibly vanilla demeanour, maybe even the fact that his voice had never ventured beyond the single tone he used to speak and laugh in. No, I wasn't not kidding. He reminded me 100% of *Squidward* from *SpongeBob SquarePants.* It was also because he had a very unhealthy attachment to my best friend, and he hung around like a bad smell (on top of his usual odour) the moment she set foot in the apartment.

By the time 5PM rolled around, I was so ready to leave that I had been sitting at my desk chair with my coat, gloves and *skeenie* on for 15 minutes already.

I headed home first to change quickly. My apartment was, well it was very *Allie*.

There was lots of wood and all the carpets were beige. As far as a colour went it was incredibly neutral and it balanced out the ridiculous amounts of colour that was splattered everywhere else.

The living room was blues and greens and yellows, but all in moderation, and it also housed a secondhand sofa that I found on Facebook Marketplace for $15. Sure, I had to have it professionally steam cleaned four times but now it was practically brand new. It was a lovely light blue sectional, so I was impressed by that particular save.

The rest of the colour came from chairs in different shapes and lots and lots and *lots* of blankets and pillows. Then there were the plants and the plant pots.

It was full, but not overcrowded and it wasn't dusty either. It was astoundingly clean, and Dean had no issues whatsoever that I took charge of the interior decoration. He got the massive bedroom with the en suite and we halve the rent so, I suppose that was our compromise.

I chucked my keys in the bowl on the hallway table and dumped the rest of my stuff on the chair right next to it. Yanked off my boots and headed straight for the bathroom. I showered, shampooing my hair twice (if you haven't tried it you should and I'll accept your thanks later), then waddled to my room in my towel.

My standard clothing of skinny jeans and big sweater were adorned and after a quick blow dry of my hair, I was wrapped securely once again in all my winter wear. Yes, of course including my *skeenie*, and I headed to Savannah's, where I had to walk by the 24-hour corner store.

A pang of unease went through me as I walked by the automatic doors and a rush of the warm air from inside wafted out to me.

I had absolutely refused to think about Dax since I had run hell for leather from the concert last night (except for just now at work, evidently). I was so convinced I was going to be able to see him up there. This guy I met at the baking aisle, this cool and really nice and *funny* guy, and be able to wave and enjoy the show and then go backstage and see him, fall in love and Bob's your uncle! But then, there he was, and there *I* was, and I had thought about it *so much* that I just, well, I ran. Obviously.

It had occupied my thoughts so much that when the stadium went dark and the big flashing lights turned on that nothing else had pierced my mind. No accident or anxiety beyond seeing him, Dax, *Wyatt,* on stage and trying to convey my coolness in the short seconds our eyes met.

This guy I had thought of nonstop since the awkward first encounter, who I was hoping I might find there again and be brave enough to get his number. But nope, Dax was not normal. He was… whatever he was. He was the frontman to the biggest band in rock and when we met, *I didn't even know who he was.* Not only did that reinforce my loner-loser status but, I felt like an idiot. Like it was all an inside joke everyone knew but me.

All his sexy side smiles became mocking as I looked back at them through my memory bank, and the brownie mix he had claimed to be his favourite didn't quite hold the same amazing taste in my mind as I had originally thought. I felt stupid, which was in itself stupid.

I call this one the 'classic Allie-over-thinker'. It's a move I make often in the comfort of my own mind.

I hit the buzzer for Savannah's apartment and a second later, the electric crunching sound notified me that she had granted me access to the building. She was on the second floor and the door was already open, letting me walk right in. I took off my shoes and winter wear and plopped on the couch where a glass of wine waited for me.

I. Love. Her.

The sounds of the oven door closing shut echoed my way

from the kitchen and Sav rounded the corner not a second later, planting a kiss on my head.

"Hey, Al."

I leaned back and smiled at her, "Hey, yourself. What's for dinner?"

"Frozen pizzas," she sent me a wink.

Hmm. Something was up.

"With garlic bread?"

"Of course," she smiled at me over the rim of her own wine glass.

Definitely up.

I made sure to find my own beverage incredibly interesting while Sav found a way to explain to me what was so important that she'd go as far as to put pizzas *and* garlic bread in the oven for me. It may not look it but that was a lot of effort for Miss T.V. dinner over there.

"I met Wyatt," she looked like a stunned deer, but it got my attention and my eyes flashed up to hers so fast that I knew that she knew I knew that Dax was Wyatt.

"Oh?" I was going to need to know exactly where the bottle of wine was to refill my glass in about 5 seconds. My ears were already burning from embarrassment.

"Mmm. It was crazy. When I went backstage, I was asked if I wanted to meet the band. Naturally I thought it was because of my incredible makeup and, let's be honest, I looked very good in my outfit of choice."

I nodded my head in agreement. Savannah was bangin'. Her platinum blonde hair darkened at the roots and ended in a bob around her chin. I'd never seen anyone able to pull off that haircut but her. She always had her lips painted red, the lipstick was called 'heartbreaker', and it made her blue eyes brighter.

Sav sported an entire sleeve of tattoos that she added to whenever, wherever. She had more that dotted her legs, too. And as if the universe owed her or something, despite this badass exterior, she was also the nicest person to ever exist.

"That's so cool! You met your favourite band," and before you ask, yes, it would have killed me to exude anymore enthusiasm than that.

"Mmm, yes that was very cool," she took a deep breath, "And, so I asked why they'd invited me and that's when Wyatt Smith said that he saw me with you and wanted to know how I knew you. He said, 'how do you know Allie?'"

Savannah took another sip of her wine and the hold she had over her expression was good, impressive even, but it was a telling sign that inside she was bursting with so much excitement she could probably pass out.

"That's so weird. Maybe my name was on my shirt or something," it wasn't. I didn't even know why it would have been.

"Maybe. Could have been, or..."

"*Or...*," I mimicked her, there was no way I was moving this conversation forward. Jeepers, it was so *hot* in this apartment. Why did she keep it so hot in here?

She took another deep breath, "Or it might have been that after I realised who he was, he realised that I already knew who he was and he was the tall, sexy guy with the red hair from the corner store with the baking powder and that's why you ran out of the concert like a headless chicken," it all left her mouth so quickly, if I hadn't lived the events myself, I would have needed her to repeat it with a lot more information.

I let out a long breath. I was caught out, but that was a new record on time taken to figure me out on Sav's end.

I'm getting better. 5 points to Allie.

"Yes, okay, that's all correct. I saw Dax, *Wyatt,* whichever his name is and I had never felt more stupid in my whole life and so I left. Are you happy now?"

Savannah's face fell in a bit of surprise, "Allie, what are you even talking about. This is so exciting!" her face lifted again, and she clutched her wine glass with both hands.

"How is this exciting? I made a complete fool of myself, Savannah! In front of someone who I've only met once and thought I had made a connection with. Who I'd actually begun *looking* for when I was walking on the street? Did you know I went into the corner store once more to see if maybe he was there? Thinking he was my *neighbour*. My neighbour!" I repeated to make sure I got the ridiculousness of this situation across.

"Only to have Craig, the check-out guy, break the news to me like the hermit-living wiener I was. And then I had built it up in my head I was going to be *so cool,* and then there he was in his leather jacket with all the buckles and it was me and *gah,* I felt like such a phoney. I don't *go* to concerts and *rock out*. I was wearing earplugs, for crying out loud!" it all came out in a huff and all of a sudden, I wanted to cry.

"Ahh," she said. Nodding her head like she was picking up what I was putting down. I knew she wasn't. She did that any time she thought I was being ridiculous, then eventually I came to the same conclusion as her and we just moved on. Yeah, well, not this time lady.

"So, that's the end of that," I nodded my head in finality. I would not think about Wyatt Smith anymore. I wouldn't think about Dax either. Because in my mind they were two different people.

One was someone who I got on with and related to – as much as you could relate to a stranger in 20 minutes – and laughed at my jokes and told me I was his *kind of person,* and the other was a buckled up, leather wearing sex-god who sang with the voice of an angel to thousands and thousands of people.

I'm not even going to acknowledge where that thought train came from. We are going to wash right over that like a river flowing around a rock.

"Yep. Sounds good," Savannah said. I was just about to sigh in relief when she dropped the next bombshell, "Except it's not because he has your number and I can tell you that he's already whipped."

"What?! Savannah!" I set my wine glass down softly but firmly. And then my next words to her even shocked myself, "He said that to you?"

Get a grip, Allie.

The smirk she wore was infuriating. She hopped off the sofa to go and tend to the pizzas as she said, "Nope. But I know how to read people and I have never been so confident in something as I am of *that.*"

11

Dax

"I'm still getting some feedback in my left earpiece," I noted to our sound guy, Noah, who was set up to the left of the stage. He held up a finger, motioned for me to first wait a second and then followed it up with a thumbs-up to try again.

I headed straight into the chorus of one of our songs. The feedback from my guitar had stopped and it all sounded perfect. I motioned back to him with my own hand gesture for 'perfect' just in case he couldn't hear me properly.

"Thank you!" I removed the earpieces and let them hang around my neck, lifting off the strap of my guitar, I set it in its stand. I made my way off stage and handed Noah the earpieces, thanked him with a pat on the back before I headed towards the back little apartment-slash-dressing-room where the rest of the guys were waiting. All their individual sound checks were done, and we'd play a few songs as a band later before the main show.

This was the last night of our stadium tour for the album. It was bittersweet but being able to stay where we were for the next few months was a relief too. We had finished recording our next album in the summer and it was coming out soon.

Once it was out, we'd set out to do some press for it and then shortly after we'd pick up and head out on our next tour for the new album. It felt exhausting just to think about it, but I knew after a few months of downtime, the itch to travel and play live would hit us all and it would be nothing but good times ahead.

I opened the door and leaned on the frame, knocking lightly. They all stood up together and we walked out to the parking lot to head home and chill before the show. Aspen drove us all to our apartment. We tended to hang out together especially before the shows. If we split off, sometimes we weren't on the same level and, well, things just always *gelled* better when we were.

I found myself flopped on a chair in our living room. Rip was in the kitchen making a sandwich when he called out to see if anyone else wanted one. Of course, we all responded with a yes to which a disgruntled "lazy assholes" was replied.

Aspen and Angus were playing Call of Duty and Luke was out on our balcony having a cigarette. I was staring at the number in my phone that was sitting under the only name I was thinking of for the past several days: Allie.

"Are you going to invite her to tonight's show?" Aspen asked while his attention remained firmly placed on the T.V.

"Why would I invite her back to the same show she bolted from? Also, she probably has work or something," took a shot in the dark with that excuse.

"Mmm," Aspen replied. I flipped him off even though he wasn't looking.

"Saw that."

But how?

"Dude you're being such a baby about it. Just call her or message her first *then* call her," Aspen went on, his attention on the TV.

"She won't reply."

"Oh, she'll reply," he was incredibly confident for someone who was constantly losing against Angus.

"She won't," I replied.

"She will," he shot back.

"Aspen," God, he was relentless sometimes.

"Dax," he said back, just as sternly.

"Okay! Fine, *fine.* I'll message her."

One text, that was all.

And if she didn't reply?

Then that was that matter settled.

Dax: *Hey, Allie.*
It's Dax, from the baking aisle.
Savannah gave me your number.

The bubble with the 3 dots popped up and vanished 3…no, 4 times.

Allie: *Hello*

Okay. I suddenly had the undeniable and overwhelming need to throw my phone out the window and pace around the apartment.

She replied.

Dax: *So, this is crazy, huh!*

Why…?

Allie: *This is...well yes, it's crazy lol*

The bubbles popped up again. Once. Twice.

Allie: *So, Dax isn't your name then?*

Dax: *No, Dax is definitely my name.*
Or else my mum has had it wrong
for the last 27 years...

Why can't I *unsend* a text message?

Dax: *I was hoping to explain*
after the show...but you left.

Allie: *I did. I know. Sorry.*
I wasn't feeling that great. It gets

really hot in the mosh pit. Did you know that? You probably did. The music was great though, you were great.

Dax: *That's good. That's awesome, thanks, I mean. Yeah it does get pretty hot down there in the mosh!*

Allie: *Yeah haha*

Dax: *Would you like to grab a bite?*

Allie: *With you?*

Dax: *I mean...*

Allie: *Yes, I'd like that.*

She said yes. I needed to go for a run or something.

Dax: *You could come over to mine if you wanted?*

Allie: *Yes, I mean, I would. I don't have a car, though. I don't drive.*

Dax: *Maybe yours, then?*

Allie: *We can do mine.*

Dax: *Okay, cool! What time suits you best?*

I waited.

I waited and waited, and she just didn't reply.

Rip handed me my sandwich and I ate it staring at my black phone screen. I finished the sandwich and she still hadn't replied.

Aspen came and got me when it was time to head back to the stadium for our last show. I didn't want to play. I had never *not* wanted to play. Ever.

* * *

We got to the stadium and jumped straight on stage to run through a few songs as a band before heading back into the back room to get ready.

"Dax, are you with us?" Aspen had his hand on my shoulder as we walked off the stage.

"Mm. Yeah, no, I'm good."

"Sure you are, bud," he left it at that, obviously not believing me.

Jenna and Marco were waiting for us to start getting ready while Phoebe and Lilly, our outfit coordinators, were on the other side of the room sorting out our clothes for the stage.

I had left my phone in the room needing to be away from it for a while. I wasn't really attached to my phone, but it could have been an extra limb after the past few hours. I picked it up and turned it over to unlock it.

Allie: *Tomorrow?*
Is 6pm okay with you?
56 Collin Street.
Apartment number 20.

My smile was stupid. It was stupidly big. I knew it and I didn't care at all.

Everyone else knew it too.

Luke who was first in the chair being airbrushed by Jenna whooped and yelled, "Yeah, baby, she replied!"

"Who replied?" asked Jenna.

"Wyatt's new girlfriend," Aspen chimed in, wagging his eyebrows up and down. I held up my middle finger to them all as I stared at my phone.

She replied.

"Oh my gosh, Wyatt! That's so exciting!" Jenna looked at me with so much excitement she was giving Aspen a run for his money. Her eyes also held this warm sympathy dashed with a bit of pity for me. It made me sick.

I sent her a tight-lipped smile before I moved my attention back to my phone.

This was good. This was really, really good.

Dax: *6pm is perfect.*

12

Allie

"Yeah, hi. Wendy, it's Allie," I said through the crackly line of the phone to my local Chinese restaurant.

"Allie! Oh, it's so good to hear from you, how are you?" she replied enthusiastically. It made me smile every time, she reminded me a lot of my mom.

"Wendy, I spoke to you last week," I corrected her. I could almost *feel* her swatting my comment away as complete nonsense.

"You should just call to say hello, Allie. Maybe even come *in* to eat one of these times."

"Yeah, yeah, I know. I'll come in soon," I wouldn't.

The restaurant had a terrible atmosphere and because it was a 'family restaurant', there were always crying babies. I loved kids, I loved babies, hopefully be lucky enough to have some of my own one day, but for now, I preferred to eat in the silence of my apartment.

"Mmhm," she replied, she also knew I wouldn't be coming in, "Alright honey, what am I getting you? The usual today?" she asked.

"Uhm, yes please. Could I also get an extra of the number 5 and number 19?" Wendy's silence was an indication that she was jotting down the order for the kitchen.

"Company tonight? Is it Savannah? Oh, she's so darling you know how much I love her. Put her on for a hello!" that also made me smile. Sav and Wendy probably got on better than her and I did. Savannah actually *went in* to eat.

"Actually no, not Savannah tonight. It's a friend," that was not the right word but I couldn't exactly tell her that it was the lead singer to *Lady Luck,* who was also the most beautiful person I'd ever met, and he was coming to my apartment, "His name is Dax. He's new."

"Oh Allie!" I had to move the phone away from my ear because if not, her ear-piercing squeal would have been the last thing I'd have ever heard from that side.

"Yes, yes. Very exciting."

Please don't mention Ben, please don't mention Ben.

"Yes, that certainly is! The last time you had a guy was that Ben fella!"

Awesome.

"Oh wonderful, you remember," I couldn't keep the disdain from my voice.

"Of course, I remember. I get so sad every time he comes in here to eat with his new girlfriend. It's just such a shame," she went on 'tutting' at the situation.

"He cheated on me Wendy; it was a blessing not a shame," I piped up. His visit from the other day still lingered.

"Oh, of course, honey. You're absolutely right. Did you want the fortune cookies?" she, thankfully, changed the subject.

"Yeah, I'll take extra if you can sneak them in," I said, the annoyance I felt already simmering away. Wendy didn't mean to; she was just a bit…oblivious.

"Sure can, sweetheart. Have fun! Can't wait to hear all about it!" she chimed.

Yeah, fat chance Wendy. I was never telling her about another romantic endeavour of mine ever again. Not that this was a romantic endeavour. I was just…dipping a toe in.

I ordered the food at 5:30PM and it arrived exactly 30-minutes later. Perfect. The food would still be hot by the time Dax arrived. That was 5 points for me in the hostess department.

I took two bowls out of the cupboard and then grabbed a couple spoons and forks. I assembled everything on the kitchen island in one big tower. It looked incredibly stupid. Just as I was dismantling the leaning-tower-of-bowls-and-C hinese-food, a knock came at my door that caught me so off guard I threw the spoons I was holding. This was going to go terribly; I could feel it in my bones.

I ran quickly to pick up the fly-away spoons, chucking them in the sink before flinging myself at my front door. I smoothed out my dress and ran a hand through my hair. I was so nervous. Why was I so nervous? Why did this feel so *important?*

I opened my front door and there he was. I was still nervous, yes, but I also felt relief. Contentment? Weird.

His hands were tucked into the front of his jeans. He wore some all black chucks with another band shirt that said '*Smashing Pumpkins*' – whoever they were – on it and the same long, thick black coat from the baking aisle.

I was just taking it all in when he spoke. He was gentle and unsure and completely like the guy I had met in the 24-hour corner store. Maybe there was hope for this yet.

Maybe.

"Hi," he said, offering an effortless smile that made his eyes sparkle.

Oh, get a grip Allie you're drooling all over the welcome mat.

"Hey!" I shouted right at him. I yelled right into his face. I cleared my throat, "Hey. Hi, sorry, Hi. Please, come in. The food just got here so you've got great timing," I offered him a smile.

"Shoes?" he asked, pointing to his feet.

"Off is good," I said over my shoulder as I made my way back to the kitchen.

You could see the kitchen from the front door, so I knew I wasn't leaving him blind and unaware of where to go in my apartment.

I grabbed a couple more spoons from the drawer and proceeded to take the lids off the food.

Dax strode into my kitchen after having left his shoes and his coat by the door. His bright red hair and dark clothes oddly fit into the colour around him, not like he absorbed it but like he reflected it back.

I grabbed the bowls and cutlery and took them to the living area where I set them on the coffee table.

This last-minute location change was completely unintentional, but it was better than explaining that while I waited for him, I was fashioning the food and crockery into a tower on my kitchen island. I didn't have to say any of that to him, but I 100% knew that I would.

"Do you want some help?" he asked.

"Uhm, yeah you can grab some of the food, I just thought maybe the living room would be more comfortable," I said as I grabbed as many of the food containers as I could after putting all the lids back on.

This was just going so great, he probably thought I was insane with the word 'idiot' stamped on my forehead.

He smiled at me like he didn't think I was an idiot at all and grabbed the rest of the food before following me to the living room. I sat down on the couch, grabbing a pillow onto my lap as he dropped down with a big exhale. Dax rubbed his hands up and down his thighs before he ran a hand through his hair and looked around, taking in the living room.

"I feel like this room was entirely decorated by you," he offered as a conversation starter.

I smiled, "You would be absolutely correct. String-bean-Dean has absolutely no sense of interior flare, so it was left in my capable hands."

His eyebrows shot up at the mention of my roommate. I thought I slid that in there quite well, actually.

"*String-bean-Dean*?" he repeated back to me with a breathy laugh.

"Yeah. He's okay. We work together and he lets me have his leftovers but he's kind of a…well, he's sort of a jock-strap," my face was scrunched up like I just downed some sour milk.

Dax's head tipped back, hitting the back of the sofa as he let out a proper belly-laugh. It was incredibly contagious, and I was laughing along with him to the point where my eyes were watering and my cheeks ached.

This was *nice.*

I grabbed a bowl and handed it to him along with a spoon and fork. I didn't know if he was the kind of person who ate his noodles with a fork or a spoon, so I kept with my top tier hostess vibe and gave him options.

He took the bowl and the cutlery – opting for the fork primarily – from me as the laughter died down on both our lips.

It might have been the instant feeling of being relaxed and comfortable that overcame me after our joined laughter at Dean's expense, but I felt bold, so I ran with it.

"What's Dax short for?" he looked straight at me then, the smile on his face faltering a little bit, like he had forgotten why he was here. That we didn't know each other, like, at all.

"Maddox. My full name is Wyatt Maddox Smith, my mum has always called me Dax and it kind of just stuck with family. To everyone else I am Wyatt. To the entire *world* I am Wyatt Smith, the frontman of *Lady Luck.* But to the people I care about, the people closest to me, I'm just Dax," he explained this all as he was shovelling food into his bowl, but my eyes were glued to his face and my entire body was frozen.

"So why didn't you tell me your name was Wyatt? I might've known who you were if you had. Instead I've babbled about meeting *Dax* at the corner store, but I didn't even really meet *you.*"

"You've been babbling about meeting me?" his mouth quirked to the side in his sexy smile, still filling his bowl with food.

"Don't change the subject," I countered immediately. His smile grew more at that and then his face became very, very serious. He brought his focus back to me.

"You did really meet me. I am more Dax than I am Wyatt. Don't get me wrong, I love being both," he added, quickly, "I love being on stage and music and the stadiums and the tours, I love it. I *live* for it. But Dax is me without all those pressures, those responsibilities."

Dax's shoulders relaxed, "I guess that's why I introduced myself like that. Meeting you, speaking to you. It felt easy.

Like I'd known you already even though I know I put my foot in it when I asked you if you knew who I was."

I gave him a knowing look that had him letting out a small laugh and rubbing a hand over his face.

"I thought so," his face was squished in a wince like remembering that part of the interaction was hard for him to do.

"Only for a second though. I changed my mind on that pretty much straight away," and then before he could say anything else, I jumped in again, "You thought talking to me was easy?"

I was bewildered. That didn't happen to me. I was always facing the *Ben's* of the world, a little too weird to be *easy.*

"It was a relief. To speak to you, someone who didn't know me and have you talk back to me like an actual person. Not because you were related to me or liked my music. When you spoke to me, you were looking at *me.* It was normal, and you were...," Dax seemed to retreat into his own mind for a second before he turned to look me in the eyes, "You completely surprised me Allie, and I freaked out because if I told you my first name, the way you looked at me might've changed."

I was not expecting that. I was also not expecting to lean forward and press my lips to his without any warning on either part, especially not with keeping my eyes completely open.

Oh fuck.

I pulled back, setting my empty bowl on the coffee table and stood up. I took a step back from the couch – and Dax. My hand came up, my finger moving across my lips that still felt warm and tingly from touching his.

"Oh, I'm so sorry, I...oh, *god*—" I said. I could feel the

emotion building behind my eyes, not because I was sad or angry but because that was entirely embarrassing.

Minus 5 points, minus 10 points, MINUS 10 POINTS.

Dax set his bowl down and stood. His chest rising and falling as fast as mine as he stepped closer, only stopping an inch from me. He was so close that every time I breathed in; my chest touched his. His eyes looked over my face as if he was searching for something, something he shortly thereafter found.

His hand reached out to hold the side of my face, "Is this okay?" he asked. His voice was whispered, and I was eternally grateful that neither of us had started to eat the Chinese food if he was really about to kiss me.

I nodded my head, probably a bit too frantically, but it was good enough for him.

His lips met mine much softer than when I had gone the distance, and I remembered to also close my eyes this time around. I melted into him straight away and was more than happy for him to take the lead. His other hand came up as both of mine landed on his chest. A small throaty sound I didn't even know I could make left me as I felt the definition of his chest beneath his shirt.

The pace picked up and his hands drifted, roaming over my curves hidden beneath my flowy dress like he had imagined every dip and was going through them all just to see if his mental map was right. It wasn't just him; I had thought about this more than I would have ever admitted as I lifted my hands and gripped fistfuls of his bright red hair, earning a throaty groan from him.

Holy shit, this was so hot. *Was this really happening? Mmhm, yep. Yep, this was happening.*

He moved us backwards the way we had come, settling us back on the couch. The Chinese food was completely forgotten on the table. At that point it just seemed like just a bad idea to have ordered such an aromatic food in the first place, but with this whole glorious liplocking moment, that was seriously not even on the horizon of my mind.

He broke away, his eyes hooded with lust and his lips edging towards swollen from the out-of-this-world smooching we were doing. I had no doubt I looked the same and I was totally present for it. He looked over me again before he asked one more time, "Is this okay?"

Translation: 'Is this too fast?' Absolutely not.

"No, no, this is— this is good. This is perfect," the smile my jumble of words earned was enough to have me pulling his face back to mine.

How did anyone know how to kiss like this? I'd never been kissed like this before in my life.

His tongue swept against my bottom lip and I'll be damned if that wasn't the sexiest thing in the whole world.

His hands continued their voyage of my body and I was burning through and through. The sounds that were starting to erupt from me were dangerously close to moans and my hands weren't nearly as satisfied with holding his shirt and gripping his hair like they were just a minute before.

Things were moving very quickly in the direction where there very well might be no clothes involved at all, and then he slowed down the rhythm. Instead of hot and heavy, his mouth on mine became slow and sweet, and then it ended in the most beautiful decrescendo I'd ever witnessed.

The only sounds in my apartment were our heavy breathing as we remained as we were on the couch, him lingering above me and me below, just taking each other in. It was almost more intimate than anything I think we could have done.

I reached up and straightened his shirt before trying to organise his hair back in the effortless pushed back mess he had come in with. His smile was small and did incredibly sinister things to my hormones.

He leaned back and brought me up with him, and just as I had done for him, he did for me - fixing my dress so it sat properly on my shoulders and sorting out my hair. His touch was so gentle. No one had ever touched me like that before.

The pads of his fingers that held proof of his musical talent, lingered across my cheek sending another shiver through my body before he dropped it back into his lap.

We were still staring, just looking. *Really* looking. He was quite beautiful, I thought.

"Chinese?" he asked, his voice still heavy with the rasp of emotion from our meet and greet just now.

"Chinese," I replied and turned to start filling up my bowl.

13

Allie

I learned something valuable during my Chinese takeaway dinner date with Dax: a good, smokin' hot make out session was the best icebreaker ever.

There was heat and want and so much need I could have sworn I was morphing into a damn butterfly. But then he was kind, and tender and a gentleman, and all I kept thinking was that no one had ever been that way with me before. Did that make me the anomaly, or did that make *him* the anomaly?

Just like our laughter at the expense of Dean before all the lip action, our…*moment* lifted any type of veil that had unintentionally settled over us when he walked into my apartment.

I wasn't sure what I expected. If you had asked me if I thought it was going to go well when I shouted my greeting right into his face as he stood in the threshold of my home, the answer would have been no, without a doubt.

The time between meeting Dax and then finding him sitting on my $15 Facebook Marketplace couch was not how any other male had ever come to find themselves there. Not that there were really many men before Dax. There was Ben, but I didn't count him, the three years of my life he wasted, or how much of that time he insulted my couch by sitting on it with his ass. There were a couple more when I was still living out of the city before my accident but, they hadn't sat on *this* couch, and none of them had ever come with a story quite like Dax's.

He'd said that I surprised him, well, Wyatt Smith surprised me right back and he paid with interest.

The date – because it was absolutely a date (squeals like a teenage girl on the inside but offers a casual smirk with hair-flip on the outside) – went about as perfectly as it could have gone.

After Dax matched me bite for bite of the mammoth serving size I gave myself (5 points for Dax on consumption support), he helped me ferry the bowls into the sink and the leftover Chinese food I would not be sharing with Dean into the fridge before we plopped back down onto the couch.

Dax chose to sit in the middle while I had taken the corner - everyone knew that the corner spot on a sectional was the place you wanted to be. He lifted my feet up and put them over his lap like he had done it a hundred times before and it made my heart do a weird little flip.

We sat for a moment and digested our food before he turned to look at me.

"How did you find out?" he asked, a small smirk playing on his lips.

"Find out what?" I asked back, even though I knew what he meant, I just wanted to hear him talk.

Allie, you're ridiculous.

"How did you know I was going to be on stage at the

concert?" he elaborated.

"Oh, you'll love this," I said, though it was bold of me to assume I knew what he'd love after being in his company for a total of an hour and fifteen minutes.

"Mmm," he waited.

"It was Craig from the corner store," I said with a grin.

Dax burst into another belly laugh, he said he had a suspicion it might've been Craig, based on the fact he had taken a photo of us like a little creeper.

When I mentioned I had then followed up the shocking revelation with a Google search, Dax dove for the pillows on the other end of the couch and groaned.

"The poses where we all fold our arms, that's never our idea, I just want that to be known," he defended his band.

"There are thousands of photos of you all like that, it sure looks like it's your idea," I laughed in response, hugging a pillow to my chest.

I moved my feet off his lap thinking he was probably over it and was too polite to move them, but then he reached back down to swoop them up into the same position before giving me a look that made it impossible to keep his eye contact. I looked down and felt my cheeks pinken immediately.

I swallowed and I was pretty sure he heard it.

He pulled out his phone quickly, tapped away for a second and then pocketed it again.

"Is everything okay?" I asked.

He gave me an easy smile back, "Perfect," he rested his hands back on my ankles.

"Okay, I have a question," I said, playing with the frilly bits that framed the pillow I held.

"Shoot," he replied.

"What inspired the red hair?" I looked up at him.

"Ah, well, I figured it was time to try something new," he said, as if that was all the explanation that was required for such a drastic colour change.

"Yes, but most people add highlights, when they 'want something new'," I did the quotation marks in the air and everything, "You went from black to blonde to red. I don't even want to know how long it took you to get it blonde enough that the red would come out as bright as it looks now." I pointed to his hair.

He looked down at his hands as he was picking at his nails and he barked a laugh, "It was actually an incredibly long process. No one has wondered that before."

"Sweet lord, how could no one wonder that?!" I exclaimed, "I've seen enough of those 'hairdresser reacts' videos to know that you would've been fighting an uphill battle."

"What videos?" he stopped fiddling with his hands and looked at me.

My inhaled gasp almost made me choke on my own spit, "Stop it! Are you saying you've never seen them?" I was already up and off the couch and making a run for my room to grab my laptop, "You're gonna *die!*" I yelled from down the hallway.

Dax had, in fact, not seen any hairdresser react videos which was shocking to me in and of itself. He sat next to me and unquestioningly watched about four videos in a row before I looked at him with what I knew was a ridiculous smile on my face. It wasn't hard to note that I loved those videos.

"I think if I had seen those, I wouldn't have ever tried to do it," he cringed a bit, "In my defence though, it was done by the hair and makeup team on the crew."

"I think you escaped unscathed. I can attest to the fact that it is still very soft. It seems pretty strong too given all the bleach," I went on before I realised I was referencing the fact that I had *tugged* at his hair. I was going to deduct 5 points from myself for that one.

Good one, Allie.

Dax, bless him, just laughed and thanked me for the compliment with a wink that came way too naturally to him.

We moved on and he told me about how he and Aspen, his younger brother and the drummer for *Lady Luck,* had gotten into music as kids and started their first two-man rock-and-roll band when he was ten and Aspen was eight.

"What was your band name?" I asked.

"Nope," he made a motion of sealing his lips, locking them and throwing away the key.

"Holy smokes, so it was bad, huh?" I got way too excited about finding out, that I moved to kneeling next to him on the couch. He just shrugged, crossed his arms and kept looking straight.

"No, that's not fair, you have to say! The suspense will truly kill me Dax, I'm not kidding, I need to know," I started bouncing. I figured if I was as annoying as possible, he would eventually relent.

He made the motion of *unzipping his lips* before he said, "Don't forget I have a younger brother. Your tactics are completely ineffective," he then rezipped his lips again, making me laugh and tip my head back.

"Dax come on. This isn't fair," I grabbed his face with both hands and turned it towards me. He looked at me with such a mischievous glint in his eyes that I knew I'd have to play dirty to get the answer.

I was gambling that this would work, but I looked him dead

in the eyes and said as seriously as I could, "Please, forgive me for this," then, I attacked him.

My nimble fingers went straight for the danger zone of his unprotected rib cage because he had, so foolishly, crossed his arms. He immediately let out a howling scream-laugh that made me laugh even harder. He was yelling out my name in a hoarse voice that had my heart do another little flip while making me laugh so hard I snorted and thought I was going to get a stitch on my side.

"Just tell me Dax, and this will all end," I said over his laughter.

He relented. My gamble paid off. I sat back on the balls of my feet as Dax's laughter faded and he was slouched, breathing heavily with his face in a pillow.

Once he managed to compose himself, he sat up and pushed his hair back.

"Okay, okay, you win," he said, his sexy side smile made a show and it was by pure will-power alone that I remained where I was.

"If you ever tell Aspen that I told you this, he will kill me, Allie," he pleaded for secrecy.

"I will take it to the grave," I placed my hand over my heart to show him just how serious I was.

"Our band was called *Socks and Sandals.*" he scrunched his eyes up tightly as he said it.

I had never cackled so loudly in my life. I fell off the couch.

I had tears in my eyes by the time I managed to confirm that the genre of their band was rock. He nodded, laughing too. It took me a good ten minutes to compose myself.

Dax told me about the rest of the guys and how they all met. They'd all gone to the same high school but were in different year groups. Dax and Rip were in the same year, Angus and Luke in the year below, and Aspen was in the year below that. They didn't all connect until they had unintentionally run into one another at a *Warp Tour,* and the rest was history.

"Do you play anything?" he asked me after we had settled back on the couch, my feet back on his lap.

I smiled, "I do," I said, "I play the piano."

"How good are you?" he said, wagging his eyebrows at me.

"I've done all eight grades. It's what I wanted to do. I wanted to join an orchestra, travel and play the piano," I said. I had never said that out loud to anyone except for Savannah.

"Why didn't you?" he asked, like it would have been the simplest thing in the world to do. I suppose it might have been.

"It's not a happy story, Dax," I said, fiddling once again with the edges of the pillow in my lap.

"Not all stories are happy, Allie," he replied, his voice not holding a single ounce of mocking or disdain for a heavy topic on a first date.

I looked at him and he looked back at me. I searched his face, trying to find anything that would tell me sharing this would backfire. I didn't see anything.

I took a deep breath, "I studied piano all through high school. If I wasn't with Sav, I was playing the piano or listening to songs that I was trying to learn," Dax smiled at that, like he knew exactly what that was like.

"It was just me and my mom growing up. Savvy and I had grown up across the hall in the same apartment building just outside the city. My mom got sick when I was sixteen. She died just before I graduated," I said. My voice wasn't more than a whisper by the time I had gotten the sentence out of my mouth.

"Allie—," Dax started.

I looked up at him and gave him a small smile, "It's okay, it was a while ago now. She deteriorated fast. I was so focused on my music through it all that I don't remember it affecting me until she was gone. I knew she was going to be gone and I just clung to my music. It was stable, it was constant, you know?" I asked. He nodded. I knew that he knew what I meant.

"Anyway, she passed away and I was left on my own, in the same apartment I grew up in and with not much else. I stayed with Savannah for a bit and then I got the job I have now."

"What do you do?" Dax asked, and I realised I hadn't even mentioned it.

"I work in the marketing department of a pet store. Nothing exciting, but it's fun sometimes."

He smiled at me like he knew that was a lie.

We were quiet again for a while. It was the most comfortable silence I'd ever been in besides being with Savannah.

"Will you play something for me?" he asked.

I looked at him again, trying to see if I could share this with him. I wasn't sure. This was mine. No one touched this part of my life except for Savannah and even then, I didn't play in front of her.

He let me look, as if he knew I was looking for a reason to say no. The truth was that I couldn't find one. I nodded my head and stood up. I took his hand in mine and led him down the hallway to my room. He sat on my bed and I sat at the piano and played for him.

I started with my favourite, the *Rondo Alla Turca.* It was loud, and lively and it pulsed through you, giving no other option but to sit and listen. I slowed it down and moved into the *Prelude in C Major.* It was a softer tune, more delicate.

I finished, lifting my hands off the piano and I turned to look at Dax.

My heart was pumping so loudly I could feel it in my fingertips, but he just sat there and looked at me with such blatant awe on his face.

"I'll make you a deal. If you teach me how to play the piano, I'll teach you how to play the guitar," his throat bobbed as he swallowed.

I looked at him, really looked at him, as I released a breath I didn't know I had been holding.

"Deal," I said.

* * *

Dax left shortly after we struck our deal. He gave me a kiss on the cheek and said he'd message me. I walked back into my apartment with the stupidest grin on my face.

I headed to the kitchen and cleaned the bowls we'd eaten out of when my phone pinged from the living room.

I turned off the water, dried my hands and walked over to pick it up.

Dax: *Is it too soon for me to text you?*

I smiled and plopped down into my regular position in the corner of the couch and responded straight away.

Allie: *Sorry, who is this?*

Dax: *Just wanted to let you know that you're the lucky winner of a brand new car!*

Allie: *You're kidding! I didn't even enter a competition. That's fate for you.*

Dax: *If you just send through your card number, the expiry and whatever that number is on the back I'll have your free car sent right over.*

Allie: *Woah, just like that? You don't need my address?*

Dax: *Nope!*

I was laughing so hard I thought I was going to pee.

My phone rang.

"Hey," I said, trying to calm down from my laughing fit.

"Just wanted to clarify that if someone contacts you for winning anything for free, please don't give away your card details," Dax said, equally as breathless from laughing on the other end as I was.

"Okay, perfect. Thank you for that clarification," I said, still wiping the tears from my eyes.

"Okay, I'm going to text you again now. Just wanted to make

sure you knew it was me," he sounded... shy.

"I knew," I said quietly.

The phone call ended, and my phone pinged a second later.

Dax: *Hey*

Allie: *Sorry, who is this?*

Dax: *Oh my god, Allie!*

14

Allie

It felt like it wasn't fair to still have an almost full week of work ahead of me, not after the world's best first date.

I groaned as I got out of bed but, surprisingly, I felt spritely.

Dax and I hadn't made any plans to see one another again, but we had talked the entire evening until I had eventually passed out. Maybe it was a rock star thing, but I would have wagered he could have kept talking all night had I not lost consciousness.

I walked back into my room after my shower, snuggled into my fuzzy robe, a hot cup of coffee in my hand and picked up my phone to check what the weather would be like.

Winter was still very much upon the world, but I wanted to be prepared for the 10-minute walk to my office.

I had a message from Dax waiting to be read that must've come through when I was in the shower.

Dax: *Question. Are you a morning person?*

He had started doing that last night, firing off questions to me rapidly like we were on a speed dating show. I had begun firing them right back, catching on quickly. Another wonderful ice-breaker tip.

I had to admit, hearing from him at almost the same time that I took my first sip of coffee for the day released so much serotonin into my body, it should have been illegal.

I replied, my face already wearing a smile.

It was probably an accurate assumption to be made that for the last 9 hours, I had been smiling continuously. I wasn't putting it past myself to have continued to smile through my sleep either, hence the collective 9 hours.

Allie: *Mornings are a good time for me, as long as I have a big cup of coffee.*

I sent it off and quickly threw on a pair of work pants and a blouse. The weather app said that it was going to be a bit overcast and windy. I didn't want to have to hold down my dress the entire walk to work for fear of showcasing my nether regions to the world.

I shot back another message before rushing out the door.

Allie: *Tea or coffee? And then to follow on from that, white or black?*

The weather app had been correct. It was a hit or miss sometimes, but it was definitely windy. My *skeenie* was wrapped around me tight and my jacket was buttoned all the way down.

I was the sort of person that genuinely loved winter. The fashion, the weather, the everything. But I found myself wishing that the warmer weather would hurry up just a little on my way into work.

I got to work and peeled off my layers as I sat at my desk. The immediate contrast in temperature between outside and inside made me immediately start to sweat as per usual and also made me eternally grateful that most of my work wardrobe consisted of dark colours.

My phone pinged.

Dax: *Coffee. Black as my heart baby.*

I snorted, actually *snorted* out a laugh that grabbed all the attention of the marketing team that worked around me. I mumbled an apology.

Allie: *You made me snort-laugh and the people I work with are not impressed.*

Dax: *Haha. If it was anything like the snort-laugh from last night I can absolutely see how someone*

might report you to H.R. for disrupting
the work environment.

My mouth dropped open like, yep, you guessed it, a bloody trout. The sass of this guy!

I was definitely not complaining.

Allie: *Watch it Mr. Socks and Sandals.*

Dax: *That information was not given*
voluntarily. I would like the jury to
be aware that was quite literally
tortured out of me.

My laugh was much more controlled, my body shaking to keep it contained. I was not going to get any work done, I could just tell.

Allie: *Ladies and Gentlemen*
we're Socks and Sandals
are you ready to rock tonight?!

Dax: *You win.*
What about you? Tea or Coffee?
Black or White?

Allie: *Coffee.*

Black as my heart baby.

Dax: *You're my kind of person, Allie.*

My heart fluttered like it had the night before. I took a leap and assumed that that was something I needed to get used to.

I put my phone away and made a point to get all the work I needed to get done as fast as possible.

The rest of my week went much the same.

Dax and I spoke through the whole day, every day, and we asked lots of questions.

His favourite colour was red. I thought if I had to, I could've guessed that one. Mine was blue, like midnight blue.

He said he could have guessed that too, but I didn't see how.

His favourite day of the week was Tuesday because the pressure of the Monday was over, and the rest of the days offered ample possibilities.

I thought that was a wonderful answer.

My favourite day was Thursday. When he asked me why, I answered honestly. It was because that was when I usually got Chinese take away. I could feel through the airwaves that he was having a good ol' belly-laugh at that. This proceeded with me sharing with Dax the fact that as a grown woman of 25 years old, I had probably cooked myself a meal once. And that was years ago, and I didn't really count it.

He was shocked, of course, but went on to assure me that 'cooking wasn't for everyone' and that Aspen was the real kitchen-goer in their household.

I knew he was just being nice.

The week was coming to a close and I felt like I was on

cloud nine. I was so *happy*. It seemed weird to me that I could acknowledge the presence of that emotion only now, when I had thought I was happy every day before that.

If this was what it was like to 'get back on the horse' like Savannah had so gracefully put it, it made me seriously wonder why I hadn't done it sooner.

* * *

It was Thursday and as I walked by the corner store on my way home from work, the ingenious idea that I had semi-regularly flowed back into my mind.

Tonight was the night. I was saying *au revoir* to the below-average leftovers from string-bean-Dean, and *adios* to weekly Thursday night Chinese takeaway deals. The conversation I had with Dax had turned on the metaphorical stove within me.

I was going to cook myself a meal. A real life, adult meal. And of course, when one thinks of real life adult meals, what do you think of?

Spaghetti and meatballs. Naturally.

The trip in and out of the 24-hour corner store was uneventful. It wasn't Craig who checked me out and I sent out a massive thank you into the world for sparing me. I knew if it had been Craig, he would have asked more about Dax, and the idea of him pawing at my personal life, *Dax's* personal life like that, made my skin crawl.

This was a good meal to start off with, it literally had three ingredients; spaghetti, meatballs and a tomato-based pasta sauce. Plus some salt and pepper, because, c'mon, I'm not a monster.

Dean got home just as I had put the kettle on to boil for the pasta. I murmured a hello back to him after he greeted me first. He asked about my week and I gave him as broad an answer as possible, then I asked about his.

I was more than happy to keep this level of distance from Dean. Until he apologised for being such a jerk, he was going to be hard pressed to get anything out of me. I just hoped for his sake that he did that before I divulged the situation to Savannah. There would be no hope for him then.

It took me ten minutes to figure out how to turn on the stove top. My mind went to fire and gas, but what was before me was, in fact, electric. Imagine my surprise.

The pasta was in the water, I even added a bit of salt like that packet said to do, to make sure that the noodles didn't stick together.

I was going to be generous. 10 points to Allie. This was a milestone.

The pan was on the biggest burner because that just felt right, and I turned the little illuminated digital heat settings up to level 5. Whatever that meant.

The oil was hot and by the time all the pre-rolled meatballs were on the pan, it was not going well. The oil was spitting and every time I leaned over the pan to try and stir the noodles, the oil hit me, and I squealed.

Then, amidst the chaos, the last thing I wanted to happen, happened.

My phone started to ring. Not just any ring but the unmistakable diddle that was a FaceTime call.

It was Dax.

I shouldn't have. The pasta was probably over cooked and there was oil flying everywhere, but I picked it up.

He was grinning like a buffoon when I answered his call and because I could see my own face in the front camera, I could tell that I looked terrified.

His face dropped.

"What's wrong?" he said straight away. Concern laced in his voice.

"I'm going to burn down my apartment," I announced. This was ridiculous.

He smiled at my dramatic answer before he asked another question, "And how will you do that?"

"No, I can't tell you," I said, shaking my head.

He was really trying to hold his laugh in then.

"Allie, maybe I can help," he said, being the voice of reason.

"You'll laugh at me," I said, my mouth turning into a little pout.

"Oh, absolutely, I will," he said, his face incredibly serious.

I rolled my eyes but relented, tapping the little icon to flip the camera around.

"I'm trying to cook a meal," I said.

Though Dax couldn't see me, I could see him, and his face lit up into the most beautiful smile. I stuck my tongue out at the screen.

"Dax! This is not funny. There's oil flying everywhere, and the spaghetti is going to be all mushy," I whined.

That finally broke his control and he let out a throaty laugh, "No, this is okay. I can help you. What number have you got the stove on? Is it electric?" he asked. Okay, so he was just being nice when he said cooking wasn't for everyone.

"It's at a 5," I said.

"Oh my god, Allie," he was enjoying this way too much. I flipped the camera around so he could see me and stuck my tongue out at him again, which just made him laugh even more.

"Turn it down to 3, it's too hot," he said.

I did as he instructed.

"Also, now would probably be a good time to flip the meatballs," he said.

I went ahead and did that too, breathing a sigh of relief when they weren't burnt on the other side.

Dax talked me through the rest of the cooking experience. And by the end of it, it wasn't that much of a disaster.

I drained the noodles and added the meatballs to the pot before pouring in the sauce. And taadaa! Allie's homemade spag-and-meatballs. I bounced around the kitchen clapping so loudly that Dean stuck his head out to see what was going on. That sobered me up real quick. I apologised and went about my business pretending to clean something until he disappeared.

"Okay, make yourself a bowl, but don't eat it yet," Dax said when I relayed that the coast was clear.

I mean, that was a weird request, but I obliged. He hadn't steered me wrong yet.

I sat down at the kitchen island with my bowl in front of me and leaned my phone on a vase with some flowers in it that usually lived in the centre of the island.

5-minutes later and Dax was sitting down like he really was across from me, except he was smaller and obviously in my phone.

"What was that?" I asked, a smile tugging at my lips at his mysteriousness.

He lifted the plate in front of him that showed peanut butter on toast.

"I thought we could eat together," he said.

There went the little flip flop movement of my heart.

"Okay, now you can take a bite."

I cut through a meatball and stabbed it with my fork before twirling some spaghetti around it too. I was just about to lift it into my mouth when he abruptly yelled, "Wait!"

"For crying out loud, Dax, I'm going to die of starvation," I said.

He shook his head, "Hold your fork down a bit and give me your biggest look-what-I-made smile."

"What? Why?"

Dax just smirked, "Please with a cherry on top."

How could I say no to that? So I humoured him, giving him the most natural smile I could manage on an empty stomach.

"Okay, go ahead," he said, finally.

"Don't need to tell me twice!" I replied and took a bite.

He watched me chew, leaning towards the screen to the point where almost his whole face was in the picture, and his face alone.

"So?" he prompted, "how is it?"

I chewed a little more and then swallowed.

"I'll give it a 6 out of 10," I said, giving him a tight lipped smile.

"That's a pretty decent score!" he said as he took a bite of his toast.

We ate together in a comfortable silence for a bit, but I had to ask, "Why did you make me smile holding my food?" I'm pretty sure I knew.

"I took a screenshot," he said, like it was no biggy.

"Dax!" I said.

"Allie!" he mimicked me.

"Do I look like I'm camera ready?" I replied, "My hair is basically a birds nest, pretty sure I have oil all over my shirt—"

"You look beautiful, Allie," he cut in.

I almost dropped my fork. I was glad we were phones apart because my face went so red, I could have been mistaken for the sauce on my plate.

"This was a big moment, I had to document it. I'm proud of you."

"For cooking a meal that required only 3 ingredients?" I scoffed, taking the last few bites.

"Yes, for cooking a meal. Will you make me this 6 out of 10 dinner sometime?" he sounded so hopeful, like he was asking to be more than just *nice*.

I picked up my phone and put it at an angle where I could move around the kitchen and Dax could still see me.

"Really?" I asked, looking at him.

"I have never been more real in my whole life," he said, the seriousness in his face and voice both a game and completely real, just like he said.

"Okay, I'll cook it for you. Thank you for your help," I said.

* * *

Dax hung out with me while I cleaned up the kitchen and put away the leftovers into the fridge. He came with me into my room and, ever the gentleman, didn't complain once as he dutifully looked at the ceiling of my bedroom because I had tipped the phone away as I got changed into my jammies.

We hung out like that for the rest of the night, until Dax was settled into his own bed and the last thing I remembered was him telling me that the first four chords he would teach me on the guitar were G, D, E Minor and C because those were his favourite notes. He also added that they were the prettiest ones.

15

Allie

My alarm woke me up and the realisation that I had fallen asleep on the phone to Dax was like being doused with cold water.

Honestly, Allie! He's going to think you have narcolepsy.

That was not exactly the look I was going for; snoring and drooling on my pillow.

I grabbed my phone and saw that I had a message from late last night.

Dax: *Good night.*
I wish I could say you snore,
but you don't.

It was becoming quite apparent to me that Dax might just be my kind of person too.

* * *

I rolled out of bed and straight into the shower. Fuzzy robe on and I was making my way to the kitchen to get my coffee when someone knocked on my front door.

Keeping in mind it was 7AM on a Friday morning, I was not expecting anyone.

I walked over and opened the door a bit, completely aware that I was in my robe and naked as the day I was born beneath it all.

For the time of morning, he looked far too put together.

Instead of his long coat, he sported a leather jacket that was different to the one he wore on stage. More lived in. Used.

His red hair was still wet, making it look darker than normal as he looked at me and held up a brown paper bag and two takeaways with a terribly handsome grin.

"Breakfast?" he asked.

It took me a minute to process what was happening, but as soon as my brain caught up with the situation, I enthusiastically opened the door wide and waved him in.

"You're my hero, Dax," I said as I shut the door and followed him to the kitchen.

"I know," He quipped over his shoulder.

We got to the centre island and I sat down as he put the stuff on the counter before he made a full 180 and headed back towards the front door.

"Where are you going?" I frowned. Was he just dropping it off? My heart sank a bit.

He looked back at me and pointed to his feet.

"Shoes off," he said with a wink.

He remembered.

* * *

That was the best send off to work I'd ever had. Not only did he bring me a chocolate croissant for breakfast and a black coffee, but he walked me to work.

Yes, you heard me correctly. He walked me to work.

I cannot be the only person who was baffled by what was going on.

I mean, this could only be compared to hitting a hole-in-one, twice in a row. I didn't play golf but I was using my imagination here. Clearly.

Firstly, it was one of my favourite crisp January days where the sky was blue, the sun was out and the air was chilly. Secondly, he walked me right to the door and kissed me on the cheek before asking if I wanted to hang out on Saturday. Talk about starting the day with a double whammy.

I gave him my most controlled nod, as to not look like a bobble-head, and waved goodbye as I walked into my building. I was still dazed by the whole morning, and then my phone pinged, and my face adopted a smile for the rest of the day. It was my most used expression as of the last week.

The day was full of more speed-dating questions.

Favourite Olympic sport to watch, would I prefer the beach or the mountains, if I had to – in a life and death situation, he made sure to clarify – choose between socks or a blanket, what would I pick?

For every answer I gave, he gave one back. I didn't think I could get sick of that. The openness. The honesty. It was so *new* to me and it was all consuming.

What we were going to do on the weekend had me stumped a bit. I knew that Dax was famous, for lack of a better word, even though he didn't seem famous when he was eating peanut butter toast with me on FaceTime and explaining with incredible passion that, no matter what anyone said, Female Ice Skating was the best Olympic sport to watch. Hands down.

So, when I asked him what we were going to do, he suggested grabbing some takeaway coffee and heading out of the city. There was a park he went to that was about 30 minutes from where he lived that wasn't very busy. He said if he sat away from the path and wore a beanie, then no one recognised him.

So that's exactly what we did.

16

Dax

Aspen let me borrow his car for the day.

I breathed into my hands as I waited for Allie to meet me at the bottom of her apartment building.

I had suggested we head out of the city. I usually went to the place we were going to alone. Sometimes Ap came with me but it was nice to get away, be surrounded by quiet.

I had been once, earlier in the week, for the first time in months. Now that we were finished with the tour, we had some down time. We had just over a month before we started our album press tour, but that still gave us plenty of time to live a little out of the limelight. Time to recharge.

Allie walked out of her apartment, wrapped in her *skeenie* as she had called it in the 24-hour corner store.

How was that only 3 weeks ago?

Her face lit up when she saw me, and my heart did something stupid.

"Hey," she said quietly. Her bag over her shoulder and a blanket clutched to her chest.

"Hey," I echoed, opening the car door for her.

She stepped in and I walked around and got into my side.

The drive was quiet, but it was pleasant. I liked that I could be quiet with Allie. That she didn't need to talk all the time and that she seemed just as comfortable to sit in the silence with me.

"Cats or dogs?" I asked her.

"Dogs," she said, not having to think about that one for a moment, "I'm allergic to cats." She elaborated, scrunching her nose up like the very thought made her need to sneeze.

"Okay, so no cats," I nodded.

"Sweet or savoury?" she asked me back.

"Both," I said, "If I have one, I need to have the other."

She nodded in complete understanding and looked over to me, her seafoam eyes sparkling as her mouth formed into her prettiest smile yet, "You're my kind of person, Dax."

The urge to reach over and hold her hand was there, but I held off. Allie was ringing her fingers and averted her eyes to her hands, so I figured that to grab one would be interrupting something.

The drive was only 30 minutes and by the time we got to the park, not only was it practically empty but the spot I had wanted was under a few trees was free of people, and to top it off, the sky was starting to dot bits of blue amongst the heavy grey.

Allie had brought two blankets, one to sit on and one to put over our legs. It made me smile and felt like a very *Allie* thing to think of.

Sitting with her in person and speaking to her over the phone were almost the same. The only difference being that if I wanted to, I could reach out and touch her. She was *right there.* So I did just that. Often.

I leant forward and grabbed her hand, entwining my fingers with hers. Allie's lips tugged into a small smile as her cheeks took on a rosy hue.

"Is it nice to have some time off?" she asked.

I nodded, "Yeah. When you're on the move so much sometimes you forget what it's like to sit still."

"I can imagine," she said, offering me a small smile.

Allie also never asked me about the band. Not because I thought she was uninterested, but because maybe there was more that she wanted to know. That's what it felt like, at least. That was new for me.

"We head off in about a month for the press tour for the new album though, then some more down time before we head to tour for the shows," I went on, feeling like telling her about my life plans for the immediate future was kind of necessary.

My heart started to speed up as I thought about what her reply could be. We weren't even dating, really. We were just hanging out, you know, casually.

"A month is still a long time," she replied softly, like she knew that I was worried about her answer, that for some reason it was important.

"Yeah, I guess it could be considered a long time," I replied, my eyes were glued to our entwined hands.

"It all depends on what you fill it with though, doesn't it?" she asked.

"What would you fill that time with?" it was hypothetical, but at the same time it wasn't. I knew the question was loaded.

"Well, I like this park, so I would probably spend some time here," her thumb started moving in circles on mine, "I also like my apartment and playing the piano, so I would spend some time there. I also just discovered that I have this urge to learn the guitar, so I would fill it with that too." Her smile turned mischievous and it reached all the way to her eyes, making them crinkle. She was beautiful.

"That sounds pretty good to me. You've got it all planned out," I said, a wash of relief passing over me.

"Cooking too," she went on.

"Ahh," I nodded my head, "Of course, your newest and possibly your greatest talent?" I enquired, teasing her a bit.

"Hey, you just wait until you have my 6 out of 10 meatballs, you'll be grovelling for seconds."

I tipped my head back and laughed, causing Allie to shove my shoulder and say my name in a whining way. It only made me laugh harder.

We were at the park until after lunch time. It went by way too fast and I didn't think I'd ever been hit with so many promising lyrics for some new songs in a long while, all of which I had dutifully listed into my notes.

I pulled my phone out so often, I had practically written a song by the end.

I caught Allie frowning, trying to lean over and sneak a look but when she asked, I told her not to worry, that it was nothing.

And it *was* nothing. At the moment. Nothing but ideas and words and phrases.

When I told her, I wanted there to be something to show.

I had a small collection of notes from almost every time I saw her or spoke to her, all safely tucked away on my phone. There was always something that came to mind that I had to get down. Every time.

She asked then too but, no, not yet. I'd show her soon. I wanted it to mean something when she read the lyrics, heard the songs.

It wasn't until Allie's stomach let out the loudest, and I mean *loudest,* growl I'd ever heard that we made any move to leave.

We packed up and headed back to her apartment.

"Would you like to stay for dinner?" she asked. She sounded nervous, "Even though I know it's still technically mid-afternoon." She frowned a bit, in a way that I was coming to learn was another very *Allie* thing to do.

I looked over at her and smiled, as if she didn't know I had been waiting all day for her to ask, "Dinner at mid-afternoon is how I hoped today would wrap up," I said.

"What a relief," she said, her hand going to her chest sarcastically, "There is one thing, though," she went on.

"Mmm?" I asked, keeping my eyes on the road, perfectly happy and content.

"Well, string-bean-Dean will be home. We're not on good terms. Don't ask, it's a long story. So maybe we could chill in my room and watch a movie or something?"

"Do I need to have a word with string-bean-Dean?" I asked, sneaking a look at her. She was smiling down at her hands and it did another stupid thing to my heart.

"Not quite yet, but I'll let you know," she said.

"Alright, I'll be on call," I said, "And pizza and a movie sound perfect to me," I finished.

"Cheese?" she asked.

"Only my favourite dairy product," I answered.

She rolled her eyes and pulled out her phone to call the pizza place, ordering one large cheese pizza and making sure she mentioned that one of the people who would be consuming their creation claimed that cheese was a favourite and that if it could be the best cheese they had, that would be appreciated.

I realised that I'd never want to put this into a box.

I never wanted to take any of the time I spent with Allie and tuck it away. I thought about everything in my life that was tucked away and organised, about the house in my mind where everything was still packed up, and I wanted there to be *more.*

I wanted Allie's throw pillows and weirdly shaped chairs. I wanted her shoes by the front door and her jacket on a hook.

It was the first time I looked at all the other boxes in my mind and thought they would all be better off if Allie went through them.

17

Allie

I finally got to see Dax's apartment.

Well, he called it an apartment, but I was going to be real, it was a freaking penthouse. It was at the very top of an incredibly intimidating building and when he came to pick me up on Monday night after work, he assured me that it was nothing extravagant.

It seemed that Dax wouldn't know what 'nothing extravagant' was if it sat on his face.

He had made sure that Aspen was out for when we got there.

"I don't want you to feel like you're being pulled in all directions. Aspen is very excited about the fact we're hanging out," Dax had said as we walked up to his massively pristine white and very expensive looking kitchen.

My eyebrows lifted at that, "Why?"

Dax went ahead and busied himself in the kitchen, pulling lots of different things out of the fridge. He was going to make me a stir-fry, since he knew of my preference for Asian cuisine.

"Aspen is enthusiastic about my happiness, to put it lightly,"

Dax went on, still with his head in the fridge.

My chest panged with something that told me there was a lot more to what that meant, that there was more than just a surface deep understanding.

He went on, "So, the idea that we've been hanging out, and that I have been happier than usual... Let's just say he's walking around the house yelling our 'couple name' out in the form of song."

I let out a laugh and the tightness that had formed in my chest released a little. "He has given us a 'couple name'?" I asked, "What is it?" I couldn't help myself.

"I don't think you want to know," he said, though his mouth was pulling up at the side while he started to wash the vegetables in the sink that was in the kitchen island I was sitting at.

"Oh, come on! I need to know. I will tickle you again, I'm not above it, Dax," I said. I got to my feet and moved around the island.

He moved away from the sink with the water still running. His hands held up in front of him and dripping with water, "Okay, okay! I'll tell you."

I squinted my eyes at him, so he knew I meant business before moving back to my spot.

"He's been calling us *Wallie*," Dax's face told me that even saying the word out loud was painful for him.

"You're kidding me," I said, a bubble of laughter erupting out of me until I was hanging over the side of the island, trying to catch my breath, "That's the worst ship name I've ever heard!" I wiped the tears from my eyes.

Dax was still cleaning the vegetables, "Well, I implore you not to tell him that. He was very pleased with himself," he smirked.

Dax loved his brother. That was very clear to me, it made me smile. It reminded me of the way I loved Savannah.

I started moving my head to get a look at the penthouse.

"You can take a look around if you want," Dax said, his eyes were on me while simultaneously chopping the washed vegetables.

Cooking wasn't for everyone, my ass, Dax!

"Okay," my voice was already far away with the wonder of what I might find. I hopped off the stool and made my way through the living room.

The ceilings were high. Like, very high. And the place was decked out with fancy lights and modern looking furniture. It felt like they had gotten someone to come in and decorate it the way they imagined all rock stars lived.

The only bit of Dax, or maybe his brother, that I saw was a faded beanbag in the corner that had the Green Day *American Idiot* Album cover on it. The one that was clenching the bleeding-heart shaped grenade. That screamed 'Dax' to me.

I walked through the living room, up some stairs to another sitting area where there was a long hallway that stretched on farther than you would have thought for a living space at the top of a building.

I walked down the hallway and all the doors were open. I walked by the first and it was a room that was just filled, and I mean *filled* with guitars, so many guitars that it would have taken me a long time to count them. They were all organised neatly in stands, except one fancy looking black one that was on display facing front on to anyone who walked in, or past, the room.

"Wow," I said softly, before I hurried onto the next room.

I kind of felt like I was illegally poking around their things, but did that stop me? Nope.

The next room was a bathroom then the following door was on the other side of the hallway. It was much the same as the guitar room but this one was clearly Aspen's, as it held a set of drums. The walls and floors were all carpeted, I imagine that was for soundproofing. The walls surrounding the drums in the middle reminded me of floor to ceiling bookshelves, but instead of holding books, they held drums. Lots and lots of different drums and cymbals.

It was freaking cool.

On my way out there was a sign on the door that said 'Warning', but under that word someone had written in a Sharpie that said, 'if I'm rocking don't come knocking', it earned one of my snort-laughs.

I continued my snooping of the rest of their home. There were a few more doors but the next one held a king size bed. The walls were all black and so was the bedding. There was a whole rack of guitars set up in this room too and one was plugged into an amp and just resting on top of it, a notebook beside it.

I knew I shouldn't, but I walked in.

This was Dax's room.

His bed was made, which earned a smile from me. I'd thought he'd have been the sort to make his bed.

On the right bedside table was a book, I didn't recognise the title, but the back made it out to be some kind of memoir of a guitarist in a band. That seemed very apt too.

I learned two more things. That Dax liked to read, and he also slept on the right side of the bed.

There was a door that led off into what I assumed was a

closet. I was just about to walk in when he called my name from the kitchen.

My heart sped up so fast, like I'd been caught doing something wrong.

I rushed out of his room and walked back down the hallway. As I was making my way through the living room, I stopped for a second and just *looked.* Took him in.

He was standing at the stove, stirring something around in one pot and then checking on something else by lifting a lid.

He was... well, I hadn't quite made my mind up on what exactly he was. But I just knew that I liked to be around him. Watching him in the kitchen making us dinner made my heart do its signature flip. Every push back of his bright red hair, every comment he said to himself about the quality of his own cooking.

He reached up to grab a couple of bowls out of a cupboard before he turned, taking a breath as if he was about to yell my name again.

As he spun, he saw me, and his face lit up. I'd never seen anyone's face light up like that just for seeing me.

"Allie," He said softly, with a smile. He cleared his throat, "Did you get a good amount of snooping in?" He enquired, quirking a brow.

I kept my face neutral as I made my way over to him. I hadn't responded yet and his expression took on a nervous sheen that made me wonder what he might have been worried that I found.

I walked right up to him, reached up and put my arms around his neck before I leaned in and gave him a kiss.

His lips were soft, and they kissed me back straight away. He put the bowls he still held down on the counter behind me and his arms circled around my waist, pulling me to him.

We hadn't kissed again like we had on my couch. Most of the lip action had been simple, and far too appropriate, lip touches or a gentle peck on my cheek.

But when he pulled me against him, I felt a rush just like I had from our first date in my apartment.

I pulled away to look at him, but he spoke first.

"What was that for?" he asked, smiling down at me.

I reached up to move some of the hair that had fallen into his face out of the way. It probably wasn't necessary, but I wanted, *needed,* to touch him.

"You make your bed." I said, as if that was the reason.

"Is that bad?" He asked, smirking a little.

"No, not bad." I leaned in to give him another kiss.

"Thank you for cooking dinner." I said, as I released him and tried to step away.

He grabbed one of my wrists as it was unlocking from my other and moved it back around his neck where it had been. He crouched down to lift me up by my waist, setting me on the kitchen island. The movement earned a squeak of surprise from me.

"Will you come over to dinner tomorrow?" Dax asked. His voice, a mere whisper as he leaned in and gave me another soft peck on the lips. My stomach burst into butterflies and I suddenly got very, very hot.

"I haven't had any food yet, what if you're a bad cook?" I returned his kiss with one of my own. I lifted my hand up, entwined my fingers into his wild, red hair.

"If my cooking is terrible then I'll improve and keep trying until I find a meal that's at least a 6 out of 10," he placed a kiss on my jaw as I tilted my head back in a laugh. I looked back down at him, still smiling wide.

"Deal," I said, "I'll come to dinner tomorrow."

Dax pulled me closer again until I was almost not sitting on the island at all but being held up by him. My hands were frantic in his hair and there wasn't one part of me that didn't absolutely acknowledge that Dax's hands were on my ass.

A loud pop came from the stove that jolted us both out of what was a make-out session that rivalled the first in every way. The stir-fry was still on the stove and it had just spat a piece of onion at us like it would have preferred us to be doing… whatever it was we were doing, away from the kitchen.

I turned back to Dax as he turned to me and I even surprised myself by going in for one more kiss, it lingered, and it was not at all light or soft.

He looked a little stunned but not in any way that could be considered bad. Like, at all.

"Stir-fry?" I croaked.

"Stir-fry," he said, letting me down gently and popping a kiss on my temple before turning back towards the stove.

* * *

Every night for the rest of the week was just like that. Dinner at Dax's, me always giving him a 5 out of 10 rating so that he would insist I come back the next night to try again for the winning number 6 out of 10.

The food was a 10 out of 10 every time, and the lip action sessions got better with every meal. Every time I saw him, I wanted him more. It was building up and driving me insane, I just wanted to scream. Scream at the people I passed on my way to work. Scream at string-bean-Dean every time I saw him walk into our shared apartment. I even want to scream right into Dax's face, because how could he not know that I was drowning in my own hormones.

Dax dropped me back off at my apartment every night after dinner, each time no matter how heated our non-verbal interaction became, he'd always leave me with a kiss on the cheek and usually after about a minute I'd received another speed-dating question.

Tonight was no different.

"What are you doing tomorrow?" he asked, as we walked into my building and he called the elevator button. He pressed it the entire time until it arrived.

Was it weird that that turned me on more than anything I've ever seen in my life?

"Tomorrow is reserved for Savannah," I said.

He gave me a little pout.

"I've not seen her in two whole weeks. I think that's a record for us. You're taking all my time," I teased.

"I won't apologise," he said back.

"Even if you did, I wouldn't accept it."

We walked up to my door and I could hear string-bean-Dean inside whipping something up in the kitchen.

"When will I meet your roommate?" Dax tried to pass it off as a nonchalant question, but I knew he was itching for an introduction.

"When you want to lose your appetite," I scrunched my nose up and frowned at the same time, earning a laugh from Dax as he reached up and tried to smooth the lines between my eyes.

"He can't be that bad," he said, leaning in to give me a kiss on the cheek.

"Trust me, he is that bad," I leaned in and gave him a kiss on the lips as a thank you for my kiss on the cheek. It veered from our standard routine, but who said the girl couldn't go in for some lip action?

Dax leaned in as I was leaning away, capturing my lips in another kiss that had my blood heating instantly.

We pulled away but he left his forehead resting on mine.

"Night, Allie," his voice was all sorts of sexy, and soft and rough and…

"Night, Dax," I said, stealing one more kiss before slipping into my apartment.

I walked straight into my room, saying hello to Dean as I walked by. I closed the door quietly and landed with an un-lady like *humph* on my bed.

My phone pinged.

Dax: *Will you go out on a date with me Sunday night?*

Not the usual sort of question he asked, but a welcome one, nonetheless.

Allie: *I'd love to.*

18

Allie

"Allie, this is so *hot!*" Savannah squeaked as we sat on her couch, wine in hand.

"I know, I can't really comprehend it," I said, taking a swig to hide my smile. I put my wine glass down and shook out my hands.

"Okay, enough about me. You're now fully up to date on all things Dax and Allie. I want to know what's going on in your world. Two weeks is a long time to be apart," I frowned at her.

"I know, but we still spoke every day," she said, taking a drink from her own glass.

"Yeah, but it's different," I said.

"It is," she agreed.

"Okay. So? Anyone caught your eye?" I asked.

Savannah just took another, very long drink from her wine.

"Oh my god! There *is* someone! I knew it! I couldn't imagine spending two weeks away from you and not have you ask me to come around once. I would like to point out I invited myself here."

"I know, *I know.* But I guess you understand what it's like.

It's so *consuming,*" she tried to plead her case.

"Is it weird that I can say that I know what you're talking about?"

It certainly felt weird to say.

"No, it's not weird, it's good. I'm glad you're back on the metaphorical horse that is Wyatt Smith," she wagged her eyebrows at me.

I threw the pillow I was holding at her. She lifted her wine glass up and out of the way just in time, "Savannah!" I said, completely embarrassed.

"Oh, Allie! Come on, you're dating a *rock star,*" she said.

"It's not like that, and we're not dating we're just... hanging out," I grabbed another pillow that was in reach onto my lap. "Dax is not only *Wyatt Smith*. I don't even see him as that when we're together. He's...," I thought about it. He was so many things, and everything about the things he was, and about how I *felt* about those things, it was all intense. My mind started to spiral.

"Allie," Savannah said, snapping me out of my inner turmoil, "Don't pull away from him now that it's getting good," she said.

"I'm not," I replied, not meeting her gaze.

"Maybe not yet, but you were thinking about it just now," her single, well defined eyebrow stared me down.

"We're only just hanging out," I repeated, more to myself than to Savannah, "We haven't even slept together yet."

"So?" Savannah asked, "You don't need to sleep with someone straight away for it to mean that the relationship will work out. Sleeping, or not sleeping, with someone on the first date means diddly-squat, Al."

I frowned to myself. I knew that she and I were both

thinking about Ben. I had slept with him on the first date.

"There's nothing wrong with that either though, Allie," she continued.

I looked up at her. I knew she could see and feel the fear that was pinging through my body. Every fear and insecurity that was carved into me by Ben, the need to run away and hide so that it never happened again.

Savannah reached out for my hand, "This is good, Allie. Wyatt is good, and he isn't Ben. Sometimes you have to see it for what it is. Feel the fear, and do it anyway," she said.

"Feel the fear?" I squeezed her hand back with one hand and reached for my wine glass with the other.

She nodded, "And do it anyway."

* * *

I gave Savannah a long hug before I left. It felt like for the first time in our 24 years of friendship we were setting off on endeavours of our own where we might see one another less. It felt okay, like she was there if I needed anything and vice versa, but it still felt weird that we hadn't set a date for the next time we'd see one another.

She told me again to feel the fear and not to run and hide, that if I did that then it meant that all the Ben's of the world won. I didn't like that idea at all. So, with a promise back to her to feel the fear and do it anyway, I made my way home.

The pull of comfy clothes and my latest piece of interest, *Beethoven's Sonata No. 14 in C-sharp minor, Op. 27,* was undeniable. It was an incredibly thought-provoking piece of music to play and I was enjoying the change in tone from the *Prelude in C Major.*

My phone started to buzz in my pocket.

I answered straight away, "Hello, stranger." You could tell by my voice that I was smiling.

"Long time no speak," Dax said back, I could hear the smile in his voice too, "How's Sav?"

"She's good. Lots of talking and lots of wine drank," I recounted.

"I hope you spoke about me."

"You remained in the conversation 90% of the time," I replied.

"Only 90%?" he asked, mock horror lacing his voice.

"The other 10% was filled with the act of drinking our wine, of course," I assured him.

"I supposed you'd need to breathe too, between sentences," he went on.

"I came to find that was a particularly important part of speaking. Who knew?"

"So, there's a catch to our date," he chimed in.

Our playful banter moved into a real-life type of conversation without missing a beat. That was probably one of my favourite things. When Dax had told me that speaking to me was easy when we first met, I never got it. But I got it now, talking to Dax was the easiest thing I'd ever done.

"I'm listening," I said, though I was a bit weary.

"The date will begin around 10:30PM," he explained.

"Like, at night?" I asked, baffled.

"That is usually the purpose of the 'PM'," I could hear him trying not to laugh.

I just rolled my eyes, "Okay, I'll be ready at 10PM then." That was very spontaneous, I thought.

Allie being spontaneous. Quick! Someone record the date and time.

"That's it? You're not scared about what it could be?" he asked.

"I'm feeling the fear, Dax, and I'm doing it anyway," I replied.

19

Allie

I should have had a nap. I was just wrapping on my *skeenie* and I felt my eyes starting to close.

It was 10:10PM and Dax had just messaged that he was downstairs. I had seriously considered making a coffee for myself before leaving, but it got too late and I was just too tired.

I tried to pep myself up on the way down. The excitement of my first out-in-public date with Dax, this was quite a milestone. I mean, we did go to the park, but this was a *date* date.

It was freezing as I walked out of my apartment and into the night. Dax was leaning against Aspen's black sedan like he usually was, looking far too cool and way too sexy and it was all made a thousand times better as I saw that he had two thermoses in his hands.

"Don't tell me," I said, my eyes focused on the hot beverages he held, and the hot beverages alone.

"I figured coffee might be required," he handed one to me.

I took it and launched myself at him and I kissed him with

equal enthusiasm. His hand immediately found my waist and held me against him. I could feel him smiling against my lips.

"Are you ready?" he asked as he opened my car door.

"I was born ready," I said, suddenly filled with so much energy I could have sprinted a mile. Dax rolled his eyes and he closed the door on my side and jumped in his own side.

He raised his thermos to me, and I *clinked* mine against his as we sped off into the quiet city streets.

We just drove for a bit, not really leaving the city but driving to a different part of it. I was sipping my coffee when Dax reached his hand over and put it on my knee. I smiled and looked at him.

"This is new," I said.

With one hand on the wheel and one hand on my knee, he looked at me from the side as a small smile grew on his face.

"Is this okay?" he asked.

"It's perfect," I said, reaching over and combing the hair back from his face before settling my hand on the back of his neck.

We drove like that for another 15 minutes until we pulled up to a little row of shops somewhere on the other side of the city. All the shops were dark except for one. The sign read '24-hour Ice Cream Parlour.'

My throat got all tight and my nose tingled like I just downed a sparkling beverage too fast. I moved my hand away from Dax as he put the car into park.

I was wearing my signature open-mouth-trout look. Again.

I knew why we were here. I looked over at him only to find him already staring at me.

"I figured, while we were on a 24-hour operating place of work streak, that we might as well try another," he sounded so unsure, like he didn't know if my silence was good or bad.

I knew I had been kissing him a lot lately, but I didn't really care. I leaned over and pulled his face to mine by the front of his leather jacket, "This is wonderful, Dax," and planted one right on him.

"Yeah?" he asked, like he thought that there was more than one way that this date could have been interpreted.

"Yeah," I said, leaning back into my seat.

He gave me the biggest grin and jumped out to get my door. He always got my door.

He held his hand out for me and continued to hold it as we made our way across the lot to the ice cream store.

Dax was wearing a beanie but there was no mistaking, as soon as we walked into the little shop, the three on-the-clock staff knew exactly who he was.

"Holy crap," one said.

"Dude. *Dude,"* another said as he was tapping his friend trying to get their attention.

"What is— oh my god," they all stared at us, and it was my first time ever seeing Dax recognised in public. It made the fact that he was *famous* a little more real for me.

"Hey, guys," Dax said, taking off his beanie.

"Dude, you're that guy!" the shortest of all the ice cream parlour workers said.

"I might be," Dax said with a smile.

"You're Wyatt Smith!" one of the others said, "I'm seriously your biggest fan, you have no idea. Your music is all I listen to." They hurtled the words out to him like they were worried the moment would end too soon.

The last one of the three just stood there in shock. The shortest one nudged his friend, "This is Remy, he's probably your biggest fan of all of us. He even dyed his hair like yours."

The short worker ripped off his friend's uniform hat.

"Dude, no way! That looks awesome!" Dax said. The boy with stage fright smiled and murmured a thanks as he ran his hand through his hair.

The one, who was his biggest fan, stepped forward, finding his confidence, "Do you think we could get a photo with you?" he looked like this was probably the best day of his life.

"Sure, if my girlfriend doesn't mind taking it for us?" he turned to me.

A lot of things happened in that moment. The first being that I became a bobble-head. Nodding my head like my neck was a spring. The second being that I lost my voice entirely, and the third being that I apparently just became Dax's girlfriend.

I took the phone from the one who was called Remy and snapped a few shots, one regular and one silly. Dax ordered us two scoops of chocolate ice cream, paid for them and led me back to the car. We sat in the parking lot on the hood of the sedan and ate our ice cream.

The silence was nice. Calming.

Dax gave me the chance to be the first to speak, content to sit in silence with me or tap away on his phone from time to time.

I could see in the corner of my eye that he kept looking at me, but it wasn't until I finished my whole ice cream that I spoke.

"Girlfriend?" I finally looked at him.

He looked back at me with such honest hope that I wanted to crawl into his lap then and there.

"Is that okay?" I saw him swallow.

"You actually make me nauseous, so I'm not really sure," I

scrunched my face up at him.

Dax tipped his head back and let out a laugh that echoed through the empty parking lot around us. He set down his ice cream and tugged me to him by my *skeenie*.

"You're such a dork, Allie," he leaned in to press a kiss to my jaw, a spot I was coming to find I liked to be kissed very, very much.

"Will you be?" he asked again, so close our noses were touching.

"If I have to," I said, adding an eye roll for emphasis.

"Allie," Dax said, whining my name.

"Yes, Dax. I'll be your girlfriend," I said. Letting every lightning-storm emotion I was feeling shine through my face just for him to see, as I pulled him in for another kiss.

* * *

I asked Dax if he wanted to stay over at mine. He said yes very quickly to the point where it made me blush. I told him he could park his car under my apartment building seeing as neither Dean nor I had a car, but the apartment had a spot that came along with it.

He sent a message to Aspen letting him know he'd be out with the sedan until morning and we made our way up to my apartment.

It was like there was an elastic band between us that was getting more taut with every passing second and it was going to snap, making us collide and headbutt into one another.

I got a spare toothbrush out for Dax. Yes, I was that person who had spare toothbrushes and mini shampoos and conditioners. I mean, you never knew what the situation would call for, right?

String-bean-Dean was fast asleep in his room, so we brushed our teeth in silence before moving into my room. I quickly put on some pyjamas that were simple but appropriate for a 25-year-old and handed Dax a pair of oversized sweats that I had.

We hopped into bed, him on the right side, me on the left and we just looked at one another for a while.

Dax's hand reached out to my knee and slowly, very slowly, moved up the rest of my body, all the way up my arm until he cupped the side of my face, and then it all just exploded.

Our lips crashed in a mess of tongues and teeth faster than you could say 24-hour Ice Cream Parlour.

Just like the time on my couch, his hands roamed over every curve of my body like it was the only thing they had wanted to do in the weeks since we'd met. Lord knew mine hadn't thought about much else.

He hovered above me and I tugged at his shirt, indicating that it needed to go, toot sweet. Dax leaned back as I leaned up, helping him remove my own shirt until he leaned down, letting me feel the weight of him in a way that was incredibly satisfying and still not nearly close enough.

The kissing continued and the feel of his skin on my skin sent shivers through my entire body. His hand drifted to the elastic of my pyjama bottoms.

I certainly didn't think that *this* would be happening tonight, which made me infinitely grateful that I had taken the necessary steps to groom the day before.

Thank you, thank you, thank you.

When he moved in again it was slower and much more deliberate. He kissed me one last time before his hand, that wasn't propping him up, moved from my cheek to my neck, over the curve of my breast and down to my waist and to my hip. His mouth followed the exact same path as his hand, kissing down my whole body and earning shallow, breathy pants of approval.

I knew what he was doing and *wowzers,* I was freaking out. All I could think was, *good god, I've been blessed with a giver. Thank you. Thank you.*

I watched him as he made his descent.

Oh shit.

After I helped him shimmy off my pyjama pants, he played with the band of my underwear. His eyes flicked up in another silent request. I nodded to him as I lifted my hips slightly to help him out. I mean, it was the least I could do.

He settled further down on the bed and had a hand flat against the plane of my stomach, trailing kisses along my inner thigh that were a little too ticklish.

Christ, Allie. Don't laugh, don't laugh, don't laugh.

The first touch of his tongue was absolutely nothing to laugh about and gave me enough of an indication of where exactly the rest of this engagement was headed.

I couldn't breathe.

My responding gasp was quite clearly exactly what he was after because he didn't stop, but rather proceeded to execute manoeuvres I wouldn't be able to tell you the names of in a million years. At this point I wasn't even entirely sure what my own name was.

My eyes squeezed to the point of seeing stars and my entire body began to shake. I didn't have any self-awareness in that moment to be concerned, or embarrassed, in the slightest about the amount of times his name fell from my lips or how loud it came out.

Dax looked up at me from where he was, his eyes twinkling with satisfaction and mischief as he let me compose myself. My breathing came back down to a healthy tempo. Dax moved up to lay next to me, bringing the blanket that was folded at the end of my bed with him.

He kissed me as he settled by my side. Still on the high of what just happened, I began to let my hands roam, eager to return the favour.

"It's okay, Allie," he said. His voice was gentle, making me stop my movements.

I looked at him quizzically, "You don't want…?" I asked. I was completely aware of the situation going on beneath the elastic of *his* pyjama bottoms and to say I was zealous to return the favour was an understatement.

"Oh, we'll get to it all Allie, believe me. But just not in an apartment that you share with a guy named *string-bean-Dean."*

I laughed so hard I snorted, my hand immediately slapped over my mouth and nose, but only made us laugh more.

Dax pulled me closer, tucked the blankets around us and pulled the pillows further down the bed. The spot we had settled in was warm and neither of us were keen on moving.

We talked for a while longer in our rapid-fire-speed-dating -questions way as the early hours of the morning ticked on.

I idly traced nonsensical patterns onto the planes of his chest, and he mindlessly played with strands of my hair.

We fell asleep like that and I couldn't tell you the last time I went to sleep feeling that happy. Just utterly content with everything, especially with the body that was laying next to mine.

20

Dax

Allie's alarm went off so loudly that it felt like someone had slapped me into consciousness.

We woke up just as we had fallen asleep - her curled up to my chest without any pants on and me wrapped around her like an octopus.

It was fair to say that that was one of the best sleeps I'd had in a long time. Cliché, but still true. Allie was warm, and soft and she smelt like cherry blossom shampoo and clean laundry. With her was the only place I had wanted to be since our date in her living room.

She groaned at the sound of her alarm and moved out of my embrace to turn it off. She looked over at me and rubbed her eyes before she gave me a sleepy smile.

"Morning," she said in a raspy voice.

I smiled back before moving across the bed to pull her to me. I was leaning in for a kiss when her hands shot up, one covering her mouth and one covering mine

"No way, José," her voice was muffled from behind her hand and she was shaking her head, scuttling back.

"What? Why?" my voice was muffled too while I tried - and failed - to pull her back towards me.

"Morning breath. Or do rock stars not have that?" she asked as she reached down the side of the bed for something to put on her bottom half.

I rolled my eyes at her before giving her a poke to the ribs. "Brat," I said.

She looked at me with mock offence and threw a sock at me.

Allie got up from the bed and grabbed her robe, "Can I request you make the coffee this morning?" she said with her sweetest smile, "I have a feeling I'm going to be late for work."

"On it," I said, giving her a salute.

She hesitated in the doorway before making a dash back for the bed and planted a quick kiss on my lips.

"Gross, Allie! Rock stars don't do morning breath, didn't you know?"

She flipped me off and then made her way to the shower, leaving me with a stupid grin and the very important task of making coffee.

Allies coffee machine was exactly what you would have thought Allie's coffee machine would be. It was small, and old and had one button that turned it on and off. It was an incredible piece of machinery, especially considering that it still worked and produced what she claimed was 'top tier brew'.

I was watching the machine drip it's liquid gold, standing in Allie's kitchen in my borrowed sweats and no shirt, waiting for her to get out of the shower.

"Woah, sorry—"

I turned at the sound of a male voice behind me. Score. I

was finally getting to meet string-bean-Dean.

"Holy crap," he said, staring at me with his mouth wide open. Maybe it was something about this apartment, but both the residents had a tendency to look at me just like that.

"You must be Dean," I said, walking over with my hand stretched out, "Sorry about being half naked in your kitchen, I was just making coffee for Allie."

Dean reached out and shook my hand, "You're—I mean, aren't you?" he got very flustered, very quickly. His hand was clammy, and it took all my energy not to wipe my own hand after I moved back from our shake.

"Totally depends on what you're referring to, Dean, but in this case, I think I could be. Or, maybe I'm just a very handsome imposter," I smiled.

My phone buzzed in my pocket.

Ap: *Dax we have to head to Jane's office for a brief about the publicity stuff for the album. Are you coming back soon?*

Jane was our wonderful, incredible and just generally badass manager. She was why we were where we were in our career as a band, without a doubt.

Dax: *Coming now be back in 30 minutes.*

Ap: *Hope you used protection.*

Dax: *You can't see me but*
I'm giving you the finger
Asshole

Ap: *Touchy touchy.*
Be back soon pls.

"Sorry, what?" I said back to Dean, pocketing my phone. He'd been speaking that whole time and I didn't hear a word.

"I was just saying that I can't believe you're hanging out with Allie," Dean repeated.

I frowned, my head cocking to the side, "Why's that?" I said. I didn't know Dean from a hole in the wall and regardless of what Allie had said, I was willing to give the guy a chance, but things were not working in his favour so far.

"Well, I just mean, Allie doesn't get out much. If I had imagined the next guy who would be standing in my kitchen was dating Allie, it sure as shorts wouldn't have been Wyatt Smith, you know? Like, how does that even happen!?" he reached up and pushed his glasses up his nose, scratching his head and laughing. Giving me a look that showed me he was 100% waiting for me to reply to that.

"I would say she gets out enough," I suddenly felt very protective of Allie, "I've actually got to go, sorry to leave so soon. It was nice to meet you though," I said with a smile, moving past him back into Allie's room. She was right, Dean was a complete string bean.

I was just pulling my shirt over my head as Allie walked into her room wearing her fuzzy robe. I handed her a mug of coffee.

She saw that I was dressed and gave a little pout, "Oh no, you're going?" she asked. I liked that she wanted me to stay.

"I am," I said, mocking her pout, "I have to go to a meeting with my manager about the dates for the press tour. It's coming up quick," I stood and pushed my hair back.

Allie nodded as she took a sip from her coffee, "Of course, that makes sense that you would have to do that."

Her response made me smile. She was so happily *Allie*. Completely unconcerned that she was an absolute weirdo and she went with it. Incredibly witty, smart, kind and very funny amongst a comprehensive list of other things, but still a massive weirdo. The thought of that made my chest feel all warm.

I walked over to her and she stretched out the mug of coffee. I took it from her and had a sip, grateful that she liked her coffee the same way I liked mine. Uncomplicated.

I then scooped her towards me, "Can I kiss you now?" I asked.

"You may," she said, smiling as my lips met hers. It was meant to be a peck, but the undeniable heat was there, simmering under the surface.

"Thank you for last night," she said, her cheeks going a bit pink.

"The pleasure was all mine," I said. Then I gave her a little smirk, "Well, maybe the pleasure was yours too, actually," I laughed as she squirmed.

"Dax!" She smacked my chest and then pulled me to her for another kiss as she took the coffee cup back from my hand. "I look forward to returning the favour," her voice was a low whisper that immediately had me thinking about puppies and the elderly to settle the stir of emotion that built up in the pit of my stomach.

The blush that rose on her cheeks was the only indication that she saw all of what had transpired just flash across my face in the brief few seconds it all went down. I would have bet you anything that she was thinking of exactly what I was thinking of.

She cleared her throat and said with a jarring amount of enthusiasm, "Okay, well, have a groovy day!"

That's a new one. My eyebrows shot up, "A groovy day?"

"Yep!" she said, popping the 'p' for emphasis. I was trying to hold in my smile. Like I said, a proper weirdo and I was definitely there for it.

"Okay, you have a groovy day too. I'll text you okay?"

"You better," she smiled.

With one last kiss, I left her place, grateful to have avoided seeing Dean again and made my way to Ap's car in the basement of her building.

Ap: *Dude?*

I will actually come over there.

Dax: *I'm leaving now*

don't get your panties in a twist.

21

Allie

I had the realisation on my way to work, at some point during the week after the 24-hour ice-cream parlour date, that it had been well over a month since I'd had the urge to buy any premixed brownie boxes. February was usually a prime brownie buying month because the hustle and bustle of the New Year died down and everyone realised no plans had been made for the second month of the year. Of course, I got the shitty end of that stick.

Had work still been shit sometimes? For sure. But I had much rather spoken to Dax about it and been pulled from that misery by his humour than make the trek to get a brownie mix in the late hours of the evening. But things were good. Things were better than good, but I wasn't about to jinx it.

Dax had continued to cook me meals most nights for the next few weeks, and I continued to rate them a 5 out of 10. We settled into a wonderful routine, alternating between his apartment and mine and it was much to my great pleasure that I got to repay him for his initial favour after our ice cream date. Repeatedly.

Savannah had asked for the details of all those encounters too many times until I called her a perv and threw a pillow at her face.

I finally got to say hello to his friends, and band mates, during one of our many FaceTime chats. I got to see Aspen a lot more than the others, and I often heard him whine to Dax about when we would all meet in person. It made me laugh. I knew that when I finally did get to meet him in person, it would feel like I'd known him forever. He had that type of personality, I was coming to find.

Aspen was also exactly how Dax had described and absolutely the sort of younger brother that would insist on calling a band *Socks and Sandals.*

I knew that Dax was going to have to leave for the press tour soon, it was hard to believe it had almost been two months since our park picnic. What I had not anticipated was that he might've had to leave earlier than planned.

We were sitting on one of the sofas in his living room, wrapped up in one another, as usual, while our food digested. Dax had made us *pho,* and yes, it was a 10 out of 10, and yes, I gave him a 5. I was starting to think that he knew that when I said 5, I really meant 10.

"How much earlier?" I hated how disappointed I sounded, how sad I felt. This was his *job.*

Way to be supportive, Allie.

Dax was playing with my fingers, turning a ring I wore around and around my finger in a mindless action.

"Not tomorrow, but the next day," he sounded equally as glum.

I decided that enough was enough. We had been down about it for about 10 minutes, but it was exciting. They were leaving earlier because they had to fit in more dates due to the success of the album so far.

"No, this will be great," I scooted up the couch from my slouched position.

"It will?" he looked at me a bit confused.

"Yes, it will. This is so exciting Dax! Your album is *killing it.* So, you're gonna have a hoot of a time promoting it and I'll be present and accounted for for all the phone calls, texts and FaceTimes," I beamed at him.

"A hoot of a time?" he sounded completely unsure.

"Like a wise owl, my friend," I combed a hand through his red hair. I had never seen it faded, come to think of it. He must be all over the dying schedule to keep it so bright. Maybe it was his hair and makeup team.

I wanted a hair and makeup team.

"It's going to be for a few months, Allie," he said it like he was trying to convince me that calling things off would be best or something. That the distance would be too big of a thing between us. What a looney.

"Oh, like... *three*?" I made sure to have it seem like that was a dreadfully long time.

He nodded.

"Bugger, well this has been great and all but maybe we should call it here," I started to move away from him, and he looked right at me, not yet catching on. "If you could move, that would be great. You're super heavy, and heavy dudes who have to travel for work are a pretty big turn off for me so...," I made a wincing face at him while shooing him away with my hands, "Not to mention you smell *awful.* What is that?" I scrunched my nose.

He finally cracked a smile and rolled his eyes, "Okay, okay.

I'll perk up."

"Months, shmonths, Dax."

He was definitely about to laugh at that, which was better than seeing him broody. I kissed his temple, "It'll be fine. We'll be fine."

He grabbed my hand and planted a kiss into my open palm, tugging me back down so I was laying next to him. He nuzzled into the side of my neck and requested I stayed the night. I did, of course, and tried my best not to think about how I would soon be without the body I had come so used to having around me.

We were in bed and I was about to fall asleep when he asked quietly, "Do you really think I smell bad?"

I huffed a laugh into his chest where I was comfortably tucked.

"No," I said, taking a big deep breath in, "You smell like the—," I stopped. There was no way to say it without it being weird. I told him just that, "There's no way to explain it without it sounding weird."

"That's okay, I already know you're weird. The damage is done," His voice was muffled as he spoke with his lips pressed against my hair, "Tell me."

"You smell like lavender and mint. Like salt water. Sort of woodsy as well, I guess. And like leather, too. All of those combined," my voice was riddled with tiredness.

"That's a lot of smells for one nose to pick up."

"Mmm," was my only response and I breathed him in again, but made it very exaggerated.

Dax's laugh rumbled through his chest, it made me smile.

"You smell *clean* and *fresh*," I finished and nuzzled in closer.

"Clean is good," his voice was barely more than a whisper.

"Definitely better than whatever I was smelling on the couch earlier," I whispered back.

His laugh was a quiet interruption in the dark. It hung around us, clinging to the shadows until sleep found us both.

* * *

When Dax said that it would be like he was with me all the time, even though he would be bouncing from country to country, he wasn't wrong.

He took me on every plane trip, taking a stream of photos and sending them all to me when they landed. I sent him photos of what I was up to as well, but there was only so much excitement that could be had from doing the washing.

I didn't realise how used to having Dax around I had become until he was no longer knocking at my door at 7AM with coffee and croissants, or I wasn't waking up way too hot but perfectly content in his python-like embrace.

It was weird, but things were still… well, I hated using the word in fear of jinxing it, but things were sort of perfect.

Dax was still many things I had yet to put a name to, but some of the blanks I'd once had while explaining him to Savannah had started to fill in. Dax was thoughtful and kind. He was considerate and sexy as hell. Dax was the person I wanted to be around most, and as terrifying as that was, I was doing just what Sav had said. I was feeling the fear and doing it anyway, and so far, it was paying off.

I was walking home from work and my phone pinged.

Dax: *FaceTime?*

That was how things were, and to be completely honest, it was working a treat. His days were my nights more often than not, but we made it work. In some ways, it was like he was still just across the city in his own apartment.

Once, he had done it more than once, but I remembered this time particularly, he had woken up at 3AM his time to have dinner with me. He had gone out and bought take-out just to put in his hotel mini fridge so that come 3AM, he could wake up to an alarm and eat with me on FaceTime.

He had been shirtless and his eyes were half closed the whole time, but I laughed so hard that I inhaled a noodle and spent most of our internet date cry-laughing at the very real and completely underrated pain of having a noodle lodged in my nasal cavity.

Needless to say, that whole situation certainly woke him up and that he, too, was laughing so much he cried. The cherry on top was when Dax admitted that the food speared to the end of his fork had been the same ready-to-go bite from an hour before, and that he was pretending to eat because the food 'literally tasted like ass'. That made me snort-laugh to the point of my abdominal muscles twitching from overuse because he had been *pretending to chew* to keep up the charade. I had laughed more than I had eaten, which was saying a lot considering the size of my portions.

We broke our fortune cookies together and our date ended when I needed to go to bed and he had to have a shower and get dressed for the day.

In my mental list of dates, it had become my favourite so far.

I spent a lot of time kissing the front facing camera on my phone. It was gross, but every time I did it Dax's eyes lit up a bit so, who was I to take away his joy?

I smiled and called him on FaceTime just as I walked onto the city block my apartment building was located on. He picked up on the first ring.

“There she is,” he said, smiling at me. I exhaled a bit seeing him on my phone screen.

“Shouldn’t you be asleep?” I pushed the door of my apartment building open with my shoulder and then proceeded to tap the call button of the elevator repeatedly.

“We actually arrived in Amsterdam today, so it’s still morning here. I am about to die of exhaustion though, so there’s that,” Dax had his head on a blindingly white and very soft looking hotel pillow, “Did you get my photos of the flight? Aspen fell asleep so we were balancing rice crackers into towers on his head. My tower was the highest,” he gave me a tired smile.

“Of course it was,” I laughed, stepping into the elevator, “I haven’t gotten them yet though.”

The FaceTime call moved to ‘paused’ for a second. Dax popped back on my screen as I stepped out of the elevator. I almost squealed with delight as he said, “They’re still sending.”

I nodded my head and tried to school my face into a mask of calm, but one thing I couldn’t do, as everyone knew, was hide my emotions.

“What’s happened?” Dax said immediately, moving his pillow up so he was propped against the headboard of his bed.

“No, nothin,.” I said, “But I have to put you in my bag for a second. Can you hold tight?” I put the phone in my tote without waiting for him to answer.

“You can’t woman-handle me like this, Allie!” I heard him

yell from my tote.

I just rolled my eyes.

"Don't you roll your eyes at me!" I heard him yell again a moment later. I barked a laugh at his uncanny ability to know me as I lugged in the massive parcel that had been sitting outside my apartment door.

No, people didn't usually get this sort of service, however, the postman, Doug, was a solid guy. He used to deliver mail in the mornings, when I first moved into the building with Dean, as I was leaving for work. When I was still using a cane to help myself walk, we had struck up a friendship and every time I had a package, he would always leave it at my door.

I made sure to give Doug a good bonus come the holidays. As far as I was concerned, the people in our postal service didn't get paid enough.

I dropped my things in the kitchen, including my large parcel, and went back to lock the door and take off my jacket. The weather had started to warm up a bit more that I had since stopped wearing my *skeenie* out and about. It was always a sad day when the *skeenie* was put back into the cupboard until the next winter season.

"Allie?" Dax called from my bag.

"Coming!" I hurried back and took the phone out of my tote.

"Please tell me what's going on, I'm going to die from suspense as well as exhaustion," he said around a yawn.

"Okay, so this is a surprise for you and a gift for me, sort of," I said as I disappeared from the frame to get some scissors.

"I'm scared," Dax mumbled into his pillow, making me laugh.

"I bought you a dildo," I said, as I came back into frame.

"Just what I always wanted, thanks babe," he was giving me his best 'real but fake' smile.

He told me on one of our many FaceTime's since he'd been gone that that was the smile he gave to the press. He also never called me babe, so that made me cackle.

I moved the phone onto the floor and set it against one of the legs of the kitchen stools.

"Now that's what I call a big package, Allie," he said as I started to cut into it.

"Yes, well I ordered something relatively large," I replied.

"I wasn't referring to your postal delivery, and how do you even know what I'm looking at?" he asked.

I caught on very quickly to what he was referring to and spent the next few minutes coming out of my laughing fit and wiping the tears from my eyes.

Just as I was about to get back into my unboxing, Dean walked into the apartment and wasted no time coming over and inviting himself into the frame of my FaceTime call.

"Hey Wyatt!" Dean said way too enthusiastically.

"Hey man, how's it going?" Dax replied politely.

I always forgot his first name was actually Wyatt.

"Yeah, not a lot, how's the tour?" Dean went on like he was not interrupting my FaceTime with *my* boyfriend.

"Good, thanks! Hope you're well! Take it easy Dean," Dax coolly ended the conversation. Dean fumbled with his farewell before making his way into his room.

"You're so good at that," I whispered as I finished cutting all the tape holding the box together.

"It comes with the territory," Dax shrugged.

"Teach me your ways," I said. I interrupted Dax's reply as I squealed, "Okay, okay, okay!" I beamed into the camera, "Are you ready?"

"I'm ready," he said, he was smiling but definitely a little nervous.

I lifted it out of the box and onto my lap. Dax's face lost all nervousness and he was looking at me like, well, I wasn't not sure. No one had ever looked at me the way Dax was looking at me.

"You bought a guitar," he said. His voice was soft and full of emotion.

I felt myself get choked up at hearing that voice, "I bought a guitar," I replied, picking up the phone and giving my front facing camera a big kiss.

22

Allie

The days started to slowly blur into one another and whenever I tried to recount something, I found that all my memories had suddenly started to replay in my head in the form of FaceTime calls and text messages.

Savannah and I still caught up almost every Friday for dinner at our favourite Italian place, but she had been busy too. She'd applied for, and received, a promotion at work which had her travelling out of the state to the other major stadiums owned by her company. She was now in charge of something I couldn't remember the name of, but it meant she needed to do in person reviews constantly.

Whenever she was home, she always made time to see me though. It went without saying that I missed my best friend, but I was happy for her. Savannah deserved all the success that went her way.

My evenings consisted of everything I always did, but Dax was usually on FaceTime. They were in Japan now after moving all the way through Europe.

Most of the time we would be doing our own routines while

enjoying one another's virtual company. I would play my piano while Dax would read or I'd be cooking (the only meal I knew which was spaghetti and meatballs, duh) while he played the guitar.

He had successfully taught me his four favourite chords and I could string them together well enough that I felt confident in verbalising the phrase 'yes, I play the guitar' and 'oh me? Yes, I can play more than one instrument, thank you so much for noticing.'

Dax had in fact enquired when I would be able to casually drop those lines into conversation. I told him he needn't worry about such trivial things. But when the time came, I would be ready. I made a point to practice them after every session I had on the piano. It didn't take too long for the calluses to form on the ends of my fingers.

My hands had always been soft. Gentle and rarely used for anything too hard or bracing. When I looked at them now, it felt silly, I guess, but I suppose that I felt like as the skin toughened on my fingertips, I had begun to toughen in other places too. Like maybe I was getting stronger as well.

Dax and I tried to have coffee together as often as possible, but as they continued moving on with their locations on their tour, the times fluctuated. I had learned the hard way that having a coffee at 1AM was not smart, so I invested in my first pack of decaf.

My midnight coffee dates with Dax had quickly become one of my favourite times and were well worth the day of yawning that followed it.

One thing was irrevocably clear though - I missed him very, very much.

23

Dax

When we left for the tour, not once did I realise that I'd never packed up any parts of my life before we set off. I didn't need to pivot, to tie up loose ends and switch mindsets. To unpack the life I lived when we weren't at home, and put away the box I delved into when we were having a break.

I didn't think about it. Not once.

I was ready for the tour to come to an end. Being away with the guys was always fun, I loved spending time on the road with them and my lack of compartmentalising on this tour was a lot easier than I had thought it was going to be.

Allie made it easy to be away though. She also made it hard. And the days that dragged because of the blinding tiredness were always well worth the nights I got to spend talking to her. So cute it was gross, right? It was still true.

The guys all gave me shit but being away had made me excited for them to all finally meet. I knew they'd love her.

It was during one of our FaceTime calls that the reality of it all hit me. Allie had mastered the G chord, and finally strung all four notes she had learned together. She was so excited, so was I.

I had taken a screenshot of her sitting there on the other end of our FaceTime, the guitar in her lap with the biggest smile on her face. It had been my wallpaper on my phone now for a while. Aspen was the first to notice and all he did was give me a big hug. I pushed him away and then ruffled up his hair, but I knew that it made him happy to see me happy. It made *me* happy to be happy.

Maybe there was something to this lack of compartmentalising thing. Or maybe it was Allie.

She had fallen asleep on our FaceTime chat after I had taken that screenshot of her holding her guitar.

She still didn't snore, and even though I told her she was a drooler, she wasn't. She was as beautiful awake as she was asleep. She just slept, soundly and peacefully. She was a very still and calm sleeper, which was probably why she never wriggled out of my hold when we did sleep together.

I watched her for a bit when, usually, I would've ended the call and flicked her a message saying something along the lines of how she had a nose whistle and that she might need to look into it, or that she had a stray booger that was fluttering in the wind of her inhales and exhales and I recorded it for later.

None of that ever happened, but she always laughed so hard, it brought out the infamous Allie snort-laugh, that I couldn't help myself.

It was that time when I watched her a little longer when I knew.

I knew without a shadow of a doubt that I was completely and undeniably in love with her.

24

Allie

People usually told you that life had a way of balancing itself out, that if you were hitting those hard days one after the other, that you would get the good times too. Well, when they issued that memo, they must've forgotten to include that it went both ways. You didn't get too many good days without a reminder of the cold hard truth; that the grass was actually much greener on the other side. That one side was far shittier than the other.

My boss was, how does one put it nicely?

Well, one doesn't. Not in this case.

My boss was the kid that never got picked for any team sport and grew up in his parent's basement until he was in his late thirties, only to be told repeatedly by said parents that no girl was ever going to be good enough for him so he took that lovely little falsity and morphed it into an excuse to grab my ass anytime he deemed the marketing corner of the office worthy of his presence.

That was the sort of behaviour that I dealt with at work, the sort of behaviour that had me always, *always*, sitting at my desk at almost every moment of the day and scuttling to the bathroom the long way so that I would have the lowest chance of running into him.

Did I still get the high and mighty tongue lashings he had to offer? Of course! All my successes were overshadowed by small and silly mistakes, but no one was ever remembered for their moments of glory, were they?

I had been in my own head while I was copying something at the printing station. I didn't hear the nauseating squeak of his too-new shoes or the chafing of his suit pants. Not until one hand was cupped on my ass. I screamed, of course, and turned so fast I saw stars, pressing myself up against the copier to get away from him.

"Good job today, Alice," he said. His breath smelt like tuna salad. "Another great campaign."

He smirked at me and walked off. He was the kind of person that walked on his toes, the heels of his shoes never touched the ground.

You'd think that was a compliment, but it wasn't. I would be met with a list of complaints tomorrow and this would have become another excuse to have touched my backside.

I felt sick, but mostly I felt angry, because no one in my office had ever bothered to stand up for me.

I walked home with my jacket off, enjoying the warmer turn of the weather and desperately hoped the light breeze would move over me and take the grime of the day with it.

I took out my phone.

Allie: *I hope your day has been much better than mine.*

I knew that they were heading to an interview, their last one, actually. So, I didn't want to interrupt anything with a call. I was surprised when he replied almost straight away.

Dax: *Oh no.*
Do I need to beat anyone up?

Allie: *Absolutely you do.*
:(

Dax: *> Photo*

I tapped on the photo and waited for it to download as I left the corner store. I had stopped in on my way home to grab some brownies. So, when the photo popped up from Dax and I saw a shot of the very same brownie box I held in my hand that he had grabbed from the internet, I let out a snort-laugh and sent him a selfie of me pouting, holding my own box.

Dax: *I'm sorry I'm not there to help you make them.*

Allie: *It's okay. This is good. You being here... well, there, but also here. This is good.*

Dax: *See you soon.*

I had typed out the words 'I love you' but quickly deleted it.

I had never wanted to send them more than I had wanted to then. I also had never wanted to hear them back so much.

I knew it the moment I realised that it wasn't the brownies I wanted. I wanted Dax.

* * *

The motions of turning on the oven were familiar. I had been preheating the oven since I was a kid. Even though the electric stove top had brought with it it's challenges, I had always been my most comfortable when turning on the oven.

I snapped the little dial to 'fan forced' and then cranked the temperature to 180 celsius.

I added the milk, butter and eggs to the premixed dry ingredients faster than you could say 'Allie can work an oven like a pro' and before I knew it, the batter was inside the oven, cooking.

While the goey-goodness cooked, I went to get changed into my comfies - a shirt that belonged to Dax that barely smelt like him anymore, and some baggy sweats. I walked out of my room and back towards the kitchen, more than ready for my brownies when my entire body went into shock. I couldn't move.

The wailing of a siren on the city street below blasted past so loud I could have been standing beside it. A window had been left open. I never opened windows, always making sure they were shut tight.

My body started to shake as the memory of my accident encompassed me like being submerged under water. A loud horn sounded in my head and bounced from ear to ear. I knew some kind of sound left my mouth, but I couldn't tell you how loud or how long ago that might have been. The lights of the truck flashed behind my eyes and my body erupted in pain. My leg and hip instantly gave out on me as I crumpled to the floor of the kitchen. I held myself tightly, my muscles refusing to unwind as I relived the moment the truck collided with my car over and over.

I didn't know how long I had been curled on the floor of my own kitchen until I was suddenly lifted and placed somewhere soft. The unfamiliar arms that had placed me there were soon replaced with strong, slim ones. A hand that had rubbed circles on my back the very same way more times than I could count, drew me from the nightmare I was reliving. The verbal commands to breathe in and out were delivered to me by a voice I probably knew better than my own.

As my body unwound, aching only now from the intensity of how tightly I had been curled in on myself, I kept my eyes closed and reached for Savannah, holding her tightly until the exhaustion took over and I fell into sleep.

25

Allie

I decided to forgive Dean for being an asshat and letting Ben into the apartment. I knew it had been a long time since it all happened and I had intended on forgiving him before now, I'd even forgotten to mention it to Savannah. But I got comfortable in my stubborn silent treatment towards him, and so caught up in Dax, that I just forgot to forgive him.

After I had woken up the next morning, still clutching Savannah so tightly my fingers ached, she told me everything that happened.

I had been on the floor of the kitchen for about 20 minutes in the end. It was almost 6PM when I had gotten home and sorted out the brownies, and by the time Dean found me, called Sav and helped me into bed, it had just passed around 6:15PM by Sav's to-the-minute retelling.

Dean had come home, found me on the floor unresponsive to anything he was saying and called Savannah straight away. Dean knew that I struggled with the lingering trauma from my accident and as far as housemates went, he had been quite accommodating, aside from leaving a window open here and slamming his door too loudly there, my triggers were never a real issue *inside* the apartment.

He'd lifted me off the floor under Savannah's careful instruction and placed me on my bed. He even tossed out my burnt brownies for me and washed the tray.

Sav had said he checked in to see if I was okay before he left for work. So, I had decided to forgive him for his prior offence. I hadn't had a chance to tell him yet, but I would as soon as I saw him next.

Sav had been home after arriving back from wherever she was for a work trip earlier in the day. I knew she had been away, and it was just stupid luck she had been at home, and even stupider luck that she had actually *picked up* Dean's phone call.

His stalkerish tendencies that overtook the first few months after they had been introduced, and his lingering creepiness after she had made it abundantly clear what she thought of his intentions, left me with no faith in her actually picking up that phone call. But she did.

Though it was a 15-minute walk to Savannah's, it was a 3-minute drive, 1.5 minutes if you put pedal to the metal. Sav knew how I felt about her driving. I thought she was too fast and too careless. I was grateful though, if it was only just for moments like this that she was such a speed demon.

She had stayed with me for most of the morning of the next day after I had called in sick to work, but I ordered her to leave eventually when she kept getting calls from her own work.

Savannah hesitated, clutching her own cup of coffee.

"I can stay, Al. Work will understand, I've been run off my feet since the promotion," she said as she perched back on the edge of my couch.

I was mindlessly trailing the rim of my mug with my thumb, "No, Sav. Honestly, I'm okay now, just tired and sore. A little foggy but I am just going to go back to sleep. I will be fine."

I gave her my best smile, but I could feel my bottom lip wavering.

Sav set down her coffee and pulled me into a tight hug.

"It's okay, Al," she said, her hand making the circle motions on my back again.

"I hate it, Savannah. I *hate* it," I pulled away and aggressively wiped my eyes.

I remembered when I wasn't like this, you know. When I could walk down the street and not have to decide whether or not I was going to brave the stroll to work without my earplugs or close my eyes as a car drove by me after dark.

When I could *drive.*

"Allie, there are things...," Savannah said, moving some hair behind my ear.

"It stopped working. You know that. I am not going to pay to see someone who won't help me," I said. I knew that wasn't all of it though, that some of the resistance had come from me. I didn't say that part, and neither did Savannah, though she knew it too.

"Okay," she said, letting it go, "will you promise me to at least think about it? There are other places. Other therapies to try too, Allie."

I had always refused the pharmaceutical side of therapy. I didn't want it.

"I promise I'll think about it," I said. And I meant it too. I would think about it. I knew there was more that I could give, but it was like nobody understood that *giving* that was almost the hardest part.

I slept for the rest of the day.

When I woke up my head felt clearer. My body still ached a bit but, I felt more like Allie.

I was just shuffling out of my room to head to the kitchen to make myself a tea when Dean walked in. We stood in the kitchen, I was fiddling with the tie of my fuzzy robe and Dean was playing with the keys in his hand.

I silently made my way over and gave him a hug.

Needless to say, string-bean-Dean and I didn't hug, "Thanks Dean."

It took him a minute, but he did eventually hug me back. He mumbled an awkward 'don't mention it' and headed into his room. At least I felt like I had successfully patched up that bridge.

The peppermint tea I was brewing called to me like a siren to the sea, and as I began to calm further I realised that amongst the chaos of everything that had happened, it really should have been a good day, the best day, really. Dax was coming home.

He'd arrive late but I had completely lost track of my phone the last 24 hours, so I had no idea if he'd even messaged or tried to call.

I immediately felt bad. We had spoken every single day for almost the last six months and then I fell off the face of the earth. I hope he didn't think I had ghosted him or something.

My mood lifted instantly. The last complete rotation of the planet on its axis brought me shit-all, but the lingering self-pity dissipated as I imagined seeing him again for the first time in three months.

I was carrying my tea to my room, set on finding wherever

my phone had gone to die, when a knock sounded at my door. My heart leapt into my throat. Surely it wasn't him, it was too early. Wasn't it? Or I could have gotten the flight times wrong, or maybe he had done one of those things where he told me he was back later as a ruse, only to come and surprise me earlier. It felt like that was a very 'Dax' thing to do. Something I felt like Aspen would have also fully supported.

I turned around on slippery socks, placed my steaming tea on the kitchen island with surprising steadiness and hurtled myself towards the front door. The soreness that hung around my limbs was completely forgotten.

I threw open my front door, only to have my smile turn sour on my face.

I had forgotten that it wasn't only good things that came in threes, because it wasn't Dax at my door.

It was Ben.

26

Dax

I couldn't stop my knee from bouncing the whole flight.

I watched the light fade into dark as our plane took us home.

The tour was a huge success. The promotion of the album couldn't have gone better, and the reaction from the fans was beyond anything we could have hoped for.

I loved it all. Speaking to everyone, talking about the songs, the different parts, the writing process.

But heading home was something I had looked forward to the moment that we had left.

The guys all slept on the flight, that was the usual.

Ap woke up a few times and we played cards until he was tired enough to fall asleep again. I alternated between jotting down different lyrics into my notebook, to reading, to listening to music, to just looking out the window in silence.

As soon as the plane touched down, I pulled out my phone and turned off airplane mode. I had sent Allie a stream of messages after our last interview, mostly asking about how her brownies turned out and a request that she kept one for me, but I didn't expect a reply because I knew she would have been asleep or getting ready for bed.

After the interview, the guys and I sent her a quick photo and then I sent her a customary series of shots of the journey to the airport.

She hadn't responded to any of them. It had already been a full day for her and as we landed, it was already close to getting late.

I had been talking to Allie every day for months and months, and she had never not replied.

Something in my stomach sank.

Moving through the airport was muscle memory. Once we got our bags and headed to the cars that were meant to take us home, I pulled Ap aside.

"I'm going to Allie's," I said, running a hand through my hair.

Aspen rolled his eyes, "Dude, a few more hours won't—"

"No, something's wrong. I haven't heard from her since she finished work yesterday."

Aspen's face sobered up as his eyes scanned my own features, "Could she just be busy?" he asked.

"Maybe," I agreed hesitantly.

My brother looked at me for a while longer before he nodded his head, "Okay, let me know when you get there okay?"

I nodded back and gave him a quick hug before waving to the other guys and jogging to get a taxi.

I pulled a hat over my head and jumped into the first one that pulled up, giving him Allie's address and asking him to get there as fast as he could.

27

Allie

It was pure instinct to close the door, leaving only a sliver open. Having something between him and me.

I'd never been hit by Ben, but I had been scared by him enough to warrant the shield of a door to me.

I could smell him from where I stood in my apartment.

Ben had been drinking.

"God dammit, Allie, give me back my shit!" he yelled, even though I was less than a metre in front of him. I held in my gag from his breath.

I wasn't sensitive to the smell of alcohol. I was, however, sensitive to the smell of *that much* alcohol.

His words fell into one another like dominos.

"What are you doing here, Ben? I told you I didn't want to see you again," I said, keeping my voice calm and steady.

You're fine, Allie. You're good.

"You always thought you were so much better than me, but who's the one keeping my stuff after they were thrown out!" He flung the words at me.

"You didn't *throw* me anywhere, Ben. I'm going to ask you

one more time to leave," I continued to keep my voice calm.

"You're such a *bitch,* Allie! You made me do it, you know that right? You *made* me do it all."

He stepped closer to the door. I shut it a fraction more in a mimic of his action until I was only looking out from a crack.

"Don't you fucking close the door on me Alice, give me back my fucking shit. I know you still have some of my stuff," he lifted his closed fists and smacked them so hard on the front door, it caught me off guard and I fell backwards, the door flinging wide open between us.

A look crossed Ben's face that might have been something like regret, but then it disappeared, and determination set into his features and he made to walk into my apartment.

"*Stop,*" I yelled.

That was the second time I had ever yelled in my apartment.

I really needed someone to explain to me why after 8 months of not seeing this guy, he showed up twice in the following six months.

I couldn't believe it, but he listened. He stopped.

"You take one step into this apartment Ben, and it will be the last thing you ever fucking do," I said as I kept his eye contact and brought myself up to my feet.

I was going to fall apart any minute, my legs were shaking, and my heart was in my throat.

Push through it, Allie, you're fine. You're good.

I walked up and grabbed the door, closing it again between me and Ben just as Dean rounded the corner.

"Allie? Are you okay? I heard—"

"I'm fine, Dean. Ben is drunk and was about to leave before I called the police."

Dean didn't say anything, but he didn't leave either. He

stood there and it felt like he had my back.

Ben's eyes landed back on me again.

"You're gonna regret keeping my things Allie. You're going to regret it all. You don't get to just *say* that you don't want to see me again. You are not the one who *decides* that. I did *everything* for you. We were weeks into our relationship when you had your accident, *weeks.* You owe me *everything* Alice!" His voice was so loud it cracked.

"I don't *have your things* Ben! Why would I want your crap in my life? Everything that was here I gave you in that box. Maybe, if you're so sure you've lost something, you should ask around all the other girls you were *sleeping with* while you were convincing me to pack up my life and move in with you," I spat at him, but that last part of what he had just said, that struck me hard.

I had always thought that quietly to myself, that I owed him something because he had stayed. It had *eaten me alive.* The guilt. It made it easier to believe him when he said that I had forced his hand to find someone else, multiple someones, actually, to help him feel appreciated. I could feel the bile rising in my throat.

"I never asked you to stay, Ben! No one made you stay. I thanked you, every *fucking* day of our whole relationship. It should have never been something you brought up in a fight to make me seem like the bad guy, but you *always did.* Every time! Like somehow, it was my fault for almost dying and I was... I was somehow, what, I don't know, indebted? That's not how caring about someone works Ben!"

I was yelling again. Yet another thing that had come in threes. I was not just yelling in my apartment though, because Ben was still in the hallway.

"You were indebted to me!" Ben screamed, like actually screamed into the crack of the door that I had open between me and him. I felt his spit hit my face.

I was about to yell back. I was so lost in the spiral of emotions and memories that this had brought up. That Ben, being in the hallway outside of my apartment, saying what he was saying, had dragged to the surface of my mind. I had thought I was growing stronger than that, with every callus on my fingertips I had thought I was getting tougher too. It seemed that was not the case.

"Is everything okay here?" An officer said as he stepped out of the elevator with his partner. I hadn't heard police arrive, had there been sirens I would have known. I turned to look at Dean who was walking up to me now. He lifted his phone up awkwardly as if to say, 'it was me'.

He came to stand next to me and said quietly to me first, "I asked them not to sound their sirens, cause… you know."

Dean turned to the policemen, opening the door wider, "Officers, this man is the ex-boyfriend of my roommate. He has come here twice, uninvited, and he's currently very drunk. He also pushed the door open and made her fall backwards. That's when I came out."

Ben's face encompassed a quiet fury as he set the full weight of his gaze onto Dean.

This might not be the moment, but what in the name of all that was orange was going on here. Who was this Dean, and what had he done with my Mac and Cheese smelling roommate?

"It's time you left, Ben," Dean said.

He exchanged a few more words with the police. They asked me something, but I didn't really absorb it, I just nodded.

Dean's hand rested on my shoulder to move me back into the apartment.

Ben was in handcuffs. I looked at him one more time, and I hoped with literally everything I had, that I'd never see him ever again.

He turned to look back at me as the doors to the elevator opened, "I hope you enjoy being alone, Alice. No one will want to pick up all your broken pieces," he spat.

Dean placed his hand above mine on the door, I was gripping it so tightly my fingers had gone bone white, and he shut it.

I didn't move, I just stood there trying to count my breaths.

Breathe in for 10, and out for 10.

When Dean touched my shoulder, it startled me so much I jumped.

"Sorry," he mumbled.

I had held on long enough and there was nothing I could do as the tears welled and started to fall down my face. I just shook my head.

I pulled myself away from the door to head to my room.

"Allie," Dean said.

I turned to look at him.

"I'm sorry I let him into the apartment. I didn't know," Dean pushed his glasses up his nose and scratched his head. I nodded back to him.

I don't know how I did it, but I managed a few words back to him, "Thank you. I… thank you."

Dean stared back at me, sort of like what had just transpired and the person he had morphed into for the last few minutes had never even happened. He scratched the top of his head and made a sound that was kind of like hocking up a loogie to swallow back down your throat again.

I didn't wait to hear what he said after that. I curled up on my bed, a pillow hugged to my chest and let the sobs wrack through my body.

It had been a very long time since I had felt like that. Like I was the size of pea in a world full of giants.

I had forgotten what it was like, the heaviness that pressed in on my chest, the helplessness. Things had been so *good.* I had been so happy for so long and nothing bad had touched those months.

Since the baking aisle, and the couch date and the picnic and the dinners and the FaceTimes. It had all been bright, and colourful. But as I lay there, desperate to calm my own breathing and clear my mind, the greyness that had encompassed everything that I was for what had felt like a very long time, washed over the colour. It dampened the blues, the greens. The reds.

My tears had dried up, and my breathing eventually measured out.

It turned out that my phone was on my side table, probably thanks to Sav, and I just hadn't noticed it. It was on Dax's side, not mine.

Dax's side. I wonder when I had started to think of that side as his.

It was going off relentlessly. I ignored it. I had nothing to give or to say to anyone.

My eyes were looking at nothing for a while until my piano came into focus. I slid off my bed and sat in front of the ivory keys. That still felt safe to me. Ben had never touched that part of my life; he had never turned the black and white keys grey.

I closed my eyes and played every song I remembered. There were a lot of them. I played the soft ones, I played the loud and chaotic ones, I played the thought provoking and cheeky ones. It always worked, always pulled me from whatever funk I found myself in. But with every note I played now, nothing eased. Nothing washed away with the rises and falls of the music. It wasn't working like it usually did. It didn't push the weight off me. I was under water, pinned beneath a rock. That's what it felt like, like I was drowning.

I smacked the keys, the loud sound of all the notes playing at once absorbed my scream. I didn't care if Dean was asleep, or if the apartment above me had heard.

That's when I heard another knock.

My head snapped towards my bedroom door. Like I could see through it, down the hall and into the hallway. I must have been playing for a long time because my body was stiff. I had no idea what time it was, but the sound of that knock on my door immediately sent my heart into a gallop.

Thoughts of Ben explaining what happened to the police in a way that got him out of trouble swarmed through my head. I hated him, I *hated* him.

I stormed out of my room and all but ripped the front door off its hinges, the rage rolling off me was palpable, "I swear to God, Be—," I stopped abruptly.

The words I was about to catapult at him along with the anger, the hurt, all died on my tongue.

It wasn't Ben at my door.

I didn't expect the baseball cap, he was always in a beanie, but I guess with the weather warming up, March brought with it the end of the winter hat season. So, I didn't know that it was him, not right away. He took off his cap and pushed his bright red hair back. His face was a mask of worry like I'd never seen before.

My hand shot to my mouth as a strangled sob escaped me and my legs gave way. It was only a second between that moment and next, when he was before me with his arms circled around me.

His smell enveloped me. It was nothing like what I had remembered, nothing like what I thought still clung to different parts of his shirt I sometimes wore to bed.

My forehead was on his chest as my hands gripped his shirt. He might have said something to me, might have placed a gentle kiss behind my ear, but I didn't hear it, I didn't really feel it. I was just focusing on him, on how the heaviness lifted and the grey receded back. How everything became brighter when he lifted me from the floor of the doorway of my apartment, closing it behind him and settled us onto my bed. He turned the lights off, tucked the blankets around us, and hummed softly while he ran his fingers through my hair.

I suddenly knew what Dax was to me, what I had been frightened to voice to Savannah all those months ago. What made me want to run and hide. It was scary to think about, but it was also the easiest thought that had ever fluttered through my mind.

Dax was *home.*

28

Dax

I woke up in what I was pretty sure was the middle of the night, still wearing my jeans, and incredibly uncomfortable.

That wasn't why I'd exited my R.E.M though. Allie had wiggled out of my hold and was shuffling off the end of the bed.

"Allie," I rubbed my eyes, my voice was still laced with sleep and where I usually would have just rolled over and headed back to dreamland, I'd woken with the painful reminder of her face when she opened her front door.

The anger in her voice I'd never heard before and, quite honestly, couldn't really picture someone like Allie being capable of producing. And then she crumpled to the floor and held onto my shirt like it was a lifeline.

I'd never been so desperate to know what to do in a situation. *What* do you do when that happens? Why did no one ever include that in any of the advice, warranted or not, that had always been shoved down my throat?

She turned to look at me, "Oh, sorry, I tried not to wake

you." Her voice was soft, but alert like she'd been up for a while.

"Everything okay?" I propped myself up on my elbows.

"Yeah, I was hoping to sneak out undetected and steal your shoes but that's okay, I'll do it next time," her voice was whispered and very serious which made me smile.

I felt a little of the weight lift, "You're a terrible robber. You're not supposed to tell the target your plans," I whispered back.

"It's part of the whole thing. Now you'll always be worried I'm going to steal your shoes," she said while standing and turning to look at me.

I tipped my head back and let out a laugh. I had missed this. The in-person stuff. I'd missed *her*.

She gestured over her shoulder with her thumb, "I was going to make tea, can't sleep," she offered me a small smile.

"Want company?" I asked.

"Yeah, but it's too late to ask anyone to come over, that would just be mean to wake someone up this early," she said, turning towards the door.

I barked another laugh quietly at her sass, grateful to see it had made a comeback and got up and followed her into the kitchen.

I sat at the kitchen island while she made two cups of tea. She turned on a few of the lamps in the living room and the light cast us in a soft glow. She sat down across from me and nursed her favourite mug in her hands. It had the question 'what the schnitzel?' on the side with a stick figure shrugging with their hands up in an 'I don't know' gesture. One of the hands held a plate with a little orange blob that I assumed was meant to be a schnitzel.

That was Allie's favourite mug and it didn't surprise me one bit.

We sat in our comfortable silence for a while. I had drunk half my tea already before she spoke.

"I'm worried about what you'll think if I tell you," her eyes remained on her mug of tea.

"Anything you say won't change what I already think about you, Allie," I replied.

"And what is it that you already think?" Her eyes met mine.

"That you're a huge weirdo with too many throw pillows." My face couldn't have been any more serious.

She cracked a smile and it pushed my worry away a little farther.

I waited for her to start. I wouldn't ask her to tell me anything she wasn't comfortable in saying, I hoped she knew that too.

She took a deep breath and started from the beginning.

She told me about her accident.

God, I swear my stomach dropped out through the floor of her apartment. She spoke through it all like it was a rehearsed speech.

It moved from the accident onto Ben's involvement in her life. My stomach suddenly reappeared and went sour.

It was like once she started to explain what her life had been like for the last few years, and what *she* had been like, she couldn't stop.

I wondered if she'd ever had the opportunity to tell someone those events from her perspective before, like she was doing with me now.

I gripped my mug tighter and tighter the more she went on. How was there *more*? Where did she keep all that stuff?

Where did she keep those memories and still find the time to joke about stealing my shoes in the middle of the night?

Allie didn't look at me once while she told me about her injuries, the time in hospital and the person that Ben was, who had been to her and the way he had treated her. Why he was around just before I had gotten back and what he'd said.

By the end of it, we sat in silence again, but it just felt *so loud.* I'd been in arenas full of screaming people and *this* was too loud for me.

Nothing deserved to be that quiet, that serene and still, while I'd just learned that the person I was in love with had endured things I couldn't even comprehend.

"Why didn't you say before? Not about Ben, but the accident? Or any of it, I guess. I could have…" I didn't know how to finish that sentence.

"I guess there were moments I could have mentioned it, but I was worried." She traced the rim of her mug with her pointer.

"About?" I prompted.

"No one has ever looked at me the way you do, Dax. I didn't want that to change, how you looked at me, laughed with me—"

"*At* you," I corrected her. A smile lit up her face immediately.

"I'm sorry that your welcome-home party after something so exciting was so drab." She tucked a loose strand of hair behind her ear.

"No," I got up and walked around the island, she swivelled on her stool to look at me.

For all our banter, our back and forth and jokes and poking fun, I looked her right in her eyes, bright and clear, and urged her to believe everything I was about to say

"You don't apologise for things like that, Allie. For any of it. For your accident or for how he made you feel. None of it has ever been, or ever will be, your fault. I'm sorry if no one has ever taken the time to tell you that. I'm sorry I hadn't been here with you. *I'm* sorry that you couldn't tell me sooner. I swear, Allie, I won't ever hurt you like that," I leaned in and kissed her forehead.

I didn't know if that was good, or the right thing to say. If it was too much or too little.

Her arms looped around my waist, and that's how we stayed until I was sure our tea was cold, and the sun was going to peak up around the buildings of the city outside soon.

Allie took a big inhale, like a massive sniff.

"Are you smelling me?" I stepped back to look at her, a smile already ghosting my lips.

"Absolutely, I am. You've been gone for three months and now I realise that I've really just been smelling myself on the shirt you left here," she explained, letting her arms drop.

"You've been smelling my shirt?" I lifted an eyebrow and clamped my lips shut. Allie hopped off her stool and took our cups to the sink.

"Like my life depended on it," she replied and I cracked, a laugh bubbled out of me. I laughed, of course, but there wasn't a single part of me that wasn't elated to hear that she had been sleeping in one of my shirts.

Allie walked down the hall, flipped me off over her shoulder, grabbed her robe from her room and went to have a shower.

It was a lot later than I thought, it was almost 6:30AM and I knew the Allie would have to leave for work soon, so I decided to duck out while she was in the shower and grab some coffees and croissants. Our usual.

I picked up her keys and locked the door to her apartment on my way out, not entirely comfortable leaving it open given all the new information I had just learned. Even if Dean had stepped up, which surprised me as much as it had surprised Allie. For all his faults, he was a good guy. I'll think about buying him something orange as a thank you.

Holding the bag of pastry between my teeth, I unlocked the door to her apartment and pushed it open with my back. I turned to find Allie standing at the end of the hallway in her fuzzy robe. I lifted the takeaways and paper bag up.

"Breakfast?" I grinned at her.

"I thought you left," she said back, her voice a little too sad to be funny. Her expression looked a little too lost.

"Oh, I did," I walked by her, planted a kiss on her temple and sat the bag and cups on the counter, "I was actually running like the wind; you should have seen me," I continued as I grabbed a couple plates from the cupboard.

"Oh?" she said, her face lifted as she finally caught on. I'd be damned though, if the tightness in my chest didn't ease at seeing her light up.

"Mmm. Olympic quality," I put a croissant on each plate.

"I'm sorry I missed it," she laughed.

I walked over and grabbed her hand. I led her to a stool and pulled it out for her to sit before I took the lid off one of the coffee cups and put it in front of her.

"What made you change your mind?" she said around a mouth full of chocolate and pastry.

"I haven't had your 6 out of 10 meatballs yet," my response was spoken around a bite equally as large which earned the biggest snort-laugh I'd heard yet.

29

Allie

Dax walked me right to the doors of my office building. His hair was tucked away tightly into the baseball cap he had worn to mine straight off the plane and with a kiss farewell, and the assurance that Aspen was on his way to grab him, I headed into the office.

I tapped the elevator call button until the doors opened and stepped inside. I was the only one going up. It was refreshing.

I swear, Allie, I won't ever hurt you like that.

Dax's words circled around my mind like a canoe with only one paddle.

It's not like I never thought someone would say that to me, like I thought I was going to be alone forever and never share with someone the ongoings of the last three years of my life. I had thought I'd meet someone, tell them of my past and that I'd hear those exact words. What I didn't realise was that when I heard them, I'd believe them.

And I did, I believed every word that Dax had said which was… weird. And sort of freeing, like I was a little bird pushed out of the nest and I had about 4 seconds to learn how to fly for the first time or *splat*. I was kaput.

This is going to sound really stupid, but I *did* feel like I was flying, or at least moving farther away from the nearing ground rather than closer to it.

Allie: *Have a good day. Thank you for breakfast and smelling so great.*

Dax: *I am going to sleep for forever. You can just transfer me for the coffee whenever.*

I huffed a laugh, taking the time to think of the perfect reply that would make him pee himself just a little, but it seemed I had taken just that little bit too long.

"Alice!" There was nowhere in the world I wouldn't have recognised that voice. Unfortunately.

For anyone who wondered or really cared, my boss's name was Bart.

Yes, exactly like the character from the Simpsons. Better yet, his full first name was Bartholomew and he used it whenever he was speaking to any other bigwigs that came in for a yarn.

I looked it up, he told everyone that it meant he was the great descendent of some important person. Anyone with two fingers and a phone could've told you that there was no version of this reality where that was true in any capacity.

I called him Bart the Fart, and I was equally excited and terrified that I would one day say it out loud to his face. I mean, could you *imagine?*

"My office," he said, pointing at the small glass square behind him. All the drapes were drawn as they always were.

I dropped my stuff at my desk before I walked in. I kept the door open as I sat down.

"Shut the door, please," he said, and I was confident he waited until I had taken my seat before he said it, just so I'd have to get back up.

That was the sort of person Bart the Fart was.

"Where were you yesterday? Take the day off when you knew you'd messed up on the campaign?" His eyebrows were raised high like he was satisfied in catching me in the act of avoiding my responsibilities.

"I wasn't feeling well. I actually spent the whole day in bed. You had mentioned on Wednesday that the campaign went well, I didn't realise there were so many faults," I replied as politely as possible, trying to keep my eyes off the sweat patches that had soaked through his blazer.

"Well, there was a shit-storm of issues yesterday with the choice of asset used for our Facebook ads, Alice." His eyebrows didn't move, like they were taped up.

"Bart, Sir, I am not in charge of the assets, that's Allegra's responsibility. I put together the plan and then monitor for opportunities of optimization through the course of the campaign," I explained.

We'd had this conversation more times than I could remember, but I was continuously impressed on how well I managed to hold myself every time. I really wanted to tell him to stick his asset up his ass.

"Alice, is your role not the *Marketing Manager*?" he said it like it was an insult.

"It is," I replied.

"Then *manage* the *fucking* marketing," his eyebrows still didn't move, but his attention did finally drift from my face.

"Absolutely," I said.

You pimple of a man.

"I'll get right on it," I stood up.

I bet you've never gotten laid.

I walked out of his office feeling a lot better with the additions to my responses I had said internally. I was a positive person. I was the sort of glass-half-full person. But even I could admit that everyone has a threshold, and I just didn't need that today.

I was thinking about all the hard days I'd hit consecutively and pumped myself up that the good days were around the corner. This world demanded balance; I could dig that. I wasn't selfish enough to believe that I was the only person alive who deserved all good days and no bad ones, but surely there was a scale or something that determined how shit one's day was and how many other shitty days they should then incur afterward.

I spent the rest of the day thinking about that. About the scale on which my days sat. I didn't just dwell on the bad ones though, I had so many 10 out of 10 days in the last 6 months that I really had nothing to complain about.

As true as that was, there was nothing that could have stopped me from picking up a box of brownie mix on my way home.

I sent a photo of them to Dax.

Dax: *I really hope I never meet your boss.*
I would accidentally sneeze in his salad.

I was laughing to myself like a mad woman as I continued down the street to my apartment, thinking about all the ways that I would one day quit and make my dramatic exit from that company. How I would really stick it to the man by throwing a stack of paper into the air and not care in the slightest who had to pick it up. Maybe photocopy my ass and print it out a hundred times and put a copy in everyone's 'in' drawers.

Once, I had walked by a little dog turd on my way to work and thought about all the different reactions that Bart would have if I placed it on his desk for him to find when he walked in.

That made me laugh even more. I hadn't entirely ruled out that particular event from ever coming to fruition. It was in the vault. Just in case.

People could judge me all they wanted, but if they had their ass grabbed by someone named Bart the Fart who perspired through his thick polyester blazer, they'd be thinking about it too.

Dax: *Want me to come round?*

Yes, a thousand times yes.

Allie: *I can feel your lack of energy from here. It's okay, you sleep. Message me tomorrow when your reserves are no* *longer depleted.*

Dax: *Save one for me.*

I made the brownies.

I made them really well too.

The top glistened and the edges had a nice crust. I sliced into them and if you were imagining a nice gooey centre, you would be on the nose. They were the gooiest, and I didn't want them.

I didn't want a single one.

I waved hello to Dean as he walked in, he asked if he could have one and I wasn't defensive at all. I even told him he could have two. *Two.*

I didn't have dinner either, I thought that maybe my body thought it needed dinner before dessert, which had never been an issue before, but it had been a weird week for me to say the least so if my body's response to brownies was altered I would understand. But, the urge to gorge never came.

By the time I looked away from the brownies sitting on the plate in front of me it was midnight.

Midnight.

So that meant I had been sitting and looking at a plate of warm brownies slowly going cold for 6 hours.

I lifted my phone from where it sat face down on the counter and it unlocked immediately when it took in my face.

My phone was still open on my messages with Dax.

I sat and looked at it for a while, at the last conversation we'd had.

I grabbed the plate of brownies and threw some cling wrap over them. Pulled on my jacket and hopped into my shoes as

I raced out of my apartment. I had the mind to close the door quietly as to not wake Dean, then I was full speed ahead.

I knew where Dax lived. It was a 40-minute walk from my apartment, but if I ran I could make it in half that time.

I didn't even know if he was going to be home, or awake, or whatever.

I ran, holding the plate of brownies out in front of me like I was in an egg and spoon race. My Chucks smacking the sidewalk and echoing back off the buildings around me.

I kept my eyes mostly on the ground and for every car that drove by, I turned my head away, avoiding the glare of their lights.

I managed to run for about 10 minutes.

10 minutes and I was so sure I was going to die. Oh my god.

My determination and my grip on the plate of brownies didn't falter, even though my stamina had let me down.

I walked and walked and walked.

I was standing face to face with the base of his intimidating building. My heart was thundering with the very idea that he might be up on the top floor, as well as from the mini marathon I'd just completed.

What was I doing here?

No, I knew.

I knew what I was doing here.

I pressed the call button for his floor.

Can we just… his *whole* floor.

Yeah, I'd get used to that when pigs flew.

I buzzed again, and again. The fact that it was now almost 1AM didn't stop me.

I went to buzz again but stopped myself. I had called up more times than what should have been required.

He wasn't home. That was fine, he might have been out with his brother or—

"Hello?" Dax's sleepy voice croaked through the little speaker.

I didn't even hesitate, "It's Allie."

He might have said something back, and I could have totally missed his response over the pounding of my heart, but I didn't think he said anything. There was a little wait and then the door buzzed and clanged, and I pulled it open.

My momentum had slowed down during the wait, but I still tapped the button for the elevator with a speed I wished I had been able to run here with.

It finally arrived and I hopped in, tapping the top button.

37.

It lit up without needing a card to scan and took me all the way up.

It was the longest elevator ride of my life.

My heart had calmed down by the time the doors pinged open, and showed Dax pacing back and forth in nothing but his boxers, his red hair askew in every direction.

"Jesus Christ, Allie. Are you okay? How did you get here, what—," he stopped, "are those brownies?" He had every right to look as confused as he did.

"I walked here," I said.

"You *walked* here?"

"And yes, they're brownies. They're like 10-points-to-Allie sort of brownies too," I handed him the plate and he took them, looking at the plate, to my face then back to the plate and back to my face.

"10-points-to-Allie?" He looked dumbfounded, "You give yourself points?" His face broke out into the biggest shit-eating grin.

I just seriously have no filter.

"Just blink twice if I'm right," he continued, lifting his eyebrows.

I knew my face was the colour of his hair, so I tactfully changed the subject.

"Did I wake up Aspen too?" I enquired, none the wiser, peering around him to look for his brother.

Dax pushed his hair back with one hand, letting out an exhale and clearly not as phased by my weirdness as he ought to be, "No, he went out with Rip. They don't really get affected by jet lag, or so they say." He shook his head, "You could have called me, I would have come over and gotten you and your 10-points-to-Allie brownies, or I could have come round to yours for the night or something."

I was sure he was thinking about yesterday, but that wasn't why I had walked all the way to his.

I rolled my eyes at me, "No, it's— well, I made the brownies," I nodded towards the plate in his hands, "But I didn't eat any."

"You didn't?" He looked at the plate that was clearly missing two brownies.

"That was Dean," I clarified. He rolled his eyes, earning a smile from me.

"I made them, and I didn't want them. I stared at them for 6 hours and I didn't want a single bite," I said, looking at his face.

"You spent 6 hours staring at brownies? How do you know they're worthy of 10 points if you didn't try any?" He was trying not to laugh.

"Dax!" I whined, "you're missing the point."

He sobered up but kept on his signature side smirk, "What's

the point, Allie?"

"The brownies weren't going to fix it. They weren't what I wanted," my voice had dropped down, and though I was speaking low and quiet, it still felt too loud for the stillness of his apartment.

Dax's eyes darkened immediately. He took in my own features as the reason why I had walked almost an hour to his apartment in the middle of the night clicked into place.

He set the brownies down on the floor just beside me, next to the doors of the elevator. His breathing had quickened ever so slightly, and I was suddenly painfully aware that he was in his underwear, and only his underwear, right in front of me.

"Mmm?" The weight of his gaze was literally like nothing I'd ever experienced.

"Yes, well, I thought about it, and then I thought of you. And I thought of you and me, well... I mean, then *naturally* I thought of us. I guess what I'm *trying* to say is—"

"What did you want, Allie?" His voice was thick.

"You," I breathed, and I reached for him.

His hands were in my hair, they roamed down the sides of my neck and continued to move up and down my body like he didn't know what to do, where to start.

My arms were locked around his neck and my own hands had found their standard place of residence in his hair.

His hair. I tugged at it a bit, earning a throaty sound that would be my absolute undoing.

He tugged at my jacket in response, not breaking from our kiss as he pushed it from my shoulders, and it landed on the floor behind me.

He started moving us backwards and, with every step towards his room, another article of my clothing was left behind. I cast a thought to what someone might've thought if they arrived here and saw my clothes paving the way to Dax's room, but I didn't care. In fact, I sort of liked it.

I'll be damned, who was this person and what have they done with the Alice Charlotte Jamison I know.

I'd admit, taking off my slacks - the same ones I had worn to work because I hadn't changed and just spent the whole evening staring at baked goods - was a definite interruption to the kissing.

Dax unbuttoned and helped me shimmy them down. I almost *fell over* which had us both laughing. Dax stopped our retreat and bent down to remove the pants entirely considering they were a health and safety hazard. His words exactly.

That moment sort of slowed everything down. I stood back up after using his crouched frame for support as he tossed the slacks away.

He placed a soft kiss on the inner side of my knee and looked up at me. He kept my gaze the whole way up to his impressive height before his eyes roamed my features again.

"Is this okay?" he whispered as his hands moved down my shoulders to my arms.

I nodded my head, "Yes. More than okay."

He bent down to lift me up, my legs circling around his waist and he walked us the rest of the way into his room, nudging the door closed gently.

Our kisses changed then, they were no longer frantic or greedy, they were exactly the sort of kisses that said the words I struggled to find the courage to say, the words I was *afraid* to say no matter how true they might have been. The sort of kisses that made it so you didn't really need to say it out loud at all, he'd just know. He had to know.

The weight of Dax settling above me was an experience in and of itself. He held himself up just enough, but I felt every inch of his skin against mine.

Our hands explored one another. We had done that before, I had traced the planes of his chest and felt the dips and lines of his back, and he knew my own body about as well as I knew it myself. But this was different. This felt new, this felt like *more.*

My whole body erupted into goosebumps as Dax traced the line of my jaw with his lips.

I was going to combust, Lord help me.

"You're so beautiful, Allie," Dax mumbled against my skin.

"You are," I said back, breathless.

"I know," he said, his mouth still lazily followed a path I couldn't see, but one he knew well, across the different surfaces of my body.

I snorted a laugh.

Of all the times to snort-laugh, that was not it, Allie.

Dax drew back and looked down at me with his sexy side smirk, "That was so hot, do it again."

I burst out laughing. He wagged his eyebrows at me, and I brought my hands up to cover my face.

"Oh *shit,* I'm so sorry," I couldn't stop laughing.

"I could pass some gas if that would make things even?" he enquired which made me snort-laugh again, louder.

"Dax! That's totally ruined the moment." The giggle fit finally dissipated as I met his eyes once more.

"Has it?" His face settled back into a mask of calm, of expectation and, *hot damn,* so much lust I could have caught on fire.

"No, it hasn't." I pulled him down to me and he settled his weight on me again. I sighed into him.

Dax reached over to his top drawer and grabbed something out of it. He leaned back and ripped open the little square pack with his teeth.

Fuck, I completely forgot.

20 points for Dax, cause that little detail completely evaded my mind during the almost hour stroll to get here and every moment since.

The pressure was slight to start, but the closer we became, the more intense it felt.

My eyes quite literally rolled to the back of my head and the little habit of mine that involved his name and my tongue popped back into existence after going dormant since our first encounter.

He halted as my eyes closed completely.

The only sound for a moment was our breathing and then Dax leaned down and placed a kiss on both my eyelids. Yes, it felt about as sweet as it sounded.

I opened them to see him there above me, looking at me in the way that he did.

My throat clogged with emotion.

I never wanted that to change. I'd never not want to have him look at me like that. I didn't even know someone *could* look at me like that.

"Hey," he said, beginning to move again.

"Hey," I whispered back, reaching for him.

I had never been more grateful for jet lag, or more accurately Dax's brothers lack thereof, and I was infinitely more pleased that we had the entire penthouse to ourselves.

30

Allie

Someone was yelling from Dax's living room.

The phrases *oh my god* and *she's here* were repeated over and over and then there was a knock at Dax's door.

"Go away, Aspen," Dax croaked from behind me.

We were curled up. Me, the little spoon to his big spoon. His breath tickled the back of my neck.

"I can't do that Dax. I have to come in," Aspen's voice held a bitter sweetness, like he didn't want to, but he had no other choice.

The dramatics of their family, I swear...

"What is wrong with you? We'll be out soon," Dax's voice, on the other hand, was exasperated. I had already started to shake with laughter.

"I'm giving you five more seconds to get decent, and I think you'll need them considering that our hallway is now Allie's closet."

"*Oh no*, my clothes," I breathed, embarrassed. I turned in Dax's arms, "*My clothes*!" I repeated in a whisper-shout.

He just took in my face and gave me a sleepy half smile. He kissed my nose and then without any warning, he grabbed me and rolled us over, so his back was now to the door. I made a very unladylike squeal, sort of like pig.

Not a second later Aspen walked in.

"Aspen, get out," Dax grabbed the pillow and threw it at his brother. It hit him directly in the face and then dropped to the floor. It was hilarious and I was properly cackling.

"The infamous Wallie, at last," Aspen let out a sigh of relief, and raised both arms as if in praise.

Finally, someone who is weirder than me. Win.

I poked my head up and gave him my biggest smile, "Hey, Aspen."

"Allie! Nice to finally see you actually exist and that Dax's wallpaper isn't a random photo off the internet," he winked at me, "I'm making pancakes, get up. It's already brunch time," Aspen said over his shoulder as he walked out of Dax's room.

"Brunch time?" I mouthed to Dax. He just shook his head as if to say, 'don't even get him started'.

Dax, ever the gentleman, gathered my more delicate garments and handed them to me before braving the hallway, and his brothers exuberant singing of our ship name, for the rest of my clothes.

As soon as Dax left, I reached for his phone. There I was, my guitar on my lap and smiling like an idiot. When he came back into his room, his arms full of my clothes, I turned his phone screen towards him.

"When did you do this?" My voice was the epitome of disbelief.

"When we were on tour." He climbed back onto the bed and settled next to me, placing a kiss just behind my ear.

"I think that earns you 10 points," I leaned into him.

"Oh? I get points too?" he murmured, close enough to feel the whisper of his words.

"Mmm," I kissed him. His phone was forgotten quickly, and I regretted starting to get dressed.

"Wallie! Pancakes!" Ap yelled from the kitchen.

"For the love of all that's holy," Dax dropped his forehead to my shoulder.

"I sort of hope he says that to us in public sometime," I winked at Dax, my head tipped back in laughter at the horrified expression on his face. I gave him a quick kiss on the corner of his mouth, "Mmm. We'll have to be faster next time," I leaned away from him with an exaggerated exhale and reached for my pants.

"You always know just what to say to boost my confidence, Allie."

Dax was beaming at me while he grabbed some pants of his own, but he chose to forgo the shirt. I just rolled my eyes at him and reached my hand out.

"Let's go get our Wallie-cakes," I led us out into the hallway.

Dax had quickly typed something into his phone and then chucked it on the bed on our way out. I couldn't help but wonder what that was about.

"Don't ever repeat that word, ever again," Dax pushed his hair back from his face and grimaced.

I got to meet Aspen properly then. *Properly* being defined as in person and not naked.

It was sort of noticeable when I saw him through video chat, but in person, Aspen looked so like his brother it took me a bit by surprise.

Aspen was a couple of years younger than Dax, and his

face showed it. Whereas Dax's natural hair colour was black, Aspen's was a dark brown. Expressive brows of the same colouring sat above eyes that were such a bright green that you *felt* warm just looking at them. They were kind. The real difference, though, between him and Dax, was their smiles.

Dax's smile, the one I saw, the one he gave just to me, was soft and small and it was almost like it rarely ever saw the light. Aspen's smile was sun kissed and unrelenting.

Meeting Aspen was just as I thought it was going to be like. We had spoken a fair amount over the last three months, and I already felt like I knew him, so when we sat down to have pancakes, it was like we'd done it hundreds of times before.

"Those were the best pancakes I've ever had," I leaned back and patted my stomach.

"Well, we have to balance each other out," Aspen replied, setting his own fork down on his empty plate. I arched an eyebrow in question.

He pointed to himself, "Sweet," and then he pointed at Dax, "Savoury."

"Ahh. Did you know when we met, he told me that 'cooking wasn't for everyone', told me that you were the cook in the family and then proceeded to whip up a storm in the kitchen?" I said to Aspen as I narrowed my eyes at Dax.

Aspen just sat there grinning like he had the front row seat to a show he'd always wanted to see.

"I never said I couldn't cook," Dax defended himself, still eating his pancakes.

"It was *implied,* and you know it!" I pointed an accusatory finger at him.

"Allie, you struggled to turn on your stove top," he looked at me, an eyebrow raised, daring me to keep going.

He had a point.

"Yeah, well, you've never had a box brownie as good as mine," I slumped back into my stool.

"That," Dax pointed his fork at me, "is very true. They're delicious," he leaned over and kissed me on the cheek.

Aspen wrinkled his nose at the mention of dessert that wasn't made from scratch.

I was rolling my eyes so much lately, I swear they were going to permanently remain looking towards my frontal lobes if I wasn't careful.

Dax sorted me out with the necessary things for a shower. He had one of those rain showers where the water stream just fell from the ceiling. It was incredible and I stayed in for so long that he came to knock on the door to see if I was okay.

By the time I had dried off, dressed and made my way out into the living room, the brothers were having a very quiet argument.

"What's going on?" I was standing at the top of the stairs, observing them from above.

"Aspen thinks he's going to drive you home," Dax couldn't have sounded more unimpressed.

"That would be great, Ap," I thanked him and tried to keep the gracious look on my features while I had a mental breakdown regarding my calling him by Dax's nickname.

At what point did you start to call someone by a nickname they had been given by someone else?

"I mean, Aspen. Sorry," I winced at how awkward I sounded.

Definitely deducting 5 points for that awesome little performance.

His face softened, "Ap is good, Al," he winked at me.

Only Savannah called me Al. I wonder what she would

think when I told her that the nickname had now been commandeered by someone else.

"I'll take her home, Aspen," Dax interrupted my little thought bubble.

"I've met her once, Dax. I just want to talk to her," he turned to look at me. His gaze morphed from casual to mischievous between one blink and the next, "Get to know my future sister-in-law better. And plus, Allie wants to get to know me too, don't you Allie?"

I'm not sure what my face did, but whatever the visual was, Aspen's turned red from the strain of holding in his laughter and Dax looked positively mortified. My entire body erupted into goosebumps and I wanted to scream and cry at the same time.

Holy sheep shearing, grandma knitting, sweater vests.

Sister-in-law.

Get a grip Allie, hold it in.

I swallowed the swarm of butterflies that threatened to fly out of my mouth. Dax spun back towards his brother and I swear I'd never seen a man move so fast in my life .

I composed myself as quickly as I could with a promise to my internal self-hype woman to die over that little moment later in the safety of my own room.

Clearing my throat, I decided I would ghost over the entire ordeal, but not before taking a mental snap of the expression still plastered on Dax's face, the man was speechless.

I had never been a good actress, so despite my own confidence that I could pretend Ap didn't just say what he said, my voice came out in a high pitched squeak, "Then it's settled."

Any handle both Dax and Aspen had on their expressions cracked and they tipped their heads back in laughter.

Ah. Must be a Smith family thing.

I walked down the stairs, a small smile of my own on my face and gave Dax a peck on the cheek and a sassy tap on the bum before I headed towards the elevator.

"Aren't we hanging out today?" he pouted at me, shirtless and standing in his living room. He'd almost completely recovered from the whole sister-in-law ordeal.

"Tomorrow? I need to clean my apartment and do washing and gross adult things," I made a gagging sound.

"Okay, tomorrow. That works," he nodded.

I ran back over and gave him another kiss before trying for a mad dash, but he caught my arm and pulled me back. I squeaked and he laughed, it was so cute that it was gross.

"You guys are so cute, it's gross. Come on, Al," Aspen hit the call button for the elevator. He only hit it once which gave me the heebie-jeebies.

Because I couldn't help it, I stole a third kiss from Dax and tossed my most casual farewell over my shoulder, "Toodles!"

I froze where I was.

No, Allie. No, no. You literally just *slept with him. You needed to wait before the accents came out.*

"Wait, wait a second, what was that?" Dax's face was the picture of flat out shock.

I turned on my heels to look at him, completely mortified that I'd just flung out my Swedish accent impression to him with zero context given. Dax didn't know about my flare for accents.

"That was nothing," I could feel my face going beet-red.

"Don't tell me. You do impressions," he lost it, laughing without any restraint.

"I do not do impressions," I said. I lifted my chin a little higher, "I do accents and that was Swedish, I'll have you know. A very good take on it, too."

"Hold on, Allie," Dax was wiping tears from his eyes, "say it again, please, do it again." He was bending at the waist with his hands on his knees.

I rolled my eyes, stuck my tongue out and headed towards the elevator. It shut with Dax, cry-laughing while apologising and I think he was trying to assure me that it was incredibly accurate as far as Swedish accents went. I couldn't be sure, but I think he fell to his knees at the end there.

I huffed a laugh as the elevator doors closed. I thought about the next time I would see him and how I'd bring out the Scottish accent that I personally thought was my best work. He was going to wet his pants. I couldn't wait.

The silence on the way down with Aspen wasn't uncomfortable, but it wasn't like it was with Dax.

I was asking him about his day as we walked out of the elevator and into the basement parking of their building. He told me about how he was going to unpack as well and that there was a new video game out that he wanted so that he and Angus could verse one another, so he was probably going to order it online.

He was still going on when I looked from him to the entry ramp.

A car had just pulled in. It was daytime, so I wasn't being mindful or careful about the headlights of oncoming vehicles, but I should have been. I always needed to remember.

So, when the car entered the basement we were in - it was much darker than it was outside - the automatic headlights snapped on. I immediately stopped hearing things and my breathing started to quicken.

No. Please, no.

I was acutely aware of being around Aspen, and that this was not something I had told his brother when I mentioned my accident.

It all started to happen - the headlights flashed behind my eyes and I felt myself flinch away, covering my ears as the horn blared in my ears. My fingers had started to go numb, vibrating with pins and needles and I knew that I called out but what I said or how loud, I had no idea.

Like there was a door and I was being pushed farther away from it, the light to the exit getting dimmer and dimmer as I curled farther and farther into myself. It was crippling.

"Breathe."

It wasn't Savannah's voice that spoke to me then. I had all but forgotten for a moment who I was with or where I was, but I listened.

I inhaled. Not nearly enough air for what I needed but it was air all the same.

The hand that tried to soothe me was not the one I was used to. Instead of Savannah's circular motions on my back, Aspen gently dragged his hand up and down.

It was different but grounding all the same.

"Breathe," he said again.

I wasn't sure how many more times he said it, or how long I had been sitting on the floor of the garage with my hands over my ears and my knees against my chest. Aspen was sitting next to me, his hand still making a gentle trail up and down my back.

I finally lifted my head up, turning to look at him. Unshed tears of embarrassment were sitting in my eyes.

"I'm so sorry," I croaked out to him.

His face adopted a look of confusion that was so like his brother's it made me yearn to run back up to the thirty-seventh floor.

"Why would you be sorry for that, Allie? You don't ever need to apologise for having an anxiety attack. You can't pick and choose when they happen. Don't apologise," he gave me a small smile that made me want to fall apart all over again.

It's not like Sav had never told me that it wasn't my fault, that I didn't need to apologise, but for some reason when Aspen said it, when *Dax* said it, it felt different.

"I had a car accident three years ago," I explained.

"You don't have to—," Aspen started.

I shook my head, "No, no. It's fine. I have PTSD because of it. Headlights are a problem for me. It's why I don't drive," I finished.

Aspen nodded his head and was silent for a moment, "Does Dax know?" His question wasn't loaded with expectation, just with an honest enquiry. Like 'if I told him about this, would he lose his mind?' sort of thing.

I nodded, "He knows about the accident. I hadn't quite gotten to this part yet. It's a lot to absorb. I *am* going to tell him. I just don't know how," I said honestly. And it was true, I didn't know how to explain to another person that this was my every day. Not everyone got it, understood it, or even accepted it.

It was why I hadn't let my work know about it. Could you imagine Bart the Fart if he knew about it?

Aspen stood up and held his hands out to me to help me to my feet.

"Thanks for your help," I mumbled.

He waved me off as we walked the rest of the way to his

beat-up sedan, "Don't mention it, Al."

"How did you—," I started.

"I had a friend in high school who struggled with anxiety. Big crowds, small spaces, that kind of thing. They taught me a lot about how to help someone in that situation," Aspen unlocked the car. It made a loud *beep* that caused me to jump, my heart rate fluttered but I kept a handle on it.

"Well, I'm grateful for your friend," I slid into the passenger seat that had become so familiar to me. It'd been months since I sat in it last, but it felt like sliding on a pair of old jeans that were just my size.

The drive back to mine was equally as silent as the elevator, but almost more comfortable.

The day was beautiful. It was warm and gave the first taste of true spring as the last of winter melted away. Despite the situation that had just occurred in the basement of Dax's building, I felt… well, I felt freaking top-dog for lack of a better phrase.

I felt like that kid at the birthday party who filled up their plastic cup with some kind of delicious beverage and then proceeded to tip it upside down then right side up super-fast without spilling the drink and everyone was like 'woah, no way!'.

That was how I felt. Like the kid who could keep their juice in their plastic cup when doing the fancy magic trick.

Not only was the sun shining, but I had just had the best sex of my *life* with the guy that I was so in love with that I was putting every rom-com I'd seen and read to shame.

I felt like a phoenix from the ashes.

Was that weird to say? Probably.

It gave me an idea.

I turned to Aspen, “Hey Ap, if I wanted to do something for Dax, like a surprise, could you help?”

Aspen’s grin was blinding, “Whatever Wallie needs, Wallie gets.”

31

Dax

I was in my guitar room when Aspen got home.

"Hey, Ap!" I called out.

I heard him dump his keys and then make his way up the small set of stairs.

"Hey, I have this new chord progression I was thinking would be good for the lyrics you—," I looked up to find him standing in the doorway, his hand rubbing the back of his neck and it looked like he either had some really bad gas or something bad had happened.

"What?" My heart jumped into my throat, "What?" I said again. I pulled the guitar strap over my head and set the instrument back in the stand, turning off the amp.

"Come sit for a second," Ap just turned away and headed back towards the living room. I was on his heels but didn't pester him until we sat down.

He told me everything that had happened. He told me what Allie had told him - she didn't know how to explain it to me and that though he didn't feel like it was his place, it might help to not have to tell me herself.

He mentioned the PTSD, the anxiety and the panic attack. The headlights.

It was like hearing about her accident all over again.

I knew of Aspen's friend from high school, so I knew that, by whatever grace, he was the perfect person to have been with her. I knew he would have known what to do, how to help her.

If it had been me, I'm not sure I would've known. I still felt like when she told me about the accident and Ben, that I should have said something more, done something more.

"Did she tell you about the accident?" I asked him after a beat. Once he had told me about the basement, we both just sat for a while.

"Just that she was in one," he dragged a hand down his face and slumped back into the couch with an exhale.

I nodded back.

"Did she know you were going to say something? Like, if I were to call her would this be crossing a line or something?" I pushed my hair back from my face.

"I think she assumed I would mention it. She didn't say not to, maybe she thought it would be easier this way too, for me to tell you," he replied softly.

"She's not broken, Ap." It came out sterner than I had intended.

I hated the way he was looking, like he felt sorry for her or that maybe how she looked changed in his eyes. Rationally, I knew he didn't think those things, but it was almost a reflex to think that. To defend her. To be angry at the people who treated her differently or less than, all because she had gone through something horrible and come out the other side still smiling.

"I didn't say she was, Dax," his response was equally as defensive. I knew he cared about her already, it was just the kind of guy he was. Aspen had a big heart and was all fun, all the time. A little - okay, a whole butt load - dramatic, but he could turn on his serious side faster than you could say 'Wallie-cakes.'

"It's okay to call her, Dax," his face had softened. His eyes then took on a glint that told me he had moved on from the heavy, that he had passed on what he needed to and that he was going to step back now, "If I hear any loud moaning coming from your room, I will not hesitate to post the photo of you, butt naked in a paddling pool, on the internet," he got up and headed for the stairs, no doubt to his drum room.

"For fuck's sake, Aspen. I was 5! It is perfectly normal to swim naked at that age!" I called after him, and just like that, the mood changed.

"We could totally just let the internet decide, if you're so confident!" he retorted just before closing the door.

I rolled my eyes and flipped him off. I stood up and grabbed Aspen's keys before heading straight for the basement.

* * *

She picked up on the first ring.

I was sitting outside her apartment building. My heart had been racing the whole drive over and wasn't letting up even after I had sat, staring at the window I knew looked into her living room, for the last thirty minutes.

"Hey," she sounded tired.

"Hey yourself, what's going on?" I tried my best to sound relaxed, or as normal as I usually did.

"Nothing too much. I put on some laundry and now I'm laying in bed. I was going to try and play the guitar for a bit but I'm exhausted," she yawned.

"How are your chords going?" I knew my smile was apparent in my voice.

"Yes, I am incredibly good at the four I know. I think I'm about ready for the next four," she sounded so proud.

"Wax on, wax off, grasshopper," I said in my most serious voice, I could practically *hear* her rolling her eyes.

"You know I saw you, like, two hours ago," she changed the subject.

"Yeah, I know." It was silent for a little while, but that was normal for us.

"Ap said?" she enquired. She knew that I'd know what she meant.

"Yeah, he mentioned," I replied. I jumped out of the car, letting the door close lightly and jogged across the street to her building.

"I'm sorry I didn't tell you. I *wanted* to tell you, I just thought between the accident and Ben, the third little nugget of truth would have broken the horse's back," she said quietly. I could picture her playing with the frilly edges of one of her throw pillows.

I knew why she would have felt that way. Now that I knew about Ben, I could get a grasp on her reasonings more easily. It still didn't change the fact that I wanted to be there for her.

The elevator doors opened, and I pressed the number to her floor, then I tapped the button to close the doors until they shut.

"It wouldn't have," was all I said back.

"You don't know that, Dax. It's one thing to hear it, and

another to see it. It's not this romantic thing where you're a hero swooping in to save the damsel situation," I could hear her heavy breathing through the phone.

"I don't think you need saving, Allie. Maybe some cooking lessons, but that's probably about it," I stepped out of the elevator and walked the few steps to her apartment door.

I heard her huff a laugh, "Dax— Oh, one second someone just knocked on my door."

I pocketed my phone. If I could have captured the look on her face when she opened the door, I would have been the proud owner of the newest viral meme image.

She was wearing a long, bright pink pyjama shirtdress. The colour was completely not Allie, but the phrase on the front, however, was without a doubt on brand.

It had a groundhog on the front of it that had a long winded explanation about how groundhogs and woodchucks were the same animal, then proceeded to write out the corrected version of 'how much wood could a woodchuck chuck' which was, of course, 'how much ground, could a groundhog mound'.

Like I said, very Allie.

If you're imagining the writing going all the way to the bottom of the shirtdress and not just the standard slogan spacing being in the middle of the chest, then you're correct. I had to ask her at some point where she even bought her clothes.

"What the shi—what are you doing here?" she asked, a little breathless.

"I figured that you might need some help with your adult things today," I explained, running a hand through my hair.

"Dax—," she started, a little frown forming.

"I know you're capable, it's not that. I want to be there for you, Allie. I don't want to do it for you, I just want to help you do it. Make things a bit easier, lighten the load, brighten the day—," she interrupted me then.

"If I don't stop you there, I don't think you'll ever stop," she said, her frown ironing out. She was fighting a smile.

I continued anyway, "Balance the scale a bit, be the fruit to your vegetables—"

"You're just saying things now," her smile broke through.

"Be the knife to your fork—," I was very quickly running out of things to say.

"If I let you in will you stop?" she said with so much sass I could have choked, but her face was mischievous.

"Only if I get to fold your delicates," I followed her into her apartment and closed the door behind me. She barked a laugh so loudly that I jolted, making myself laugh.

It made me think of something that was completely unrelated.

"When's your birthday?" she turned to look at me as I asked.

She was familiar with our questions game, so she just went with it, "Start of December," she said, "Just before we met, actually. When's yours?"

"End of November," I walked up to her and pulled her to me. "Let me in, Allie. I can handle it all. All the parts you're worried might be hard to take, that you think are a lot. Let me decide that, okay? Let me in."

Her eyes scanned my face. She nodded, "Okay. You have to let me in too, though." Her hands rested against my chest.

"I already have," and I meant it. I knew it like I'd never known anything before. I didn't want the boxes anymore; I didn't want anything in them. Every part of my past that was locked up and sealed shut. Every part of my life I kept separate. I didn't want it.

It was exhausting, I realised.

Why had I never realised that before?

I wanted to start fresh; with Allie, the band, the guys, my life on the road and off the road, the cooking and movies and trips to the park.

I moved in and pressed my lips to hers as everything that had cluttered my mind before Allie completely disappeared.

32

Allie

"I *love* surprises, this is so exciting Allie!" Savannah jumped up and down in her living room clapping.

I couldn't help but smile back at her. This *was* exciting. Spending Sunday with Dax was almost impossible. I had this issue, and I wasn't entirely sure if there was a scientific name for it, but if I had exciting news, or I purchased a gift for someone too early before the time it was supposed to be gifted. I *had* to tell them.

So, keeping quiet about my plan to surprise Dax and not let anything slip... I would have preferred to wax everything from the eyebrows down, to put it plainly.

But I pulled it off. He had no idea and we spent the entire day relaxing on my Facebook Marketplace couch. We started to watch all the Marvel movies from the beginning. I had seen on my Instagram feed while scrolling this photo of all the Marvel movies and the order you were supposed to watch them in. We were probably the only people who didn't realise that they all joined into one, long, comprehensive story.

We got through two and then fell asleep. Dax woke me up

in the early hours of the morning and we shuffled to my room. It might've been the early morning or the way he looked half asleep but let's just say we didn't immediately hit the hay once we settled into bed.

I practically convinced myself to forget about it to make it through the week.

All the dinners at his apartment, the coffee and croissant breakfasts, the walks from my apartment to my office were everything, all those moments and the moments in between, I had spent months thinking of.

I had pictured him at my door almost every day, pictured him at my kitchen island while I made us tea. Now that I could reach out and run my hands through his hair or wrap my arms around his waist, I refused to be taken from the moment by anything, even a completely awesome and super amazing surprise like I was planning.

Now, if that wasn't the most obvious display of personal growth and self-control ever then you could slap my ass and call me Sally.

10 points for Allie. Hell, 15.

"Okay, okay, tell me the plan again but from the top," Savannah sat down on her couch and looked at me with big, excited eyes.

"So, on Friday afternoons Rip and Angus play some kind of indoor soccer scrimmage and they've organised for all the guys to participate. Don't even ask me what or how, it was just what Aspen put forward as the reason to get Dax out of the house.

That will go until about 7PM, so I will have plenty of time to get up to their apartment, make my impressive spaghetti and meatballs and set up a cute little date thing. Aspen gave me his second elevator card swiper so that we can get up with no issues. I just need you to drive me to their place and maybe help set up the little table all cute and lady-and-the-tramp like."

When Aspen had handed me his back up elevator card, he had unhooked it from his keys.

"Aspen. Don't tell me you keep your spare elevator swiper on your keys," I commented, worried.

"Of course, I do. If I put it anywhere else, I'd lose it," he said back with so much conviction I choked on my response. I wouldn't be the one to take that from him, he'd have to learn that lesson on his own one day.

"Allie, that is so cute, he is going to love it," Savannah gave me that look like she was about to start crying. Right on cue she started to fan her eyes.

"Sav! Stop it," I sat down next to her and grabbed her hand.

"This is just the best. I am so happy for you, Al. You deserve all this, all the good stuff," she lifted my hand that was clutching hers and kissed the back of it, I did the same thing back to hers.

"How's your secret guy going? You haven't said anything more about him since you told me there even *was* someone," I leaned back onto her couch.

"It's incredible, Allie. He's just, he's so *good*," she was picking at her nails, "I was thinking we could all have dinner here next week or something, and you can meet him properly too."

"Why are you so nervous? If you like him, I like him. All this secrecy has me scared though," I admitted.

"Don't be," she smiled at me, "It's all happy times, we just agreed to keep things on the downlow, and we wanted to tell you together," it was Sav's most genuine smile, so when she told me it was all good, I believed her.

I leaned over and kissed her cheek before standing and heading to the door to slide on my shoes, "Sounds perfect."

I slung my light jacket over my arm. It was warm enough outside that I would be fine in my t-shirt.

"Okay, I'll grab the ingredients on my way home from work. Will you come get me at 6?" I opened her front door.

"I will be so on time; you have no idea," she bounced where she sat and clapped her hands again.

Let him in.

I could do that, absolutely, I could do that. It might be that I already had, but now I just needed to tell him.

* * *

I wasn't sure if I was nervous for the cooking, the whole purpose of the event or for the fact that I didn't know if Dax did or did not like surprises and I couldn't imagine Aspen divulging that information anyway.

If Dax hated surprises, Ap would have loved to see it all play out and then piss himself as he recorded Dax's face. Out of love, of course.

I stopped by the corner store after work and picked up the three ingredients I required. I also got a couple of candles that apparently smelt like 'pine trees and the alpine wilderness' whatever that meant, and speed-walked back to mine.

Aspen messaged me just as I finished up at work that they were leaving for the soccer game. Dax had also messaged me saying the same thing.

I didn't even take my shoes off at the door. If that didn't accurately convey my nerves then I didn't know what could.

I quickly shoved the whole shopping bag - pasta and all - into the fridge and ran to my room.

I wanted to look nice, but also like I didn't even try. I opted for a mustard pinafore with a white shirt underneath that had these cute frilly details on the neck and sleeve. I felt pretty when I wore it.

I quickly threw a few curls into my hair and barely missed burning my eyeball on the barrel as I tried to pick my phone up.

It was Savannah.

"Hey chicky, I am here! Let's get surprising!" She was 'wooing' and 'ahhing' over me while I tried to tell her I'd be right down. I seriously doubted she even heard me.

I took one last look at myself in the bathroom mirror then triple checked that I'd turned my curling iron off at the wall, cause we all knew how it felt to leave the house and think it was still on. Yep, no thanks, didn't need that today.

I grabbed the bag from the fridge and went down to Savannah. She was parked at the curb and as soon as I started walking towards her, she started to chant 'yes, yes, yes!' prompting me to put on my best catwalk display. A few more hyping phrases - 'work it and spin, spin, lunge' - were thrown my way for which I classily obliged. I landed in the passenger seat of her car with about as much grace as a hippo.

"Ready?" she asked.

"Born ready," I replied, a look of determination set into my face. These would be the best 6 out of 10, letting him all in, meatballs he'd ever have in his life.

Sav parked under the building taking the spot that Aspen's sedan usually sat in and we walked over to the elevator. I pressed the button until it arrived, and we rode all the way up.

"Holy shit balls," Savannah gasped, taking in the penthouse, "It's totally surreal to me right now that I'm in *Wyatt Smith's* penthouse. Pinch me, someone...*ouch!* Allie!" She smacked my arm.

"You literally asked me to," I shrugged in earnest before walking to the kitchen.

"Toad," Savannah mumbled as she continued to snoop around.

I set about the process of boiling the kettle for the pasta and found a pan big enough for all the meatballs. They had a gas oven and I'd seen Dax use it plenty to know how to safely turn it on to the right heat. I mean, I thought so. I guess we'd find out.

Savannah came bounding into the kitchen after the pasta water had been salted and the raw noodles added, her face the picture of complete and total happiness.

"Allie, this is so *cool* I could *die,"* she collapsed onto the island before me.

"Can you help me make this cute please? I'm worried if I take my eyes off the stove top, something will catch fire," I kept my eyes glued to the heating oil in the pan. Putting my hand just above it to see how hot it was like I'd seen Dax do, too.

Savannah took her job in lady-and-the-trampifying the kitchen island with so much gusto I struggled to keep my composure. Her tongue was poking out her mouth in concentration the whole time.

Sav had brought a tartan tablecloth and a little basket with breadsticks for the middle. I had no idea she was going to do any of that so my whole body was about to split and leak gooey love everywhere, but again, my attention had to remain on the meatballs that were now happily sizzling away.

By the time I turned around, the island had been transformed into a table for two at what could have been the cutest, hole-in-the-wall, family owned Italian restaurant you'd ever seen.

"Sav," I exhaled, my eyes went a bit glassy, "that's so top tier, you have no idea."

"Yeah?" She double checked.

"Absolutely perfect," I reached out my hand for her to come over and gave her a big squeeze.

"Okay, I've gotta run. I'm having dinner with *my* guy tonight as well. He will be at the restaurant soon so I'm gonna jet. Call me if you need anything, I won't be too far away, and good luck!" She kissed my cheek and waved at me from the elevator.

I turned back to my meatballs. They were now completely cooked through and appropriately seasoned with salt and pepper. I dumped them into the strained pasta that was sitting in the pot and added in the jar of sauce.

I mean, it looked the same as always. I was smiling to myself as I grabbed a couple bowls out of the cupboard, mentally going through what I wanted to say.

I was toying between 'hey Dax, things have kind of levelled up lately, you know, with you learning all my deep dark secrets and the awesome sex, I guess what I wanted to say was that I love you'. I didn't think it was half bad, there was also 'these meatballs might be a 6 out of 10, but yours are a 10 out of 10'. It wasn't an immediate winner, but I was keeping it in the bank, just in case.

Aspen had messaged letting me know they were on their way back so I started to dish out the pasta portions.

I even found some cheese in their fridge to sprinkle on top just as the elevator pinged, indicating someone had arrived.

Oh, what? They're not supposed to be here yet, shit, shit, shit.

"Dax! Aspen!" A voice called. A *lady* voice, and not one I knew.

What the...?

"Boys?!" They called again.

She hadn't seen me. She had walked straight through to the living room and stood at the base of the stairs that moved into the hallway.

She turned around and spotted me. As soon as she did, she let out a yelp and her hand flew to her heart.

"Oh, holy pine nuts, you scared me so bad!" Her hand moved from her chest to fan her face.

My mouth opened and closed but nothing came out. I clutched the serving spoon, still piled with spaghetti and meatballs.

"Wait, *wait, wait, wait.* This is crazy. *Stop it!"* She covered her mouth and sort of pranced over to me, her heels clicking loudly on the marbled floor. I, all of a sudden, felt very short wearing my Chucks.

"You're Allie, right?! This is *so cool.* It is the best to meet you! I'm Jenna!" She said enthusiastically, pulling me into a hug. Her perfume stung my nose and made my tummy roll a bit.

"I—," I started, but she cut me off straight away.

"Oh. My. Gosh. This is *so cute.* Well, I know this absolutely cannot be Daxy, I think we both know he needs to learn a thing or two about romance, am I right?!" She knocked me with her elbow.

"What?" My heart was picking up pace. Who even was this

person?

"I mean, he has no issues with the physical stuff - but you don't need me to tell you that!" She laughed and then tapped my arm, like *I* was supposed to know that *she* was supposed to know that too?

How did she know that? Why was she talking about it like she knew about it recently?

Please, no. Please, please, please, not Dax.

"I'm sorry, but how did you get up here? You need a card." Was that rude? It felt rude.

I couldn't help it though, I thought I was going into shock. My heart was racing, my palms were sweaty, and my hands were starting to shake a bit. Dread coiled in my stomach, my mind was racing with every possibility, but there was only one that made sense.

Please, please, please, no, no, no.

She held up a swipe card with a look of confused astonishment.

I should have known. Every time he was on his phone, every time, he was talking to someone else. Stupid Allie, you're so stupid. He never let me see, he always said it was nothing.

"I have a key, silly! Like you, I would imagine, or else how did you get up here! Did Dax give you his main one? I thought I had his only spare," she looked at me. Her eyes bright and unblinking, the picture of satisfaction oozing from her features and all while I felt my brain have a power outage and my heart suffered an earthquake.

I dropped the spoon I was clutching with a white knuckled grip back into the pot and dashed for the elevator. I'd never clicked a call button so fast in my life. I could feel the tears welling and spilling over one by one. The click of her heels echoed from behind me and I think she might have been calling my name, but everything was so muffled. The smell of her perfume clung to my shirt. I was going to throw up.

My chest hurt. *Everything* hurt.

I threw myself into the elevator, prompted the doors to close as fast as they could and pulled my phone out of my pocket with shaking hands. Savannah picked up on the second ring.

"Allie? Are you okay?" She sounded worried, like she knew, like she might have had a feeling.

I choked a sob, "I'm so stupid Savannah, so, so stupid. I should have known. I should have just *asked* who he was speaking to every time. He was always talking to someone. God, how could I believe him? Everything he ever said, how could I have *believed him?*"

"Allie, calm down I can't understand you. I'm coming. I will be there in 5 minutes, don't walk anywhere, okay?"

"He's just like Ben, Sav, just like Ben. How am I so stupid? How could he—," I broke off into a strangled sob. The sort where you can feel yourself about to be sick. The ones that make you want to curl into a ball and never move.

"I'm coming, Allie. Okay? 3 minutes."

"Don't hang up," I managed to say, though I couldn't for the life of me see how she understood a word out of my mouth.

"I won't hang up. I'm right here okay? 2 minutes, Al."

I could barely see in front of me, my eyes just pouring with tears. I didn't really care if someone saw me, heard me, whatever.

I had clicked the button to the basement without even thinking of it.

"I'm in the basement," I sounded calmer. I didn't feel calmer.

How could this be happening? How?

"1 minute, Allie," Savannah said.

I let the phone slide from my face as I walked into the basement and slumped against the wall next to the elevator. The waves of painful realisation continued to crash over me, everything I had worked so hard to move past was coming up to meet with vengeance. With a questioning cruelty like 'how dare you move on from those feelings? That place?'.

When slender hands reached out to grip my forearms, it scared me so much, I screamed.

I properly screamed.

"Allie, it's okay, let's go. Come on."

"Savannah, how could he? *How could he?"*

She never replied, she just helped me into the back seat and took off, getting us as far away from Dax's place as possible.

33

Dax

Ap and I were almost home when Jenna's name popped up on my caller ID and I remembered she needed something for Phoebe.

"Hey Jenna, sorry I know you need the stage—"

"Wyatt, I'm so sorry," she interrupted, sounding frantic, "So, so sorry. I had no idea what I said, what she might— I was just trying to be nice." She sounded like she was about to cry. I was completely lost.

"Woah, slow down. What are you talking about?" My knee started to bounce. Aspen gave me a nervous look.

"I didn't know she was going to be here, Wyatt. I swear. I was just trying to be nice, find common ground. I wanted to be her friend," Jenna pushed all the words out all at once, like saying them faster would make things better.

"You didn't know who was going to be where, Jenna? Where are you?" Aspen's eyes widened as he sped up, mumbling curses under his breath.

I shot him a look of confusion.

"Allie. I didn't know Allie was going to be here or I wouldn't have come. You're always home on Friday nights, always," she explained.

My heart stopped. I felt it stop.

"What did you say to her, Jenna?" I didn't recognise my voice.

"I… well… I was just…," she was fumbling with her words.

"What the fuck did you say to her Jenna, what did you do? *What did you do?"* I didn't even wait to hear what she said before I hung up the phone.

"What's going on Aspen?" I was breathing so fast my lungs were burning.

"She wanted to surprise you, Dax," Aspen started as he picked up even more speed, "She wanted to cook you something, something about meatballs. I don't even know. She wanted to make it like a dinner date at a restaurant but at ours because you can't really go out. She wanted to surprise you."

Aspen flew into the basement parking of our building and I was out of the car before it had stopped. The elevator had never taken so long to come down to us, or so long to take us to the top.

I stopped in my tracks. The whole set up. The island, the food.

She made her spaghetti and meatballs, and her bag was still sitting on one of the chairs of the island like she'd had only one goal when she left and that was to leave as fast as possible.

I didn't even notice Jenna walk up to me, "Wyatt, please, I am so sorry, I didn't think."

"You don't ever *think,* Jenna! Ever." With that I turned on my heels. Grabbing the keys from Aspen and heading back down to the car.

Pick up, pick up, pick up.

Allie's number went to voicemail every time.

"Dammit!" I smacked the steering wheel, a zap of pain went up my arm.

I drove straight to her apartment, threw the car into neutral and ran to her building. I didn't even bother with the elevator, taking the stairs two at a time to her floor.

I wanted to bang on the door, I wanted to break it down. But I didn't.

I took some deep breaths. Calmed myself down, swallowing the emotion lodged in my throat.

I knocked on Allie's door lightly.

"Allie?" I called, "Allie, please. It's not what you think. Let me in, let me explain."

No one answered. I didn't even hear any shuffling behind the door.

I went to knock again when the door cracked. It was Savannah.

She looked behind her and then slid out into the hallway. She just looked at me and the warning from the first time we met crept back into my mind.

"Savannah, I swear it's not what she thinks," I pleaded.

"I know," she nodded.

"I mean it, Sav— what?" I was trying to process what she'd said.

"I know it's not what it looks like. Angus told me. He's inside with Allie now," she inclined her head towards the door, "He explained it to her, too."

What a relief.

"Can I see her then?" I went to move towards the door, but Savannah stepped in my path.

"No," she crossed her arms. Savannah was slight, she was

shorter than Allie and slimmer too, but for all of that, the look on her face made me step back.

"What?" I knew I looked as confused as I felt.

"You didn't tell her about Jenna, Wyatt. You *work* with Jenna, she's the person who freaking touches up your *hair!*" She whisper-yelled the last part.

"That doesn't mean anything to—," I started.

"To who, Wyatt? To you? Or to Allie? She told you *everything.* Do you know how hard that was? She even plays her piano for you, Wyatt. She doesn't even do that for *me. Me!* For all that you know of Allie, how could you not know that while she was opening every single part of herself up to you, because you *asked,* the fact that you weren't doing the same, that it wasn't even a consideration, malicious or not, how do you think that would make her feel? After everything you know. Ben? Her mum? The accident? The trauma?" Her face told me she could keep going, but she was choosing not to.

Savannah took a deep breath like reliving all those parts of Allie's life were hard for her too.

"She's not damaged, or incapable, or... or meek because of any of it," she went on.

"I know that. I've never thought that." For all that I was falling apart on the inside, those words held strong. I'd never thought anything different. How could I? Allie was probably the strongest person I knew.

"But she is not invincible, Wyatt," her voice had dropped down to where I could barely hear her.

"If I could just *tell* her, explain why I hadn't said—," the words were hollow as they waited to be spoken.

Why didn't I tell her? Why didn't I just unpack all the boxes, all the things I placed neatly together. It was because Allie was more than all of it, she was better than all of it. It didn't make sense to bring it up, to show her all those things.

"She needs time," Savannah reached for the door, she gave me one last look and then closed it gently, leaving me in the hallway. In a spot I had stood more times than I could count.

I could walk to the exact place before her door with my eyes closed, but I had never felt more desperately lost in my life.

34

Dax

I had nothing to say.

Nothing to say that would make anything revert to the way it was last week.

That was the first time in my entire life I didn't feel like I had anything to put to paper. Nothing to type into my phone or scribble into my notebook.

I sat and stared at my phone all weekend. If I wasn't watching my phone waiting for it to ding, I was staring at my guitar, wishing for something to shove me towards it. Something that I could do, or write, or play that would help.

I didn't know what to do.

The elevator pinged to our floor late Saturday afternoon. I didn't know who it was, but I knew who it wasn't and that was enough to not really care who it was at all.

Angus sat down in the chair across from me and placed the little elevator swipe card on the coffee table between us.

I looked over at him, I could feel the pleading expression on my face. My skin tightened and I suddenly felt like I couldn't get enough air into my lungs.

"Wyatt—," The tone of his voice said it all.

Neither he nor Savannah had said anything about why he ended up with her and Allie in her apartment. I had guessed he'd found someone, was seeing someone, now I knew it was Savannah. I was happy for him. I was. More than that, I was glad he had been there to explain, as selfish as that might have seemed.

I leaned forward and rested my elbows on my knees. I let my head hang for a second before I met his eyes again and pushed my hair back with both hands.

"She's not coming," I said what I knew he was dreading having to relay, "I didn't keep it from her because it meant something to me, because I didn't want her to know," I said to him, even though he already knew.

"I know," Angus said. The look in his eyes was the look they all gave me every time I ended up alone again. Like they wanted to help, to fix whatever it was that always made me end up back at square one.

"I'd tell her anything she wanted to know, anything," I said to him again.

"I know," he repeated.

"This wasn't how it was supposed to happen," I said softly. I think I was probably talking more to myself than to Angus, and not to Aspen who I knew loitered in the hallway behind me, forever unable to restrain himself from eavesdropping.

"Is she okay?" I asked.

Angus gave a small shake of his head and I swear my whole body pulsed in a shudder of pain.

I did that. That was me.

"Sav is with her now, still. She won't speak but I told her Wyatt, I explained everything to her. Just give her time to digest it. To process it," Angus walked over and placed a hand on my shoulder.

Time.

He bid Ap farewell on his way out, but I couldn't move my gaze away from the key card he had left on the coffee table. Aspen's spare indicated by the little 'A' he had written into one of the corners with a sharpie.

I knew that it was meant for his name, but I couldn't stop thinking that it should have been for Allie.

* * *

I lasted until Monday midday before I messaged her.

Dax: *Hey*

She never wrote back.

She didn't write back in the afternoon or the evening, not even through the night. I stared at my phone all night just waiting for the screen to illuminate, but it never did.

I lasted until Wednesday morning before I called her.

*Heyo, this is Allie, I'm probably busy learning a second language or maybe just on the toilet but leave a message and I'll get back to you toot-sweet. *Beep**

I hit her message bank every time. I called her three times, three times in a *row* and every time I got the same voice recording.

I knew she wasn't going to pick up, and though I had hoped, I knew I wouldn't hear from her at all on Thursday.

Friday morning came and went, so did midday and then the little digital clock on my phone ticked from 4:59PM to 5PM and I couldn't wait anymore.

The time she needed, I couldn't give her anymore. I needed to see her, hear her voice, hear her say something. *Anything.*

Aspen was out with the sedan, so I grabbed the keys to the Jeep that we had and made my way to the basement.

When we had a lot of time off, we liked to go camping. Hiking and trails and the outdoors. The quiet. That's what the Jeep was for, but it would do for a cross city sprint.

I parked in the regular spot outside her building. It was 5:20PM and I knew she would have probably just gotten home from work.

I wanted to know if she was making brownies. If she had made them at all during the week.

Did she get takeout and give some to Dean? What were the leftovers she had felt she needed to pay him back for?

Did she start to learn a new song on her piano?

Was she still playing her guitar?

I felt like I knew the answer to that last one already.

I walked across the street to her building and walked in. Grateful, for the first time ever, for her terrible security that didn't prevent anyone from walking in the front door or calling the elevator.

I stood before her door. I didn't want to knock. I wanted to just open it and walk in like I had before, when she knew I was coming and left it unlocked. I knew that if I tried the handle it wouldn't turn open like it did then.

I knocked on the door softly.

There was shuffling and then the door opened to show Dean standing there in something that wasn't orange for a change.

A pair of sweatpants and a shirt, they were both grey.

"Dude! How are you?" He stuck his hand out in a shake.

I reached out my own hand, "Hey Dean, how are you?" I asked him, giving him one of my most special 'press smiles'.

"Yeah, I'm actually pretty good. Heading out of town this weekend," he nodded his head as he spoke, "Bro, I'm sorry, but Allie said, if you showed up, not to let you in."

My chest ached at that, "I just need to speak to her for a second, Dean."

Dean must have learned from Angus how to pass on the pity look fast, because his eyes cast the same saddened stare at me.

"Wyatt—," he started.

"Sorry Dean, but I'm coming in," I pushed by him causing him to bump back into the door. He called after me and I threw an apology at him over my shoulder and rushed down the hall. He didn't bother following me as I saw him dawdle into the living room.

I stood outside her door. That was the closest I had been to her in over a week and I had a sinking feeling it might be as close as I'd ever get again.

I had to explain though, I had to try and let her know *why*.

I lifted my hand, freaking the fuck out the entire time. I was terrified.

I knocked.

"Allie," I said, "God, Allie, please. Please let me explain," I whispered through her door.

I couldn't hear anything on the other side, nothing.

But then there was some rustling, like the covers were being thrown back and I stepped back from the door, backing up the hallway a bit the way I'd come in.

Allie opened the door to her room gently, peaking at me through the crack in her door before she opened it wide.

I already felt how this was going to go.

Please, no.

She stepped out into the hallway, wearing the oversized sweatpants I had once borrowed from her and an oversized shirt. My shirt.

One of the many band T's that cluttered my closet, the only thing I ever really wore, when wearing a shirt was required. The one Allie had on said *The Smiths* across the front.

I couldn't move my eyes away from the shirt, I couldn't stop looking at *her* in my shirt. I tried to swallow and found the emotion that had clogged in my throat made it near impossible.

Allie moved her eyes from my face down to the shirt that she wore, she was gripping the bottom of it tightly.

I moved my gaze back up to hers. Her seafoam green eyes were made impossibly bright by the heartbreaking redness that surrounded them. I knew she had been crying. I knew she had probably been crying while I waited for her texts and her calls.

I swallowed again, "Allie, I swear there is nothing going on. Jenna and I dated *three years* ago. I haven't even had another girlfriend since her. Until you." I was impressed at how steady my voice sounded.

"But you didn't tell me, Dax. You didn't tell me anything. And you were always...," she trailed off, like she remembered something and got caught up in the memory of it.

"Always what, Allie?" I took a small step towards her.

She just shook her head.

"I'm trying, Allie. I'm—," my voice cracked; no steadiness

left, "I'm not good at this. I've never done more than one thing before. It was either one or the other for me. I could never *mix*. Something always suffered. I was never *good* at this," I motioned between her and I, hoping that she knew what I meant, "I'm trying, Allie," I said again.

Tears slid down her face as she looked at me, as she took in my face. Her eyes scanned my features like they had done on our very first date, when I knew she was looking for a reason to say no, but she didn't find one. I could tell as I watched her, watching me, that she had found a reason this time.

My chest was pierced with the most aggressive sort of dread I'd ever felt.

No.

She nodded at me, a small, sad smile ghosting her trembling lips. I lifted my hand, I wanted to hold her. To wipe her tears, to do anything. But I didn't, I let it drop back to my side.

"You're rock. Rock and roll. Electric guitars and drums and, and hard notes and rough edges...," she sniffed, wiping her checks of their tears, "I am classical. Sweeping, and gentle. Strong but soft." She looked back at me again, "They are too different. They don't mix, Wyatt."

I flinched. I actually *flinched*. I don't think I'd ever flinched in my life. I took a step back away from her.

Wyatt. Not Dax.

She wasn't finished, "This isn't fair for you or me, I can't do this silence. This in between. I think... I think we need to figure some things out."

I'd never nodded my head so fast, "Allie, I'll—," I started but the look on her face silenced me.

"Apart," she whispered, fresh tears falling down her face.

"What?" I said.

No.

"Apart," she repeated.

I couldn't move.

"I can't— I can't *believe* you anymore. Everything you've said, every word I want to believe but it sits in my stomach like lead weights and I can't—"

"Allie, I told you already, there's nothing—"

"I know what you said, Dax. I heard it from you, from Savannah, from Angus. I can't believe it though. I told you *everything*, you know *everything*. I thought I knew everything too, but you kept that to yourself. All the parts of me that I can't face, you saw them all. I never saw any of those parts from you. I thought you just didn't have any, not that you were *keeping* them from me. I think maybe you need to face those parts yourself. Like I need to face mine," her voice was so calm.

I didn't know how her voice was so calm, even as she couldn't stop crying, yet my entire world was being shaken.

"I thought I could do that with you," she said.

I looked up to her eyes again.

"I don't think I can do that anymore," her bottom lip started to tremble again, "Please, Dax. You need to go." It wasn't more than breathy words, but they rang clear as day as they moved right through me.

I wanted to scream.

I wanted to grab her and make her see, tell her I knew, *I knew* that I fucked up. That I didn't mean to, that I didn't even know. That I thought I didn't have to compartmentalise things to function, to do good. To *be* good. That I thought I could have it all, that for a second it felt like I *did* have it all.

But none of it came out, I didn't say any of it as I turned

around and walked away.

35

Allie

As soon as he turned to walk away, I wanted to pull him back.

Every word I had said to him, that I had spent days and days planning to say, I wanted them all to disappear like smoke in the wind. I wanted to take back every broken look that crossed his face, every hesitation that he had. I wanted to take it all back.

But he turned to leave, and I didn't move. I didn't call after him.

Even if I did grab him back, I knew the words he'd said would still sit heavy like they did when I heard them just before. I knew that anything he'd ever say would sit just the same. I knew I'd never be able to look at him with such a clear knowledge that he was right there with me.

I didn't know if he had ever been right there with me, I felt like I didn't know him at all.

I just watched him leave, saw him round the corner and disappear from my sight.

I scrunch my eyes up and prepared for the loud bang of the

front door that would come as he left. I stood there as tense as ever for longer than I realised, because the *bang* never came.

He had closed the door so quietly, I hadn't realised he'd left at all.

36

Dax

Every step away from her was harder than the one before.

I took the stairs because the thought of waiting for the elevator… I wouldn't have been able to do it.

I could feel myself losing grip, losing whatever leash on my composure I had. So, I did the only thing I knew how to do.

Everything that was Allie, that was scattered around my mind like a well-loved home, I gathered it all up. All the bits of her, the brightness, the everything, I gathered it all with every step I took and placed it all into a box I didn't realise existed. A box I never wanted to exist. The one that was clearly labelled 'Allie'.

I packed every single piece of her up, the throw pillows, the shoes by the door, the coat on the hook, and sealed it in that box in my mind. Then, carefully, I moved it to a place I would rarely ever go looking for it, to the back corner where there was hardly any light. I placed Allie's box gently there as I got in my car and sped too quickly, as far away from her as I could get.

* * *

It had been dark for so long by the time I got home, I was honestly surprised that the sun wasn't up yet.

I had driven out of town, going nowhere at all, only knowing that I was *moving*, and that was good. That if I stopped moving, I would fall apart.

Then the storm that had raged in me settled, and I had packed every part of Allie left in my mind up too well, too tight, that things looked normal. They didn't look *right*, but they looked like they did before I met her. And so, I drove home.

Aspen was asleep on the living room couch when I walked out of the elevator. Well, he had been asleep, but the ping of the elevator had caused him to stir.

"Dax?" His voice was laced with sleep.

"Hey Ap," I went to walk by him and head straight to my room. I dumped the keys for the Jeep on the hook where I had grabbed them from.

"So?" He sat up a bit.

"So what?"

"Wyatt." He stood up.

"It's done. She asked me to leave, so I left," I kept walking to the steps that lead up into the hallway.

"So, go back?" He said it like it was the simplest thing in the world, and maybe it would have been.

"No," I stopped at the base of the steps, "it's over, Aspen. Leave it alone."

"No, you need to go back. Tell her again, explain it to her again," he walked towards me. He raised his voice, determination and worry rolled into his words.

"No!" I turned and screamed at him, "No, Aspen. It's over. Did you not *hear* me? It's fucking *finished*. So, drop it."

"Dax—," he started again, and I knew what he was going to do, he was going to keep pushing.

"Jenna was right, Aspen. I'm closed off. I can't *do* more than one thing at a time. I can't be good for Allie and for the band and for me all at once. I can't let people in. I couldn't even let Allie in, she had free rein while everything else was packed up tight," I pointed to my temple.

"You can go back, Dax. Go back and fix it," he said again, so resolved like he thought I was an idiot for not having that idea first.

"Aspen, stop," I continued up the stairs, praying he would let it go.

"Dax," he said my name louder. I turned around to face him, standing outside my bedroom door, the words left my mouth before I could stop them.

"Aspen. Just stop, you never fucking *stop*. It's done. It's finished," I pushed my hair back from my face, "God, you're just so… just focus on your own fucking life for once, leave mine alone. Dammit, Aspen." My voice hurt from the strain of the volume I spat the words out at.

I didn't wait for him to say anything else, couldn't bear to see the look on his face, so I walked straight into my room and I put that in a box too.

37

Dax

Aspen didn't speak to me for a whole week after I had yelled at him. We'd even rolled into April and, every month without fail, he came up and gave me a 'pinch and a punch for the first day of the month'. This was the first time I could remember that he didn't do that.

I didn't speak to anyone that week at all.

I had woken up well before the sun. Sleep, as usual, had refused to find me again and all I could do was think about what I had said to Aspen.

I had shoved that encounter in a box labelled 'do not open' but it rattled around and made so much noise I couldn't ignore it anymore.

I had decided that enough was enough, I needed my brother back and I needed to apologise in a way that I knew he would accept without a doubt.

So, naturally, I decided to bake him something.

I made him cinnamon rolls, with extra icing. They were his favourite and there was literally nothing he wouldn't do for one.

Usually he made them himself, with sweets being his specialty and savoury being mine, but I knew that if I concentrated, I could whip up a batch that he would hoard in his room.

It took me two hours.

Two whole hours and I couldn't even let the dough, that I'd already rolled out into perfect little swirls, rise a second time. I knew the second rise was important because Aspen always said 'second's the best' as his baking motto.

In a pinch, to accelerate the whole rising process, you could put your baked goods somewhere very warm, or so I heard, and so I turned the oven on high and set them right in front of it. I wasn't really in a position to be taking those kinds of risks considering the weight of apology these buns would hold, but beggars couldn't be choosers. I had to put all my eggs in one cinnamon dusted basket and hope for the best.

By the time Aspen wandered out of his bedroom, yawning and unstable, just emerging from sleep, they were ready, glazed and placed in the middle of the kitchen island.

He stopped in front of them and then looked up at me.

"I was wondering how sorry you'd be," he said, swiping a finger across the top of them and tasted the frosting. He lifted his eyebrows and irked his head to the side slowly before picking up one of the rolls and taking a mammoth bite.

He was chewing for about 15 seconds before a grin broke over his face and he said around a mouth full of food, "You're forgiven."

I looked at him and I seriously had never wanted to cry so much as I had in the last week. This was shit, everything was just so, *so* shit, but things were always less shit when Aspen was on my side.

"Yeah?" I asked.

"Yeah," he took another bite, "You're a massive wiener, but yes." His smile grew even wider.

"I'm sorry," I couldn't quite smile back.

Aspen finished the cinnamon bun he had shoved so gracefully into his mouth before he wiped the icing on his cheek away with the back of his hand.

"I focus on your life because I love you. When you're happy, I'm happy. When you're good, I'm good. That's why. I will always try and do what is best for you, even if that makes you angry," he picked up the tray and held it gently, like it was the most precious thing in the world.

"I know," I matched his stare. He held my gaze until he was satisfied, nodding his head slightly before turning to leave.

"Good, now let's stop talking about this stuff before I barf," he flopped down the couch and turned on the TV.

I smiled and followed him, feeling a little lighter than I did before, and desperately wishing I had taken a bun out of the tray for myself, because there was no way he was sharing.

* * *

All the shows sold out for our tour.

They all sold out within an hour of the tickets going live.

I was so proud, so unbelievably proud of my friends and what we had achieved. We were living our dream and it was incredible.

In the month that led up to the start of our tour, we planned and then replanned the set list.

The new album had gone nuts, but our others had crowd favourites that we needed to incorporate into our performance as well.

Aspen had really let his freak flag fly when planning out what we would wear on stage. He had bombarded Phoebe with phone call after phone call as well as individual links to different Pinterest vision boards that he had created for everyone.

We practised for hours. Every day. Hours and hours and hours until the calluses on the ends of my fingers and on my hands had started to form their own calluses.

We landed in London for our first stop. It was one of our biggest shows and the crowds were insane. The way they welcomed us onto the stage - there was no feeling like it. It was amazing. Luke walked right up to the edge of the stage and screamed right back. Then we all followed suit. That's how we started our tour, it was euphoric. It was humbling.

Our shows were set out to be three per city and they were spaced with a day in between. Our previous tours hadn't always been like that, but considering the size of this one, it was planned with more time and made longer.

The shows, I mean, we nailed them, one after the other. And only once so far had Rip spun around, smacked into me and caused me to fall on stage. I finished the song on the ground, and we didn't miss a beat. After that particular show, none of us could stop laughing.

We still yelled and screamed before and after every performance, of course, and getting to spend time with my closest friends was everything I could have wanted.

I repeated it to myself every day.

This is all I could have ever wanted. The guys, the road and my music. The fans, the stadiums. I didn't need anything more than this.

You eventually missed the quiet and the down time, but those memories we made on tour, everywhere we got to go together; it made the fast pace and long days worth it.

A couple months of hopping from city to city, saw us making our way through Europe slowly and surely on what was the first leg of our tour, and I was perfectly fine.

I was perfectly fine not thinking about anything other than what I needed to do.

The routine was simple.

Get up, get dressed, either do something or don't, sound check, get ready, concert, do something or don't, the next day would come and be filled with either doing something or not doing something and then we did it all again.

The box that was unpacked in my mind was the one that was clearly labelled 'tour'. It always sat just within reach and it was never taped shut but only ever closed very lightly.

Everything in that box had a place and I knew where to put it. I kept it in the light where I could always see it, even if the things were packed away temporarily.

I didn't look to the corners of my mind that were dimmer, dustier.

There was nothing for me there anymore.

"Dax?" Aspen waved his hand in front of my face.

"Mmm?" I looked to him quickly before picking up my forgotten fork and diving into our takeaway food. The consensus had been Chinese food, but I had requested something else. Anything else.

I was eating Greek food. It wasn't so bad.

We were in the hotel room that Rip and Luke were sharing, a movie was playing, and we were all eating.

"Did you hear anything that I said?" Aspen took another

bite of his food, but his expression darkened.

"Sorry, I was thinking about something," I mumbled around a bit of food. I wasn't hungry, to be honest.

"You're not dealing with it, Dax," he said.

"Dealing with what?" I asked.

I knew what he was talking about.

Don't say it, don't say it.

"Allie." Once her name left his mouth, everyone stopped talking and all eyes were on me.

"I'm dealing with it fine, Aspen," I pushed my plate away. I was sitting on the ground in front of the couch and moved back to lean against it.

"It's been over two months and you've been on autopilot," he set his own fork down.

"I'm fine. The tour is going great, the shows are awesome. What more is there?" I looked at him. I shouldn't have made the non-verbal dare for him to say it because if there was anyone who would take it on, it was Aspen.

"I didn't say anything about the shows, Dax. That is one part of everything. You've done it again. Picked one box and only opened that one, everything else is suffering," Aspen was still looking at me. Before I could even reply he spoke again.

But that wasn't true. Things suffered when I *didn't* do that.

"You haven't written a song since the press tour, and that was three months ago, over three months even," his eyes flicked to Rip.

"You were doing better before, bud. You seemed happier. Brighter, even. We're just—" I cut Rip off this time.

"I was happier, Rip," I looked right at him. Not angry or mad, just showing them exactly what they were fishing for. "I had absolutely everything I had ever wanted and now, I don't have it anymore. So, now that it's been said out loud, let's move on, okay? I'll be fine," I looked at Aspen and tried to convey to him that I heard what he said, but I just didn't *want* to hear it. Not right now. Maybe not for a while longer.

In his defence, he'd said nothing to me about any of it until now. About me or about her.

He nodded his head a bit before he looked at Angus briefly.

Alright, that's enough for today.

It was hard to be around them when someone mentioned her name. Angus had struck a friendship with Savannah so it happened a lot more than you would think. He said 'friendship' but I knew they'd been seeing each other since before we'd gone on the press tour. I also knew that everyone knew except for me, that he'd told everyone but me.

Well, I knew, of course. I wasn't blind. But I also knew that he hadn't said it to me out loud yet because he thought it would bring Allie back up in conversation and it would suck for me.

It did suck.

It was the fucking worst, but I wasn't going to tell him that.

I got up and said goodbye to everyone before I headed back to my own hotel room.

Me, Angus and Aspen all had our own, where Rip and Luke shared a suite. We all took turns sharing verses getting our own space. Whoever had the foresight and patience to organise that schedule deserved a medal.

The walk down the hall was long, but it was nice and quiet.

I always had a thing for hotel hallways. The carpeted floors and the silence that sort of pressed in on you from either side. It was reminiscent of a recording booth at a studio, the way it felt. I liked how everyone whispered when they were walking from their room to the elevator even though they never had to. It was like being in a little pocket of the world in between different moments. It was calming.

There was one good thing that came from all this, if you were one of those people who really dug deep until you could pull anything together that resembled a silver lining - Jenna had stopped speaking to me.

That sounded mean, I knew that. But I was relieved.

She smiled and I smiled, and we were civil when we had to be. She did her job and fixed me up to be stage ready and that was it. She didn't tell me that I was emotionally closed off anymore. That I needed to be fixed and that my behaviour wasn't normal.

Phoebe tried to talk to me a few times while she was getting my outfits ready. About how sorry Jenna was, how she had read the situation wrong, how she had read *me* wrong.

I obviously told her it was fine, I was over it and no hard feelings.

I knew that Jenna was sorry. Her apology was there and so I took it and got on with my day, but it didn't change anything. It didn't bring Allie back or remove the fucked up situation I found myself in.

I took a very long and very hot shower.

I had just finished trying to dry my hair and cringing at the red colouring that stained the white towel when someone knocked at my door.

I opened it to find Angus on the other side, "Hey man, come in," I left the door open and walked back to throw the towel into the bathroom, "I'll be surprised if they don't charge us for all the towels I have ruined with this freaking hair colour," I laughed as I walked over to him and threw myself onto the bed.

"You're the one that thought red hair would be cool," he snickered.

"It *is* cool," I countered.

He waved me away, his face returned to a more neutral expression.

"What's up?" I tucked a hand behind my head.

"I wanted to talk to you about something," he rubbed the back of his neck with his hand. It was a habit we all had, I wasn't really sure who started it, but we all picked it up.

Ah, he was finally going to spill the beans.

"Shoot," I smiled at him.

"Alright," he took a deep breath, "Sav and I, well, we've been seeing each other for a while. Since before the press tour, actually," his eyes got a little wider like he was watching a scared animal that had been cornered against their will.

"I know," I said.

"What?" He looked dumbfounded.

"I know. Of course, I know, Angus. I think it's awesome," I chucked one of the pillows that was next to me at him. He caught it.

"You do?" He clutched the pillow to his chest.

I suddenly felt like the worst friend ever, that I had been so in my own head about my own situation that I had made my friend feel *bad* or scared to tell me something this exciting.

"Of course, I am. My situation has nothing to do with you. Savannah is awesome, Angus. I'm genuinely happy for you. I'm also glad you finally told me," I laughed.

"Okay," he smiled a bit, then cleared his throat, "How would you feel about her coming to visit for a few weeks. Maybe a month," he spoke slowly, like he was worried I was going to crack and go insane.

I wasn't going to lie. It could have still happened.

"You don't need to ask me that, Angus," I felt my own smile slip away.

"I do," he nodded.

"You don't. I'm not any more important or in charge than you are."

"No, you're not. But that's not why I'm asking," he gave me a knowing look.

I took a deep breath, "I know why you're asking," I looked down at my hand and started to pick at my nails, "And it's okay. Thank you, but it's really okay. I'm fine, Angus. Invite Sav, it will be a relief to have someone else besides you four around," I looked back at him and beamed a smile.

A smile of his own had begun to spread across his lips, "Okay. Alright, I'll ask her. You're sure that you're sure?" he asked one more time.

"Yes, I'm sure that I'm sure," I huffed, "you don't need to worry about me, I'm all good," I said as he chucked the pillow I had thrown at him back to me.

He got up and reached out his hand for one of our traditional slap-shakes, grunted and walked back towards the door to leave my room.

He hesitated like he was going to say something, then he shook his head to himself.

He opened the door and threw a wave back to me and just when I thought he was really going to leave he turned around and looked at me, like he had to really build himself up to that moment.

"We all worry about you, Dax. All the time," he said quietly before he left, the door clicked shut softly behind him.

Well, I didn't expect that.

From Aspen? Always. And Rip was the only other one that was ever vocal about anything to do with what the guys thought about me and my… I don't know, my life, my business. Angus though, he had never said a thing to me.

His words ran through my head.

We all worry.

What was I doing?

I think maybe you need to face those parts of yourself. Like I need to face mine.

That's what she had said to me.

I wasn't facing anything, I had gone over and over every box in my mind, every compartment and made sure that things were tucked away tightly where they needed to be, there was no overlap, none at all.

I couldn't bear it. Because suddenly, Allie had touched every part of my life, and I refused to face any of them because of that, everything I had worked toward would cease to exist.

I had always done this. And when the band took off, there was nothing I wasn't prepared to do to get it where it needed to go. The rest of the guys were just the same. But everyone, slowly, had started to let life in as the years moved on. Aspen was like me, focused and unrelenting, but the more I looked, *really* looked, the more I saw what he did outside of the band.

There had been no event that happened where I let someone in and I lost everything because I spread my attention too thin, because I had too many fingers in too many pies. I had never let anyone in. I had never wanted to and then, all of sudden, I never could.

It worked in my favour, eventually, because I learned all too quickly that when fame came into play, people often wanted to skip the queue from acquaintance to blood relative in a matter of moments. That everyone looked at you for something that you could give them, that no one ever really wanted to return the favour because they didn't care.

But then there was Allie, and she hadn't wanted anything except to show me where the baking powder was. She hadn't wanted anything other than me. And still, *still*, I couldn't let her in.

But wasn't that why I was where I was anyway? Because I couldn't, because I *refused* to face anything, everything.

I looked at my guitar case that sat against the wall next to my bed. I took a deep breath and on the exhale, I launched for it. I grabbed it and put it on the bed quickly. I unlatched the buckles on the side and lifted the lid.

I looked at it.

I stared.

I took another deep breath and lifted the instrument out of the case and onto my lap. I took out my phone and set it in front of me. My hands were shaking a bit but I kept going, kept breathing.

I opened the notes app and selected the one I hadn't opened in a long time. I hadn't touched or thought of in over three months.

I opened it then and slowly scrolled through the notes. It was full.

I read every single line, every word and phrase. I read them all over and over again and with another deep breath, I fit my hands onto the frets of my guitar, an action that was as familiar as saying my own name, and I began to write her song. Finally.

38

Allie

It had been almost three months.

June stared back at me from the little calendar that sat on my desk at work. And not even the start of June with its start-of-the-month, endless-opportunity-for-growth vibe. We were glaring frighteningly close to the end of the month and I felt like I'd been sleepwalking through life.

Or maybe like I'd tripped on a hill and just gave up on stopping myself and rolled down to the bottom. That was probably more accurate.

You also didn't need to tell me how ridiculous it was that I seemed to be considering the starting point of all time as the last time I saw Dax.

I was completely aware of how the entire situation looked.

Have you ever said something when you were mad, and wished that you'd just counted to 10 like all the 'control your anger outburst' articles online told you to do? Yeah, well, I felt like that was where I was at.

The classic Allie-over-thinker scenarios had resurfaced and I'd gone through every single moment from meeting Jenna

- still wanting to replace her sugar with salt - all the way to what Angus had said, to what Savannah had said, right up to the moment where Dax flinched from my words.

I knew I was in the right to say what I said, I knew that I still had every right to hate that I was kept in the dark. That I was the last to know about everything. That I was spilling my literal organs out while he kept all his dirty laundry tucked away.

But you don't just stop loving someone, no matter how much they might have sucked in a certain moment.

I wanted to hate him, but I didn't. I was glad I didn't.

So, it had been almost three months since I wished I could have had the courage to explain to him why I did what I did. Why I said what I said.

Why I felt the fear in probably the scariest moment I'd experienced with him and decided to turn around and run away instead of face it. Because that's what I did at the end of it all, wasn't it?

I ran away.

I might have hated myself a little bit for that, but mostly I hated Ben. Beyond that though, I hated that I let him win all over again.

I had been standing strong for months. My arms stretched above me and holding the metaphorical world above my head.

It took two seconds to feel it come down around me. To climb out of the rubble was exhausting. It had taken weeks and even then, it was only because I had used up the entirety of my three years of sick leave staying home.

The clock on my phone finally ticked to 5PM. Letting out the world's largest sigh, I packed up my stuff and headed out of the office, straight to Sav's.

Summer was in full swing and as much as I loved the cold, it was refreshing to leave the office while the sun was still up. Even as boots remained a staple, though they were about ready for a replacement, I swapped my work slacks and sweaters for skirts, brightly coloured tops and the occasional cardigan that offered no warmth but emphasised modesty.

I lingered outside Savannah's building while I waited for her to get home. When she arrived, she pulled me in for a bone crushing hug.

"Wine?" She pulled back from our hug with a knowing look.

"Isn't that what Friday afternoons are for?" I wagged my eyebrows at her.

Sav dialled a number into a keypad and then scanned us through another door before we made it up to her floor. The security at her building never ceased to amaze me but she had assured me on multiple occasions that it was normal, and my building was the odd one out.

It was within mere minutes that I found myself on her couch, a throw pillow in my lap, and taking a huge gulp from my glass of wine.

"Sweet petunia, *yum,*" I grabbed the bottle off the coffee table to get a look at the label. "This is new?" The enthusiasm in my voice should have been shameful, but it wasn't.

"Someone at work recommended it and of course nothing can be labelled unbeatable until it has the Sav and Allie stamp of approval," she said.

"Very true," I took another sip, "How was your day?" I set my glass down, thinking I needed to moderate myself or else I'd have to crawl home.

"My day was… well, it was good but stressful," she said, looking at me.

"Stressful how?" I enquired. Savannah's job involved a lot of travel and I knew it wasn't always easy for her.

"Stressful about the day coming to an end, not really about the work," she clarified.

"Oh?" *Oh no*. Something was coming.

She set her wine down and did the hand-rub-clap thing that indicated her internal hype session had concluded and she was ready to talk.

"Shit," I mumbled, grabbing my glass of wine and throwing caution to the wind. I'd roll home if I had to at this point.

"No, no, this is fine. It's fine, it'll take two seconds to say," she straightened her posture and turned to face me.

I groaned and took another big swig of my drink.

"Angus and I are dating," she pushed the words out quickly.

I started to choke on my wine and a little came out my nose. It wasn't a pretty sight.

Sav jumped off the couch to grab me a tissue before she settled back slowly into her original spot.

"Are you kidding me, that's what you had to tell me?" I was still dabbing my nose with the tissue, "Freakin' flapjacks, Savannah, I already knew that! Don't scare me like that, I thought you were going to tell me you were getting a cat or something," I sneered at her.

"What do you mean you know? How could you know, we've not told anyone!" she countered, looking completely shocked.

"Wait, are you saying that you didn't know that I knew?" My eyebrows hit my hairline.

"Allie, come on this is important," Sav looked as exasperated as she sounded.

"You're darn tootin' this is important. I outsmarted the people reader of all people readers. What's the date and time?

Quickly let's take a photo," I twisted and held my phone out in front of me; Savannah looked positively distressed and I looked a little crazy.

"Perfect," I smiled at her and put my phone away, "You can continue now," I took a sip.

"Thank you," Savannah rolled her eyes, "How did you know?" she asked, her face getting a guarded look like she thought I might have accidentally walked in on something.

"Good grief, whatever you're thinking, stop it. I figured you two were together when he came with you to get me from Dax's," I said. It started off strong but by the end you could hear my voice drain of any type of enthusiasm.

"Allie," she reached out for my hand. I just waved her away.

"Was that the big news?" I asked.

"No, well, not entirely," she took a deep breath, "I'm leaving to go visit him on tour."

"You're what?!" I squeaked.

"Tomorrow," she added on quickly.

"What?! Savannah! How could you only tell me now?" It was an ode to me that my eyes didn't fully pop out of my head.

It would have usually earned me 5 points, but I didn't really think about that rating system anymore. Not since I had added an extra column to the scoreboard.

"I know," she cringed, "I was worried how you'd react."

I felt my face soften, "Savannah, you know I'm always happy for you. If you're happy, I'm happy."

"I know, I just—," she hesitated, "you seem better. I didn't want to ruin that." She gave me her standard Savannah pity eyes.

I was about to tell her to knock it off when she really hit me with a stinker.

"I think you should come," she sounded so resolved.

I just stared at her while I composed myself.

I swallowed, "I'm not going with you, Savannah."

"Allie—," she started.

"No, Sav," I cut her off, "I won't go. It's not even a possibility. Plus, I am almost entirely sure that I am the last person that he wants to see." I picked some invisible fluff off the pillow in my lap.

"He would, Al. Of course, he would. You don't know that," she replied softly.

"I do know. You weren't there, you didn't see his face. I was so mad. So, so mad at him, at everyone. I felt like a joke. I was hurt, and at the time it felt worse than Ben, so, so much worse," I still didn't meet her eyes, but she sat and listened anyway, "It doesn't really matter now, anyway. He left. He heard everything I said, he knew everything, and he left." I said.

"You told him to leave, Allie," Savannah said.

"I know. I thought he would have maybe fought a little more though," I took another sip.

"You would have hated that," she leaned over the coffee table, grabbing the wine bottle and topped up both our glasses.

"I know," I nursed my now full glass.

"You have to tell him, Allie." Savannah settled back into her spot.

"No, I don't. But you go, have fun. I am so happy for you Sav, honestly," I looked up at her finally, "You deserve all the happiness. So, go. I'll be right here when you get back."

"Okay," she said but sounded unsure and her voice was thick.

I put my glass down and shuffled towards her, "Don't do that, Sav."

"I don't want to leave you," her eyes glazed over.

Sav had always looked after me. I never tried to make things difficult, but I knew that she had always worried, especially the last few months.

"You're going to have the best time," I replied.

"I know."

"Didn't you once tell me to feel the fear?" I lifted an eyebrow.

She rolled her eyes, "That was different," she retorted.

"Maybe, but it still applies. I'll be fine. I have string-bean-Dean and Wendy from the Chinese place."

"Allie!" She pushed me away from pulling me into a hug.

"I'm so happy for you, Sav," I hugged her back tightly.

"Thank you," she whispered.

That's how we stayed for a long while.

"This is good. Let's hug for a long time so we get sick of each other and you spend the night at the airport," I patted her back

Savannah laughed and pulled away, "You sure you won't come?" she asked one more time.

"He won't want to see me, Sav," I picked up my glass of wine.

I don't think I could have conveyed accurately just how much I wanted to get on that plane with her.

39

Dax

Savannah arrived with no less sass and flare than she had the last time I saw her.

Maybe not the last time, seeing as that was when she stopped me from seeing Allie. I didn't blame her though. If I was her, I probably would have stopped me too.

Angus' laugh was deep and rumbling and I hadn't heard it as much as I had since Sav had joined him.

It was no surprise that we saw him for only the hours that he was required to have an instrument in his hands for the first three days after her arrival, but once they got *that* out of their system, they had come to join us for our usual evening hangouts.

We'd landed in Spain and Aspen and I were sharing a room during this particular stop.

The crowds hadn't let up once this whole tour. Every show and every signing that followed was bigger than the last. We had thought that the first show of this entire tour was the biggest we'd get. We were wrong.

I hadn't been nervous about seeing Savannah, at least I didn't think I would be, but my heart jackhammered while we waited for their arrival and as soon as they walked into Luke's hotel room, where we had all taken residence for the night, she walked right up to me and gave me a hug.

"Hey, Wyatt," she said, stepping back.

I rubbed the back of my neck with my hand, "Hey, Sav. It's nice to have you here," I smiled at her. It was no word of a lie.

"Good to be here," she smiled back.

And that was it, no more and no less.

We sat down and chatted for a bit. We all took turns versing each other at Mario Kart and when I finally won a race, I stood up.

"Where are you going?" Angus frowned at me.

"Early night for me. Today's show wrecked me," I patted him on the shoulder, "I'll see you guys tomorrow though. Have a good night," I turned to Sav, "Night, Sav," I passed on to her separately.

"Night, Wyatt," she smiled back at me.

I welcomed the hot shower and took the time to wash my hair. Tomorrow we had a day off and I had to go get the red touched up before our next show, it had faded to a weird orange colour. I never usually let it get that bad.

After ruining another white towel, I pulled on some sweats, forgoing a shirt, and pulled out my guitar.

It was liberating. Like a flood gate had been wrenched open. Anytime I could, I reached for the guitar.

I had started five different songs, but there was one that had stuck out to me, one that I worked on the most.

I had just begun reworking the bridge when someone knocked at my door. I thought it was just Aspen. He almost always forgot his key card to get in which surprised absolutely no one.

It wasn't Ap, though.

"Savannah, hey. Everything okay?" I moved back from the door and grabbed a shirt to quickly pull over my head. She walked in and shut the door behind her.

"Yeah everything's okay, I just thought I'd come and chat," she said, moving to sit on the bed that didn't have the guitar on it.

"Are the guys okay?" I sat opposite her on my own bed.

"Yeah, they're still playing Mario Kart," she smirked.

We sat in silence for a bit, it was incredibly awkward if I was being honest.

I rubbed my hands up and down my thighs and just as I went to speak, so did she.

It broke the tension at least.

I cleared my throat and decided I would approach the conversation like ripping off a band aid, "How is she?"

I couldn't even meet her gaze as I leaned my elbows onto my knees and let my hair fall in front of my face a bit.

"She's okay," Savannah replied quietly. I looked up and found her staring right at me.

I tried to read her face, but I knew that Savannah had a good hold on people, meaning she probably also had a good hold on herself. I doubted I would be able to pull anything from her expression even if I tried.

"Is she happy?" I asked, just as quietly as she had spoken. Like if I spoke any louder, the very building around us would crack and fall to pieces.

Sav's eyes searched my face a moment before she spoke again. I wasn't entirely sure what was there anymore.

"I would say that she's trying in that department too," she

replied evenly, she really had a lock on her expression.

We sat there looking at one another for a while, trying to pull something out of the other that neither was willing to give up. Of course, Savannah knew what I was doing.

"I won't tell you anything that she's said about you, Wyatt. There's a friend code with that type of stuff, and anyway, it would be breaking her trust."

"No, I know." And I did.

I kept my eyes on Sav, because it became very clear that she had just let slip something slip, and knowing Savannah, she didn't do it by accident.

Allie had spoken about me.

She's spoken about me.

My heart was pounding so frantically, if I looked at my shirt close enough, I could see it beating. If I thought about that for too long it gave me the heebie-jeebies.

I knew that I was done living my life out of boxes. I had known it even when I wasn't doing anything to try and change it.

I wanted 24-hour ice cream stores and early breakfasts and facetime calls. I wanted shoes off at the front door and 6 out of 10 spaghetti and meatballs.

Mostly, I wanted to tell it all to Allie, I *needed* to tell her. Even if she heard it all, saw all the dusty boxes and taped up memories, and asked me to leave anyway. At least I would have told her everything I should have right from the beginning.

I wanted the constant stream of messages, the rapid-fire questions. I wanted to know if her day was good or bad or in-between. If she needed brownies or if she needed me, like she had once said she did.

Like I needed her.

A small smirk started to appear on Savannah's face as her eyes tracked every thought that passed over my face. Everything I wanted to say I knew she read clear as day.

"I need your help," I said and I knew she knew exactly what I meant.

"Perfect, I already have an idea," she beamed.

40

Allie

Savannah had been gone for an entire month and I'd never been so happy to see the end of July in my life.

Not only had the romantic notion of leaving my place of work with the sun still up melted away in the relentless heat, but I was hot, and sweaty, and blubbering like a baby while I waited at the gate that Savannah's plane had just arrived at.

I couldn't pick her up and bring her back, but Savannah had actually driven herself to the airport when she left, so I caught the train, then the bus, and made the short walk into the terminal I knew she would be at. The plan was to see her after she had gotten back, but patience wasn't really a strong quality of mine.

I spent most of the day reorganising my wardrobe, as most 25-year-old city dwellers did on a Saturday in the summer, and then I got to the airport two hours early.

She walked out of the double doors that were held open and as soon as she saw me, her face scrunched up in an ugly cry, just like mine did.

I ran up to her and pulled her into a hug so tight I even struggled to breathe, but she didn't shake me off for air, she just hugged me back.

Savannah told me all about it. She arrived in Spain and then travelled through with the band to all the major cities they were playing in that country and flew out the same time they did to head to their next stop.

I focused on nothing else except for her experiences and she was so happy. She'd even gotten a tan.

Of course, we had spoken while she was away, but this was different, hearing it in her words as opposed to text messages and photos.

It was amazing, every single part. And Angus was amazing too, for him to have caught Savannah's eye, of course he was.

"What about you?" she turned to me from the driver's seat. We had collected her bags, found the car quickly and were already on our way back to hers.

"I joined a gym," I said to her, looking straight.

"A gym?" she asked.

"I've already run an entire kilometre without stopping. It took me almost two weeks of going every day, but I did it. The first time I tried to run, I almost wet myself," I snorted, turning to her.

Savannah kept looking from the road back to me.

"I also bought a CD. It has a range of different siren noises on it," I kept looking straight ahead.

"What?" Savannah's head whipped to me so fast, I was surprised the car didn't swerve.

"I have listened to it on the lowest volume, with my earplugs, three times," I said.

"And?" She looked dishevelled.

I maybe should have waited to tell her about this until she'd parked the car.

"Dean had to come in the first time and turn it off. The second time I managed to listen to it for 12 seconds before I had to get up and turn it off, but no attack. The third time I managed 30 seconds and I could breathe clearly through it. Sort of." I was staring at my hands.

"Allie," Savannah's voice broke, causing me to look at her. Her eyes were brimmed with tears and she gripped the steering wheel tightly.

"I figured I could try it myself, the whole exposure thing, little by little. I read about it online," I mumbled.

Savannah just nodded her head and wiped her tears away.

"I'm so proud of you, Al," she tried to say, but her voice came out as a strained whisper. I reached over and she grabbed my hand.

"Next is moving on from the brownies," I said with a smile and Sav choked a laugh, letting go of my hand to wipe her cheeks again.

"Step by step, let's not get carried away," she retorted.

Step by step was right. This was good, I felt good, like I was moving back into a version of myself I might have known once upon a time.

I huffed a laugh, "Maybe you're right, maybe not the brownies yet." I went back to picking my nails, and absolutely refused to think about the fact that the brand of brownie mix I bought had changed rather suddenly 7 months ago.

And maybe it wasn't the brownies that I wasn't quite ready to let go of.

41

Allie

If the month of August was a real person, I'd kiss its feet - not considering the Roman Emperor for which the month was renamed by and in representation of, of course.

The tail end of summer was finally upon us and the cooler nights were dropping their fractions of degrees with every day that passed.

I had managed to rope Savannah into coming to the gym with me from time to time, and the day she also ran a whole kilometre without stopping, we celebrated by getting totally shitfaced in her apartment while watching *The Office*.

We'd both called into work 'sick' the next day, as I'm sure you could imagine.

A lot of things had started to change, actually.

Change wasn't really something I yearned for. I was a planner and I liked to know what was happening. I was the sort of person that had to Google suspenseful parts of movies so I could know what happened *before* it happened.

So even the *notion* of change was completely out of my

comfort zone.

I had finally run an entire 3 kilometres on the treadmill. I did celebrate with a family sized pizza for one, but all in moderation, you know.

It might have been the adrenaline of that accomplishment, but the next day, when I walked into work with my head held high and Bart the Fart decided to cop a feel as a way of praising my last campaign launch, I turned around and grabbed his chubby little wrist.

There were two different ways that the whole situation could have gone, but I decided to run with it.

I looked him in his beady eyes and said with the most steadiness I'd ever had, "Bart, if you touch my ass one more time, it will be the last thing your sweaty little sausage fingers ever do," I maintained my attention on his face. "If you like the work I do, you can thank me in an email. Have I made myself perfectly clear?" My heart sped up and pressure started to form behind my eyes at what I'd done.

It took him a minute to come to, but he nodded his head so aggressively that his whole face wobbled before he tried to pull his wrist out of my grip.

I let go, turned around and carried on making copies at the printer. I had absolutely no idea how I managed to keep my composure for the rest of the day.

I went straight to Savannah's and broke down on her couch, but she couldn't outline a bad thing about what had transpired.

"If you lose your job, then fuck them, Allie. It's time you moved on anyway. God, you're just— I am so proud of you. Who are you and what have you done with the Allie I know? I'd like to send a postcard wishing her well on her new endeavours, but this new, confident version is amazing."

She grabbed both sides of my face and planted a big kiss on my lips.

I shoved her a way, "Savannah!" I wiped away her slobber, she just laughed and tried to come in for another one.

But it was true, everything she said.

I liked this version of me better too, and also, Bart the Fart could shove it where the sun don't shine.

* * *

Sav: *Are you sure we have to go to the gym today?*

Allie: *Yes. No backsies-outsies.*

Sav: *What if I'm sick?*

Allie: *I saw you yesterday...*

Sav: *It came on suddenly, and it feels contagious.*

Allie: *I'll see you at 5:30PM!*

Sav: *I've changed my mind, I want my postcard to request the old Allie to come back. The one who thought running was a waste of bodily fluids.*

Allie: *That's the spirit!*

* * *

The gym was closer to Savannah's house than it was to mine, but it was close to work which made it a good fit for both of us.

I walked in to find her already there, geared up and ready to go.

"This is an incredibly drastic change of tune," I walked by her and headed to the change rooms.

"I decided today was going to be my 3 kilometre day," she yelled after me.

Savannah did in fact run 3 entire kilometres without stopping once.

I had done 3.5 and we decided that the best thing to do in that circumstance was have wine and pasta.

String-bean-Dean was MIA for the entire rest of the week. He was on some tech conference retreat thing that ran until Sunday, so I was halfway through my Dean-free week and though we got on, I was *loving* it.

"You can have a shower first. I'll order the food," I said to her as I unlocked the door to my apartment, kicking off my shoes.

Savannah mumbled her agreement and kicked off her shoes too. I chucked my keys in the hallway bowl and dumped my gym bag on the chair next to it. I started to make my way to the kitchen, and it took me a second to realise that someone had been in my apartment.

My walking slowed down, and I reached out to grab Savannah's arm.

"What?" She looked at me confused.

I put a finger to my lips to tell her to be quiet and then pointed towards the kitchen island, "Someone put that there, and it wasn't me," I whispered.

"What? The card?" she asked, her voice was just as quiet but she was humouring me, like I was completely overreacting.

"Yes, the card!" I whisper-shouted.

She just shrugged at me, pulled her arm from my grasp and headed down the hallway to the bathroom.

My heart was pounding like crazy as I walked right up to the card and picked it up.

It was white and completely blank on the front. I couldn't help but note that it was incredibly good paper stock.

Not the time, Allie.

I flipped it over.

I held on to the edge of the island for balance. My heart was galloping, and my nose started to sting from the sudden dump of emotion that crashed through me.

On the back of the card was a messy scrawl in black sharpie. It read:

"My favourite type of music is Classic Rock. – D"

Oh my god.

A shuffle from the hallway caught my attention. My eyes were blurry from the tears that made their descent from my rapid blinking. My brain was frantically, desperately, trying to figure out what was happening.

"What?" I looked at Savannah. She leaned casually against the wall of the hallway, "What's this?" I didn't even recognise my own voice. It broke my own heart a bit, I could tell that it might have broken Savannah's too.

The devastating hope that tumbled out was everything I had made the decision to move past. To better myself; take those feelings in my stride, and get on with my life.

It was only then that I realised the door to my apartment had been left open, and in the threshold stood the same boots with too many buckles. The jeans that were tight and black and moved into a worn and faded band T - this one had *AAR* on the front of it.

There was no jacket, but there was the same face that had no right being in the 24-hour corner store that was a 1-minute walk from my apartment in the late hours of a freezing December night. And the bright red hair.

But most of all, I had no idea how he came to be standing in the doorway of my apartment, looking at me like I was absolutely everything he needed. Looking at me in the way that only *he* had ever looked at me. In the way I never wanted to be without.

I, on the other hand, was looking at *him* like an opened mouthed trout. Wonderful.

"What—," I started to say, looking back at Savannah for help. For *anything.*

She just walked over to me and grabbed my hand, placing a soft kiss on my cheek.

"Feel the fear, Allie. And do it anyway," she looked right into my eyes, and she kept on looking until I nodded.

She picked up her shoes and patted Dax's chest on her way out.

I was left standing in the middle of the kitchen, watching as he moved into my apartment and closed the door behind him.

He sat down and took off his boots, like he was in no hurry at all, before he walked toward the kitchen. He came to a stop just that little bit too far away. If I reached out to him, I might have been able to graze his shirt with my fingertips.

I looked up at him, still blinking through the tears that spilled, still trying to piece together what was going on. I'd forgotten how much taller he was than me, even without the boots.

"How are you here? Shouldn't you be in Europe, or, somewhere not here?" The words came out in a strangled whisper.

"Yes. Technically," he pushed the hair back from his face, "We had a week break, so I flew back for a few days," his voice was equally as soft as mine. He tucked his hands into the front pockets of his jeans.

"I don't understand," I tried to clear my throat, but it wasn't really helping, there was no way to hide the absolute shock I was in.

Dax walked right up to me then, like it was a split second decision, and it took every ounce of willpower to not move a muscle. To not grab onto him and bury my face in his shirt, not to run my hands through his bright red hair.

He stopped so close to me that if I took a big enough breath, my chest would touch his. I had the feeling that we'd been right in this moment before.

He reached up slowly and moved the back of his finger down my cheek, wiping away the onslaught of tears that wouldn't stop falling.

I felt like I was always crying lately.

"Allie," his voice was a whisper, heavy with the same emotion that was wrapped around my own vocal cords, "I was stupid," he frowned as he spoke, looking at me but sort of *through* me. He grabbed a piece of my hair and moved it behind my ear. I wouldn't have been able to move, even if I tried. My eyes were glued on his face.

How is he here right now?

"And scared, I think," he went on, "I only knew that everything I'd ever wanted was right in front of me, in everything you said and did. The things we did together. I wanted *that* to be my whole life, I wanted to forget everything else. I mean, I've had girlfriends, Allie. And I will tell you anything you want to know." He looked so serious but as per Allie, a bubble of laughter erupted out of me followed by the biggest eye roll I'd delivered in, what felt like, a very long time.

Dax's face broke out into one of his signature side smirks. It would take some getting used to again, I thought, as my stomach did a flip.

"I don't care about your girlfriends, Dax," I gave him a small smile as I sniffed, but it fizzled quickly, "I was so mad, and hurt and just wanted to disappear. I had always been the last one to know about everything and when the going got tough, really tough, I ran away." I wished that I was wearing something other than gym gear, wished I could have the hem of a shirt to grab onto for support.

"You didn't run away, Allie. I did," his face held such openness, it made me wonder why I ever thought I'd never be able to believe anything he said again. How that, in a million years, could have ever been true.

"I asked you to leave, Dax," I retorted quietly.

"I shouldn't have though. I put every single thing that we did, every memory of us, I put it in a box, and I sealed it up. I refused to look at it. That's what I do with everything and everyone in my life," his voice was shaking, drawing my eyes up to his face, "But I had never wanted to do that with you. With us."

"You were always on your phone," I blurted out.

"What?" His eyebrows lifted a bit.

"Every time we were together, you were always on your phone. You never let me see it, and every time I asked you said it was nothing. On our first date, at the ice cream shop, even the day after we, you know, *got it on* for the first time. That one really rocked my boat, let me tell you," I gave him a look that said 'you couldn't even imagine my inner turmoil because I held it together like you wouldn't believe' look, "I thought that it was Jenna, or someone, who you were speaking to. I wasn't prepared to go back to that reality Dax, I'd—"

"Allie," he cut in gently, silencing my babble of an explanation. I didn't really know where it was going to go, just that there was so much I needed to say to him. Three months of stuff.

"I was writing you a song," he said simply.

"You were what?" It was my turn to look a little lost by his words.

"Whenever I was on my phone, I was writing you a song," he just stared at me.

I stared back. I traced the lines of his face like my life depended on it. I never thought he would be standing in my kitchen again.

"I'm—," my apology was cut off by his own.

"I'm sorry, Allie. There's nothing in my life that I don't want you to know about. There's nothing in yours that will ever be hard to face. I honestly don't think I could go another day without trying your 6 out of 10 meatballs, or hearing you snort-laugh right as we're about to *get it on,* as you say," he wagged his eyebrows and I couldn't stop the laughter that poured out of me along with the tears. They weren't sad though, they were happy.

I was a big, snotty, hiccuping, laughing mess. *This* was what happy looked like.

Dax reached his hand up to the side of my face and I wasted no time leaning into his touch.

"Is this okay?" he asked, slowly leaning down to me.

"I mean, I thought I would be able to move past the nausea, but you really just have this *odour*...," I offered him a small shrug and my best 'don't look at me, I don't make the rules' expression.

Dax tipped his head back in laughter. A sound that hadn't filled my apartment for months, but was quite clearly the exact thing that was missing, the thing that made it a *home* for me.

Before his hand slipped from my face, I grabbed it and tugged it back. Dax looked down at me, his face drunk on happiness and I wasted no time pulling him down to me.

"This is perfect," I said and I pressed my lips to his.

42

Allie

Just because I had used up my sick leave didn't mean I didn't have any annual leave saved up. I hadn't taken a holiday in the entire time I'd worked for the pet store, so when Dax asked if I would go back with him on tour - I had never sent my request for leave to HR so fast, the action wasn't even visible to the naked eye.

We packed up an entire suitcase filled with things that Dax was certain I'd need, or come to want. If there was anyone who I would be taking packing advice from, it was a guy who travelled the world most of the year.

It was clearly no surprise that I was flying back with Dax. Everyone had been waiting at the concert venue that we had to go straight to from the airport and I received hug after hug after hug. Aspen refused to let go and it took Dax, Rip and Luke all chipping in to peel him off me.

I saw Jenna, who rushed over and apologised to me repeatedly, she spoke so quickly it sounded like pig Latin.

I had forgiven Jenna a long time ago, so I passed that knowledge onto her. I mean, I wasn't about to invite her over for a sleepover but, I didn't hold her accountable for the downfall that happened.

I gave Dax a kiss on the cheek and reached into my bag for my earplugs.

"Okay, I'll see you after the show!" I waved over my shoulder at the guys as I left.

"What? Where are you going?" Dax tried to look at me as he was having his hair styled.

I honestly didn't really know why they bothered. They got so sweaty, and Dax ran his hand through his hair so much, that anything that was done to it prior to getting on stage in terms of style was a lost cause.

"I'm heading to my spot at the front of the stage," I answered, holding up my earplugs to him, "I am, after all, your biggest fan." I threw a wink over my shoulder and made my way to the mosh pit.

43

Dax

Allie had been on tour with the band for two months, she stayed with us through the end of our Europe leg and all through our South American one.

Two things had never worked so well together. Allie and the guys got on like they'd been friends their whole lives.

Autumn had set in completely and the weather was cooling down everywhere we went. I smiled to myself often about the fact that Allie would be whipping out her *skeenie* when we got home, something she was quite verbal about in terms of her excitement.

Every show we played; she was in the front row.

Every city in every crowd was different, but she was always there. The constant that would always be.

She sang every word to every song.

"Alright guys, how are we all doing tonight?!" I asked the stadium on one of our final shows. Their response was so loud that, of course, Luke had to yell right back at them.

"We want to thank you all for coming out here tonight, you guys have been awesome!" They yelled back at that too, and

Aspen threw in a little beat on his drums as emphasis of what I said.

"There's one more song we'd like to play for you tonight. It's brand new, so you've never heard it but—" They screamed and screamed.

My eyes found Allie's and hers were already on mine, along with the biggest grin ever, as she threw in her 'woos' and 'yeahs' with everyone else.

"This one is called 6 out of 10. I hope you like it," I said as I looked right at her and God, I wish I would have taken a photo of the look on her face.

Every song I ever wrote had become about Allie. It sounded cliché, but it was true. Everything could now be tied to her, and it made every show we played that much better.

But this song. This song was really *about* her, and I finally got to play it for her. Telling her everything, from every moment since the baking aisle, how there had never been any doubt that she was everything I'd ever been looking for. The person who could finally help me unpack all my boxes.

Epilogue

"Did it go in?" Allie yelled as she twirled around.

The penny sat to the left of the fountain after what was now her fifth attempt at tossing it over her shoulder into the water.

"Oh, crap," she huffed as she went to pick it up again.

Two years.

Two whole years, and another two albums later, and Allie had been there for all of it.

She fought me on it first, but eventually she agreed to move into the marketing team for the band and ditch her job at the pet store with Bart the Fart.

It was two years of songs written about Allie. Of her at her piano and me with my guitar.

We were currently in Italy and she insisted that every fountain within a 5-kilometre radius of our hotel had to be visited and she had to make a wish in all of them.

I wasn't one for questioning her motives, so I went along with it.

I had ditched the red hair the year before, reverting to my natural black. Allie had been devastated when I told her, she said she'd paced all day waiting for me to come home.

As soon as the elevator doors pinged open and I walked out… let's just say that Allie wasn't disappointed in the slightest and I was hard pressed for time on moving us both to our bedroom before she got the upper hand.

"There's something wrong with these pennies," Allie pouted as she returned to her position to try and toss it in again.

"There's nothing wrong with the pennies, Allie. You just have terrible aim," I smirked at her from where I stood to the side.

She turned to me and stuck her tongue out.

Getting her composure, she closed her eyes and murmured something too low for me to hear and flung the coin behind her. She turned instantly and was already jumping up and down when the little *plop* indicated that her wish had been accepted.

"Alright, where to next?" She beamed as she walked over to me, grabbing the map I held of the area of the city we were in.

"Are you sure that we need to go to every fountain?" I asked, trying not to sound like a drag but this was our fifteenth fountain. *Our fifteenth fountain.*

She even found all the little ones that weren't huge tourist attractions and insisted they were probably the most important ones to go to.

"Uhm, do turtles have shells?" She gave me a look that said 'I think you've lost half your brain. Of course, we have to go'.

I barked a laugh and followed as she grabbed my hand and headed, with absolute certainty, to our next destination.

We had doubled the amount of fountains, bringing the grand total to 30, when Allie flicked her last coin in.

I watched her every time, and every time I couldn't help but love her more.

She turned to me, opening her eyes with a smile already on her face. She walked over, completely content with what she had achieved for the day.

"What?" she asked, trying to read my expressions.

I knew what my expression looked like; her cheeks had started to redden as she dropped my gaze.

"You know," I started, and she looked back up to me. Her eyes widened a bit at whatever she saw on my face, "I have travelled the world more times than I can count," I said.

"Hello, Mr. Humble," Allie countered and poked at my side.

I grabbed her hand and pulled her towards me, earning a yelp of surprise from her.

"I meant that I've been here, to this exact city more times than you've probably been to the public toilet in your nearest shopping centre," Allie scrunched up her nose at my analogy making me laugh, but I kept going, "and this is the first time I've done this. This is the first time that I've walked around the city on my day off, or seen literally any of the fountains we went to today."

I kept my eyes on her and her face softened a bit as she listened to what I said.

"You opened my eyes, Allie," I tucked one of my arms around her waist and pulled her even closer. I just couldn't stop looking at her.

Her face was getting redder and redder, "Dax, if you keep looking at me like that, I might actually combust," she groaned, hiding her face in my jacket.

I smiled into her hair, planted a kiss on the top of her head and waited for her to look back up at me.

She did look up, eventually, and there had never been a more perfect time.

"Marry me, Allie," I asked her.

She didn't hesitate, didn't even wait a second to reply.

"Yes," she breathed and pressed her lips to mine.

About the Author

Celine L. A. Simpson was raised on the Mid-North Coast of Australia and now resides in Melbourne, Victoria. She graduated from La Trobe University with a bachelor's degree in creative arts, majoring in Creative and Professional Writing. Growing up with a passion for reading, she began writing at an early age, moving into content creation as a career path before writing and publishing her own novels.

Also by Celine L. A. Simpson

Terraleise
(The Lost Child of the Crown #1)

Terraleise turns 18, only to discover she is now gifted with the elemental power of Earth. The thing about elemental gifts is that only those with royal blood possess them.

Terraleise is thrown into a life she never dreamed to be a part of, discovering all of the secrets entwined with her past, and her future. The heir to a kingdom overthrown by a corrupt branch of her own bloodline, Terra will see what it means to have courage and be brave, learning that the fate of the four kingdoms of Vaashaa rests on her shoulders.

Finding a life to fight for only to be faced with sacrificing it all, Terraleise will have to risk her love and her life to keep the world from falling into darkness. Will the Lost Child of the Crown find her rightful place?

Heir of Vaashaa
(The Lost Child of the Crown #2)

The land is dying and the promise of war is thick in the air. With Terraleise still held captive by the enemy, Silas is forced out of his grief to move forward, to march on and ensure Terra's sacrifice, her life for his, doesn't go to waste.

The threat to the World of Vaashaa is more horrific than anyone could have ever anticipated. A long-forgotten dark-ness has crept back into the hands of the wrong person and time is running out to stop it. The Kingdoms of Vaashaa will have to come together to save their world from the bleak future it is heading towards, all while hoping for aid to come from the truths laced within myths and legends.

There is only one who stands to be a force between the darkness and the light, only one who can save them all. Will the Heir of Vaashaa rise from the ashes?

Lightning Source UK Ltd.
Milton Keynes UK
UKHW011103060223
416537UK00009B/2129

9 780645 161106